SOILED DOVES 1

SUGAR ELLIE

SARAH EDWARDS

DEDICATION

*For Miss Kitty, because you're script writers never gave you Matt,
and you deserved him.*

COPYRIGHT

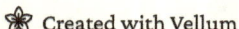

CHAPTER

ONE

Kitty's voice split the hot, still summer afternoon, so loud the horses at Gus's Livery next door snorted and kicked. "Sweet baby Jesus, Maisy! I will kill you dead for damn sure this time."

Ellie stopped reading and prayed that would be the end of it. Not that God was doing much listening to a girl like her, but it didn't hurt to try. Fifteen soiled doves in one house could raise more hell than a summer stampede, and all it took was one to stir the pot.

A few moments of peace and quiet before her busy night began, that's all Ellie wanted. With the second-floor windows open to the afternoon air, from her special place on the porch, Ellie couldn't escape what was happening up there.

"You dirty heifer!" Maisy yelled. A tooth mug sailed out the window and crashed on the hard-packed dirt about six feet away from Ellie.

Damn, Maisy was the kerosene to Kitty's match.

There went her reading time. Ellie wasn't going to find out

what happened to Moll Flanders today, and just when Moll was back in England and heading for Bath.

"What did you call me?" Kitty's voice rose higher.

"You heard. Now, what you gonna do about it?"

Maisy was heading for a butt whipping. Kitty could do plenty about it. Ellie sighed, closed her book and got her butt out her rocker beneath the back porch of the Four Kings and a Queen Saloon. Perspiration slid down her sides as Ellie quick-stepped it toward the escalating fray.

A hummingbird darted into view and then disappeared into the Mexican sage bordering her hideaway. Ellie didn't know how anything could move that fast in the heat. The heat was getting to the girls as well, making them more fractious than normal.

Her oldest brother, Theo, had built her porch hideout for her so she could put some distance between herself and the girls when she needed it. These days, her hideout got more of her company than ever.

"I'm gonna yank every last bit of that dead yeller hair outta your head!" Kitty bellowed.

Yanking it all out would probably do Maisy's dead yeller hair more good than the constant dyes she bought from the traveling medicine man who made it into Rattler's Gulch every three months or so.

"You can try it." Maisy didn't sound in the least deterred, which was part of the problem. Maisy didn't back down for anyone.

A scream led to flesh hitting flesh and more screaming.

Kitty didn't back down either.

If Maisy and Kitty got all the way into it, there would be blood on the walls before they quit.

The back door flew open and Silas trotted out still shoving

his shirt over his round belly and into his britches. His few remaining hairs stood up on his glistening pate.

"Miss Ellie." Silas's cheeks were pink from the effort of running in the infernal heat. "We got a problem."

Ellie had pretty much figured that already. "I hear it."

"Whoee!" Silas dropped into step beside her and snapped his suspenders into place. "I was havin' my nap, you know I likes to rest up before things gets busy, and they bust right into my room, yellin' and hollerin' fit to wake the dead."

Double darn it. Ellie had told Jake and told him they didn't need more girls. More girls meant more trouble, and they were full up on that already. Then Kitty had stepped off the stage from Cheyenne with her bold copper hair and flashy curves and Jake went deaf and hired her anyway. Flash a good pair of tits in front of her brother, and his mind went walking.

Of course, Jake didn't run the girls. Nope, that was Ellie's job. Fast walking through the kitchen, she glanced at Pearl.

Pearl looked up from the pot she was minding and rolled her eyes. "The cats are getting into it today."

From above, a loud thump damn near shook the walls, followed by more shrieking, a door slamming and then glass shattering. That sounded like one of the mirrors Ellie had brought in at great cost from Denver.

Lifting the skirts of her simple day dress, Ellie ran up the stairs and left Silas panting in her wake.

On the top landing, several of the other girls milled around, clucking together like hens as they peeped into Maisy's room.

Something heavy crashed to the floor.

"Silas?"

"Yes, Miss Ellie."

"Get me a pail of water." The wall shook as something big, Ellie was betting a person, banged into it. "Make that two."

3

"Yes, Miss Ellie." Wheezing a chuckle, Silas trotted off again.

Ellie slammed her hands on her hips and scowled at the gawkers. "You girls got nothing better to do?"

Girls stepped back and let her through. They might all tower over her and most of them could pick her up and toss her down the stairs, but like Theo always said, it wasn't the size of the dog in the fight. Ellie liked to remind them she was the dog with the biggest fight.

"What are you all standing here for?" Ellie met each gaze in turn. "I know you have plenty to do to get ready for tonight." She locked on to Ruby's night black eyes. "And I know you aren't thinking of going out there with your hair like that."

Ruby looked shocked and touched her tangled hair. That girl needed to make good friends with a hairbrush. "Yes, Miss Ellie, I mean, no Miss Ellie."

"Mona." She rounded on the plump, apple-cheeked blonde who was a big favorite with the miners feeling a long way from home and missing their wives and mothers. "You need to take yourself a bath before tonight. I don't want more complaints about your smell."

Mona blanched, opened her mouth to argue and then shut it and scurried away. "Yes, Miss Ellie."

"Silas!" Ellie eyed the other girls until they dissipated.

"Yes, Miss Ellie."

"You got that water?"

"Right here, Miss Ellie."

"Bring it."

In the room, Kitty was squatting on Maisy's back, one hand in her hair yanking for all she was worth, while the other was around Maisy's throat.

Ellie tossed the contents of one pail over the combatants.

Ellie didn't bother with a warning anymore. Warnings got you slapped and scratched for your trouble.

Gasping and screaming, Kitty clambered off Maisy.

Hands over her head, Maisy cowered on the floor in a puddle, her white shift soaked to her skin.

"You want more?" Ellie kept her eye on the main danger.

For a second Kitty looked like she might take her on and then she shook her head. With a scowl of disgust Kitty swiped water off her face.

Ellie turned to Maisy who was now sitting up. "How about you?"

Maisy shook her head.

"Silas."

"Yes, Miss Ellie."

"You stand right here with that second bucket. The first floozy to give me lip, you let her have it."

Silas chuckled. "Glad to, Miss Ellie."

"Or do I need to get a switch?" Ellie would do it too. That defiant gleam in Kitty's eye meant Jake favoring her all the time was giving her big ideas.

"No, Miss Ellie." Maisy sniffed and rang water from her shift.

Kitty took a bit longer before she said, "No, Miss Ellie."

"What happened here?" The girls had made a mess of the room. The chamber pot was broken—thankfully it didn't look like it had been full—and the dresser leaned drunkenly, one leg snapped in half. And, darn it, they'd smashed the beveled mirror into a thousand tiny pieces all reflecting the harsh afternoon sunlight. The mirror was coming out of their wages for damn sure.

They'd made an even bigger mess of each other, and that meant she would be two girls down tonight.

Maisy touched her split lip. "She started it."

"No, I didn't." Kitty bunched her fists and got ready to start right up where she'd left off. "I brought your dress back, like you asked, and you got all bent outta shape."

Kitty looked to be wearing the beginnings of a black eye and had a good few nail gouges over her cheeks and down her neck.

"You gave it back with man juice all over it." Maisy touched her swelling nose and winced. "I can't wear it with man juice all over it."

From the way it canted to one side, Ellie would bet Maisy's nose was broken. "Don't touch it." She slapped Maisy's hand away. "Go and see Pearl later and get her to straighten in."

"But it's gonna hurt." Maisy pouted.

"Not as much as my boot in the seat of your pants when I kick you outta here." Ellie turned back to Kitty. "Got anything more to say?"

"She can hardly complain about man juice when she gets herself a belly full of it every night. It's one mark." Kitty tossed her head and stuck her impressive bosom out.

Kitty needed to learn who was boss here. Ellie held Kitty's gaze. "Wash the dress and do a good job or you'll answer to me."

"But I have to get ready for tonight." Kitty scowled at her.

"Not with that fat lip you don't." Kitty would be unmanageable before much longer. Ellie had been doing this for too long not to recognize the gleam of ambition in a woman's eye. "You won't be working until you stop looking like a beat-up cat."

"I don't—" Kitty caught sight of her reflection in a larger piece of splintered mirror and gasped. She turned on Maisy like a rattler. "Look what you did, you bitch!"

"Me?" Maisy scrambled to feet. "You broke my nose."

"Don't make no difference to your ugly face."

"Silas!"

"Yes, Miss Ellie." With a grin, Silas doused the girls.

Both shrieked but shut the hell up.

"You're going to get your nose fixed," Ellie said to Maisy. She turned back to Kitty. "And you're going to wash that dress."

Still sullen, Kitty gave a jerky nod.

"And as both of you can't work, you're going to be scrubbing dishes and washing floors to earn your keep." She held up her hand to stop any budding arguments. "And then you're going to see about fixing what you broke in this room."

Ellie turned on her heel and stalked out. Waiting around to see if they obeyed her would only make her look weak. She reached the top of the stairs and took a deep breath. Now came the worst part, breaking the news to Jake.

Descending the stairs from the rooms where the girls worked, she took the corridor beyond the kitchen to the family section of the rambling building. They each had a bedroom and shared the two offices. Lately, Jake had taken over the larger office. If Theo had been about, Jake wouldn't have dared, but Ellie's favorite brother wasn't here, and her least favorite was in charge.

Ellie tapped on Jake's office door and took a breath. No chance he hadn't heard the commotion, and if he didn't hear what had happened from her, Kitty would be more than happy to fill him in.

"Come," Jake called from inside.

Ellie pushed open the door and walked into a cloud of cigar smoke. Jake's taste ran expensive and flashy. Drawn red velvet drapes made the room stuffy and dark.

Jake lounged in his big leather chair with his feet up on his massive desk that took up half the office. Jake had raised the biggest fuss about that desk. It had taken the carvers months to get it exactly like Jake wanted it. The whole thing was an overly ornate waste of money, but Jake could do what he liked with his cut of the profits.

Draped over the red velvet sofa in her drawers and corset and not much else was his fiancée, Minnie. The last woman Ellie wanted to see now. Pretty much the last woman Ellie wanted to see on good days as well.

Minnie had moved into the house the day she had accepted Jake's proposal. Ellie reckoned Minnie was protecting her investment from the other girls in the cathouse.

The heavy musk of Minnie's perfume competed with Jake's cigar in the stifling room.

"We've had some trouble." Ellie got straight to the point. She didn't fancy being here any longer than she had to.

Jake lifted one dark brow. He'd taken to doing that, like he was too important for words. It got right under Ellie's skin, but these days she had to pick her battles with Jake. Jake had Minnie, plus the twins always sided with him over Ellie. When Theo had been here, the twins had stood with him, but with Theo's continued absence, Paul and Patrick had thrown in with Jake.

"Kitty and Maisy got into it over a dress." She braced for the Jake explosion. "Neither of them will be working tonight."

"Dammit, Ellie!" Jake slammed his feet on the floor. "I told you to get rid of Maisy. She's washed up."

Ellie took a deep breath and instantly regretted her mouthful of cheap musk and cigar smoke. Since the day they'd expanded operations from a simple saloon, the girls had been hers to run as she saw fit.

"Maisy has been here since the beginning." Jake knew that, but Ellie explained it anyway. "She was one of our first girls. I can't get rid of her like she doesn't matter."

Minnie yawned and stretched her long, slender arms over

her head. Her bosoms heaved and nearly spilled over her corset. Like a dog on a rabbit, Jake's eyes went straight there.

Nothing so predictable as a man when his pecker was interested.

"Maisy is a whore," Minnie said in her slow, raspy drawl. "She knows how this goes."

If Ellie resented discussing her girls with Jake, that went double, triple even, for discussing them with Minnie. Since Theo had lit out to San Francisco six months ago, Minnie had been flapping her gums more and more.

"Maisy may make her living on her back"—Ellie hated using the word whore—"but she's family now, and we don't turn our back on family."

"No, Ellie, she ain't." Jake got the end of his cigar between his teeth. "She works for us, same as Silas behind the bar and Chester running the tables. And if she can't work, then she needs to find somewhere else to stay."

"She can work." Ellie stuck to her guns. If Theo were here, he would tell Jake to leave this with her. "She just needs a couple of days to get rid of the bruises."

Jake growled and glanced at Minnie. "So now it's a couple of days she's not working. And the worthless bitch has taken Kitty off the floor as well."

"I believe Kitty started the trouble." Ellie tried to get the facts straight. Jake wouldn't listen to anything where Kitty was concerned, but she still had to try,

"I don't care who started it." Face pinched and mean, Jake leaned on his desk and jabbed at it with his finger. "I'm a businessman, and this is a place of business. I care about money and who's making that for me."

Minnie undulated to her feet and padded over to Jake. "You knew Kitty was worth it the moment she stepped off the stage." Standing behind him, she draped her arms over Jake's shoulders. "You know where the money's at, Jakey."

Ellie wanted to gag as Minnie sucked on Jake's earlobe, pressing her huge breasts against him. Even worse, Jake grew hot and flushed, and Ellie had run a cathouse for enough years to know what that meant. Watching your own brother getting randy was all kinds of wrong and disturbing. "Maisy stays. The girls are mine to run."

"Mama's bored Jakey." Minnie ran her nails down Jake's chest. "Mama wants to play."

Ellie was standing right there and wanting to throw up more with each passing second.

Jake twitched like his britches had caught fire, which they probably had. "You run the girls, Ellie, but only for as long as you keep them in line."

"I do keep them in line."

"It sure don't look like that to me." Jake looked dazed as Minnie kept snuffling on his neck and scratching up his chest. "You get them in line, Ellie. Or someone who can will run the girls."

"Are you threatening me?" Theo would never have tolerated Jake and his cheap, bold hussy of a fiancée trying to shove her aside. Theo would have started by slinging Minnie out on her round ass.

"I'm just saying." Jake grabbed Minnie's arm and hauled her onto his lap. "And which of the girls is going to make up the money we're losing with Kitty and Maisy not working?" He looked at her over Minnie's shoulder. "You?" His cold, hard gaze let her know he meant it too.

Ellie got herself right out of there.

She made her way to the kitchen on shaky legs. Jake had threatened her. Not only with taking the girls away from her, but also with the possibility of her turning into one of the girls.

Theo would have Jake's head, but Theo wasn't here, and none of them had heard from him in six months.

"Sweetie?" Pearl looked up from kneading bread as Ellie walked into the kitchen. She stopped and dusted her hands on her apron. "What happened? You look like someone scared years off your life."

"Jake." Ellie dropped into the nearest chair and propped her elbows on the table. "He's mad about Maisy and Kitty."

"That woman is trouble." Pearl slammed her hands into her dough. "I saw it the moment she walked in here. Some whores live for stirring up trouble."

"I didn't want Jake to hire Kitty."

"Sweetie, I'm not talking about Kitty." Pearl pointed her floured finger toward Jake's office. "I'm talking about Minnie."

Ellie traced patterns in the flour on the table. "She says she's not one. Jake swears she isn't."

Snorting, Pearl flipped the dough on the table. "I made my living on my back for long enough to know a whore when I see one." She slammed the dough again. "And that's one all right. Now, she's got it as has her spreading for only one man. That kinda situation, she's gonna hang on to, and she's gonna be mean as she does it."

From the moment Minnie had come into their lives, she'd set her sights on Ellie. "And I'm in her way."

"You sure are." Pearl shook her head. She had come to them years ago, too old to work and starving. Ellie had taken Pearl on as a cook, and she had become the closest thing to a mother Ellie had ever had. Needless to say, Jake wasn't fond of Pearl either. Pearl spoke her mind, and she didn't care who you were when she did.

Leaning forward, Pearl caught her hands. "You watch yourself around that one, sweetie. She don't got no sense of right and wrong. All she got is a sense of what Minnie wants."

"Ugh!" Ellie wished with everything in her she was still sitting under her shady porch and reading her book. Not that she had said anything to her brothers, but Ellie had never loved running the girls. Lately it had been getting harder and harder to care. "Maybe I should step aside and let Minnie have at it."

"You could do that." Pearl shaped her bread into loaves. "But that don't mean she's not gonna come after you anyway. That girl don't want anyone near her patch."

"I wish Theo was here."

Pearl sniffed. "But he ain't, and you're gonna have to get through this on your own."

"Jake even hinted at me working." Saying it aloud sent a shiver of fear snaking down her spine. The look in Jake's eyes as he'd said that had put the fear of God into her.

Going still, Pearl looked at her. "Working?"

Ellie pointed upstairs to the bedrooms and nodded. "Working."

"Ah hell, no!" Pearl ruffled up like a chicken. "You didn't spend all these years guarding your treasure to have that Minnie bitch give it away."

"Treasure?" That made her giggle. Pearl could sound like a church matron sometimes. "One thing's for sure. I'm the only virgin in this house."

CHAPTER

TWO

C ole pushed open the doors to the Four Kings and a Queen Saloon and took a moment on the doorstep to let the unadulterated gaudiness of the place assault his eyeballs.

Gold, tassels, red velvet, mirrors and gleaming wood all fought for dominance amongst the beat-down miners, dirty cowboys and hardened characters who came to Colorado to escape a past it would earn you a gut shot to ask about.

Despite his sore ass from sitting a horse all day, the huge gold-framed painting of Sugar Ellie, which hung behind the bar, made him smile. His days of living in the saddle were over, and he'd grown soft.

Silas caught sight of him and gave him a gap-toothed grin as he called across the bar. "Well, lookee here. It's Cole "Whisky" Mansfield alive and kicking. Guess that was a bad wind blowin' in trouble all right."

Heads snapped his way. A couple of those faces he knew.

He nodded in the direction of a couple of greetings as he made his way to the bar. Tapping his hat on his leg, he created a miniature dust storm around him. It looked like they were badly missing some rain in these parts.

A big mean looking son of a bitch at the bar locked eyes with him. The lessons learned when he was a greenhorn out west were instinct now, and he didn't flinch, not so much as a twitch to let big, bad all dressed in black know how Cole felt about him.

Big Bad looked away.

"Silas." Cole held out his hand. "You got fat. Sugar Ellie feeding you too much?"

Silas hissed a chuckle from between his missing teeth. "You know Miss Ellie."

"Sweet as the day is long." Cole gave him the expected response. "You got any decent whisky behind that bar?"

"Not for the likes of you." Silas winked but bent and pulled out a bottle of the decent stuff. Cole had spent a lot of time in the saloon during his wanderings. Enough time to earn him his own bottle behind the bar, and he never drank the cheap cat piss Silas served up to everybody else.

Including Big Bad at the end of the bar.

Cole lifted his glass and toasted the man. "Give one to my new friend," he said to Silas.

From the painting above the bar, Sugar Ellie gazed at Cole over her shoulder, an impish smile on her pretty face like she knew what those curves of hers did to a man.

Theo had commissioned the painting years back. That's how long Cole had been coming here. There used to be some lewd knockoff of an overblown Titian up there before Ellie had taken over.

"Sugar Ellie." Cole raised his glass to her. The reason his ass ached from spending all day on a horse.

Silas filled him up again. "Ain't nobody sweeter."

The second one went down easier than the first.

Sugar Ellie perched on a chair in the painting, her bare legs to the side, the curve of her ass visible above the chair's cushion. The long, ivory sweep of her bare back was creamy and smooth, and Cole had not been the first man, and he wouldn't be the last, to want to stroke that flesh.

"She real?" Big Bad gestured to Ellie with his glass.

Cole took a moment to answer. "Yeah." Ellie was real enough, only he had never gotten over the sense that Sugar Ellie kept the real Ellie well out of sight. "If anything, it doesn't do her justice."

Big Bad whistled through his teeth. "I'd like to get me some of her."

"You're outta luck, mister." Silas got there while Cole tried to master the violent streak of possessiveness that shot through him. Silas turned and gazed up at the painting. "Sugar Ellie ain't for nobody to taste."

Silas's protectiveness toward Ellie had always mystified Cole. The woman ran a whorehouse, for God's sake. She'd probably had more men between her thighs than he'd had hot cups of coffee. She also had four mean brothers to back her up when she said no.

His jealousy probably had more to do with the vexing fact that he'd never gotten between those beautiful thighs of hers, not for coaxing and charming, and not for an outrageous sum of money either.

Silas leaned his elbows on the bar in front of Cole. "Where you been?"

"Busy." Cole shrugged off the question. Silas knew better than to press for details.

"It's been a while." Silas wiped the gleaming bar and went to pour two beers for a cowboy.

Cole worked out how long a while was. Damn! It had been near enough a year since he'd made his way to Sugar Ellie's door. He hadn't lied to Silas. He had gotten busy. Business in Denver was booming and taking up more and more of his time. Finally, though, his hard work had paid off enough for him to reap the rewards.

After his goodbyes, he was heading back east. He had twelve years to make up for and to get back what he'd lost by being young and stupid. Some part of him might miss the dusty trails and blazing heat that had made a man out of a spoiled boy.

This country had come close to breaking him more times than he could count, but it had also hardened him, fused his purpose and straightened his backbone.

Silas returned and leaned his elbows on the bar. "Sure has been hot."

"The trail was dry as bone."

"Yeah." Silas shook his head. "Word is there's been some fires starting up on the front range. Dang things raging for days before they burned themselves out."

Cole shared Silas's concern. Fires were disastrous and could wipe out a town before you even blinked. After another sip of whisky, Cole voiced the question he'd been dying to ask and jerked his head at the painting. "How is she?"

"Why don't you ask her yourself?" Ellie poked Cole in the back. "You yellow bellied snake. Slithering back in here like you've never been gone."

Cole turned and snatched the fan Ellie had jammed in his back like a six-shooter. "Hey, Sugar Ellie. Miss me?"

"Don't know if I'd go that far." Her velvety brown eyes laughed up at him. "But I did wonder if you were dead."

"They'd have to catch me to kill me." He leaned close enough to whisper in her ear. She smelled like roses. "And that's not going to happen." Being near Ellie made the blood pound thicker in his veins and gave him that sense of wild and free that he'd craved as a younger man.

Ellie leaned her elbows on the bar. Her breasts swelled white and plump over the edge of her bright red corset. "I got the book you sent me."

"Moll Flanders?"

"That's the one." She slipped open her fan and waved it in front of her face. "It's good, although I enjoyed the last one more."

He had taken to sending her books years ago, when they'd both discovered a mutual love of reading. Of course, Ellie had taught herself to read slowly and painfully. "Which one was that?"

"Pride and Prejudice." Ellie sighed and looked incongruously young and innocent. "Such a romantic story."

Cole didn't know how old Ellie was. Whenever he'd asked, he'd gotten the same answer. "As old as my tongue and a little older than my teeth."

He always got the sense she was much younger than people realized. If she was younger, that would put her in her early twenties and meant she must have started selling her body when she was still mostly a child, and he didn't like thinking too hard on that. "I wouldn't have taken you for a romantic."

Gaze sharpening, she cocked her head. "Because I own a cathouse?"

"Mostly."

She sniffed. "You'd be surprised what we whores like."

Although nothing showed on her face, he got the sense he had offended her, and he needed to lighten the mood. "Speaking of. How much are we up to now?"

"More than you can afford."

Her gamine grin stirred his libido. Sexual tension crackled

in the air between them. For the life of him, Cole never got why she kept saying no. He wasn't a conceited man, but he'd gotten his fair share of female attention over the years. "Try me."

"Twenty," she said.

"Thousand?"

"Yup." She giggled and pressed her breasts against his chest. "And it still won't get you a night in my bed."

Cole let his gaze feast on her tempting flesh. His body woke like it always did to Sugar Ellie.

Big Bad choked on his whisky and stared at them. "Twenty thousand dollars to fuck her?"

Cole wanted to shove his fist down the man's throat, but Ellie had been doing this for enough years to know how to handle herself. "Well, sure, sweet britches." She batted her lashes. "And he would still be getting a bargain."

Big Bad laughed and went back to his whisky.

Cole leaned closer and whispered in her ear. He brushed the smooth curve of her bare shoulder with his mouth. "Is that a yes?"

They'd been playing this game for so long he didn't know what he'd do if she ever said yes.

"As if." She stepped out of his reach and blew him a kiss.

Strike that thought; he knew exactly what to do with her if she said yes. He'd start by kissing the hell out of that pretty, pouty mouth. Then he'd let his hands find the shape of her breasts, the indent of her waist and the slight swell of her belly. He'd take his time with her ripe ass, learning its shape by touch before his hand found its way straight to heaven, waiting between Sugar Ellie's firm, white thighs.

His cock liked that idea fine and he breathed deep. Their game had started in earnest the first night he'd come in. He'd been playing poker at the table over by the window when Ellie had sashayed her pert, round ass into the saloon.

It had been so long since a woman had turned him down, he'd almost forgotten how rejection stung, but Ellie had smiled her wicked smile, flashed those eyes at him and said no thank you.

He'd doubled his offer, and she'd laughed and still said no. And kept right on saying no every time he drifted into her saloon. Now they were at twenty thousand dollars and it had become a joke. What Ellie didn't realize is that he might pay it anyway. If she ever said yes.

"You're leering," she murmured.

He followed the flare of her hips and down her legs, a good deal of which were visible due to the hitch in the side of her skirt. "I know."

"So, stop it and tell me what you've been up to that has kept you away for nearly a year."

He liked that she knew how long he'd been gone. "Mostly business. Getting myself set up."

"For?"

He shied away from the truth. "Consolidating."

But Ellie wasn't listening anymore and had her attention fixed across the room. Tension kept her body dead still.

Jake strolled down the stairs with a voluptuous redhead in bright blue satin on his arm. Her breasts threatened to spill out with every breath. As it was, the edge of her nipples peeked over her bodice. "New girl?"

Ellie snorted. "Don't let either of them hear you say that." Her face tightened. "That's Minnie, and she and Jake are engaged."

"Engaged?" Cole couldn't believe what he was hearing. "Are you joking?"

"Nope." There was no mistaking the tension in Ellie now. "I wish I was, but Miss Minnie has moved herself in, and Jake doesn't change his mind without checking with her first."

Cole could believe it. Minnie had the shrewd look of a voracious harpy. He'd met her kind many times, even tangled with one or two before he had learned his lesson. They wrapped themselves around you like a velvet ribbon, all smooth and pretty to touch, and before you knew it, that ribbon was making up your noose. "I would have thought Jake was sharper than that."

"So would I." Ellie sighed and took a small sip of his whisky.

Ellie's brothers were all big bastards. Theo was the biggest, but Jake ran a close second. With his coarse, brutish features and cunning eyes, it was hard to remember he and Ellie shared blood.

Minnie wrapped her arms around Jake's neck and whispered in his ear. With her breasts pressed into him and her hand snaking to his belt, Cole could guess the gist of her whisper. "What does Theo make of her?"

"Theo's not here." Ellie grimaced. "He went to San Francisco on business. We haven't seen him for over six months."

Damn! That couldn't be good. Theo was the oldest and the brains of the four brothers who ran the saloon with Ellie. In addition to being Ellie's favorite, Theo watched over Ellie like a papa bear. "Are you worried about him?"

"Yeah." Ellie nodded but she didn't allow any of that to show on her face.

Cole made a note to make enquiries on her behalf. California was a big place, and it was easy to disappear in its vastness. It didn't necessarily mean bad news that Theo hadn't been heard from in so long. Theo could take care of himself.

Ellie's twin brothers joined Jake and Minnie. Called the Triggers because of their hair-trigger tempers and where those tempers led, Paul and Patrick took care of the rough side of owning a saloon. They shared Theo and Ellie's more refined features, but their manners were all Jake, mean as a grizzly out of hibernation.

Cole had spent most of his adult life relying on his gut, and his squawked at him now. The way Jake, the twins, and Minnie stood over there like a team with Ellie over here on her own smacked of no good. Even though he guessed she wouldn't give him the whole truth, he still asked. "Are you okay?"

Sugar Ellie tossed her dark curls and threw him a bright smile. "I sure am."

Cole didn't believe her, and he wasn't leaving town until he found out what was causing those shadows in her eyes. "Sure you are."

THREE

Ellie had missed Cole, and she hadn't realized quite how much until she had seen him standing by the bar sipping a whisky that was the same color as his eyes.

"Shut it down, Silas." Her feet ached, and since Cole had left a couple of hours ago, the night had dragged on and on. A few stragglers nursed the dregs of their drinks, but Caleb, their hired muscle, was making short work of getting them up and moving.

Bets and Delilah hadn't had too many takers tonight and sat at one of the tables sharing a last drink before bed. A couple of the girls still had customers, but they wouldn't be much longer, and once Caleb was finished down here, he'd start clearing the rooms.

This was a cathouse and not a boarding house like some seemed to believe.

Ellie piled glasses on a tray and took them over to the bar. None of her brothers were around for cleanup.

Before Theo left, this had been her favorite part of the night. She and Theo used to work with Silas and Caleb to shut the saloon down for the night. She and Theo would talk about their day, sometimes books they were reading.

Theo had taught her to read. Jake, Patrick and Paul had seen no reason to learn. They also saw no reason to clean up when they paid others to do it. But after a long night, the cleanup could be backbreaking work, and Ellie couldn't sleep with the idea of Caleb and Silas still hard at it.

Caleb expelled old Dave Withers for the night and put the chairs atop the cleared tables.

While Silas wiped down the counters, Ellie tallied up the sales for the night and compared them to the bottles. Silas was honest to a fault, but Jake insisted on an audit every night.

"Sure was good to see Whisky tonight." Silas replaced the bottles as she finished with them.

Ellie nodded. "Yes, it was. Did he say where he's been?"

"You know Whisky." Silas shrugged. "Alls he ever says is that he had business."

"Right." Ellie couldn't help but scoff. "Business that involved a deck of cards, I'll bet."

"Surprised nobody's shot him by now." Silas shook his head. "Not a way to make a living, that."

The idea of Cole being shot stabbed at her, and she shoved it away. "He's been at this for long enough to take care of himself." At least, she dearly hoped so.

"Ellie." Patrick stood by the arch leading to the family area. "You need to come."

"What for?" Patrick had gotten mighty fond of issuing instructions. Mostly because people in this town were scared of him and Paul. Patrick had a hair trigger temper that Paul was happy to back.

Patrick scowled. "Just come."

"Tell me what for."

He growled. "Family business meeting, that's what for. Now come."

"Can you finish here, Silas?" Only Jake would call a meeting at this time of night. Of course, he'd been holed up with Minnie since about midnight so his feet weren't aching, and his back didn't feel like it could snap at the waist. Getting her corset off had become Ellie's priority.

Silas nodded and patted her hand. "You go ahead, Miss Ellie, and then take yourself straight to bed."

"Thank you." She went past Caleb. "I think Honey has someone with her, and I saw Dusty take that miner she likes so much up about an hour ago. They should be done by now."

Caleb grinned. "Iffen they ain't by now, they're about to be."

Ellie turned down the main lamps and left a couple for Silas and Caleb to work by. "Good night."

They spoke together. "Good night, Miss Ellie."

ELLIE FOUND HER THREE BROTHERS, and Minnie—of course—in the small parlor they used for themselves at the back of the house. Unlike the garishness of the rest of the saloon, Ellie had decorated this room in greens and creams and tried to keep it looking like a regular family's parlor.

Perched on the arm of his chair, Minnie had her boobs near enough in Jake's face. They certainly bought Minnie Jake's undivided attention.

Patrick strolled over to the floral sofa and wedged himself in next to Paul. It was a tight fit for both of them, and Ellie suppressed a wince as Patrick slammed his booted feet on the delicate walnut table.

Ellie chose a small armchair near the window and as far

away from Minnie's cloying perfume as she could get. Jake had that stuff brought in from Paris especially for her. Ellie reckoned Paris must be full of an awful lot of cat pee that they were bottling it up, slapping something sweet in there and selling it as perfume.

Patrick lit a cigar and added smoke to the close air.

The window was open, but the night breeze provided no respite from the heat.

Looking up from Minnie's cleavage, Jake scowled at her. "We've been waiting for you."

"Then you could have come and helped me close up."

Minnie put her black lace mitted hand on Jake's arm to stop his response. "We've all been talking."

"All of you?" Ellie looked at Patrick and then Paul shoulders hunched as they sat jammed together on the sofa.

Patrick dropped his gaze and Paul picked at his boot.

This wasn't looking good. She turned to Jake. "What about?"

"The girls." Minnie hooked a stockinged leg over Jake's thigh. "We think some changes are in order."

The *we* was really starting to nip at her drawers. "What sort of changes?"

"We think the girls are taking advantage of you." Minnie glanced at Jake and then the twins. "You're so sweet, Ellie, everybody says so, and the girls ride right over you."

"I don't think—"

"They don't respect you," Jake said and sipped his whisky. "They do what they want, and you let them."

Ellie couldn't believe what she was hearing. "That's not true, Jake. I run the girls, and I do it as I see fit. Theo said so."

"Theo isn't here." Jake's face grew hard. "And I don't think he's coming back neither."

"Don't say that." Ellie couldn't bring herself to admit the

possibility of never seeing Theo again. "People don't always find a way to contact their folks when they're out in California."

Minnie clicked her fingers, her gold bangles jingling. "I suggest we get back to the important part of tonight."

"Right." Jake kissed her hand. "We've decided"—he tilted his head toward the twins—"that someone else should handle the girls. Someone with a firmer hand on them. Someone older and more experienced."

The floor disappeared under Ellie's heeled boots. She didn't even have to guess who they were thinking of replacing her with.

Then Jake said it anyway. "Minnie will take over the girls. Once we're married, that will give her my authority as well her own."

"And what do I do?" Ellie looked at her brothers, but not one of the cowards would meet her eye. "Cook? Clean?"

"Ellie, honey." Minnie smiled like a cougar with its prey in sight. "You're far too special for something like that. You ask around, and everybody from Denver to Cheyenne has heard of Sugar Ellie."

She and Theo had done that on purpose, as a means of protection. They let the myth of Sugar Ellie cover up the truth of Ellie Pierce, a dirt-poor miner's daughter who had never so much as kissed a man.

Minnie spread her fingers through Jake's hair. "It really is a blessing that you're so darned pretty." Minnie twinkled at her. "We know you're going to have your pick of the customers out there. First prize, Sugar Ellie, and with a price to match."

A strange buzzing set up in her ears as Minnie continued to speak. The stink of Patrick's cigar turned Ellie's stomach. Minnie's mouth moved. The words made sense as collections of sounds, but Ellie's brain lagged in putting meaning on them. "You want me to do what?"

"It's not a question of want." Jake stood and loomed over her. "We've all busted our asses to get this place where it is today. Now it's time you do your part."

She wished her brain would start working because her future depended on it. "But I have been doing my part. I run the girls."

"And God knows how much money that stupidity has cost us." Jake folded his arms. "Now you can make it all up to us, and Minnie has the right idea. Everybody knows Sugar Ellie, and everybody knows she don't take no man to her bed."

Ellie had never fainted, but she rather suspected she might now. She shifted closer to the window and tried to breathe. Her corset pinched at her lungs and dug into her waist. Her brain was slow in catching up with her ears. They'd planned this, the four of them, an auction to sell her virginity to the highest bidder.

"You'll fetch the best price of any whore in the Territory of Colorado." Jake rubbed his hands together. "And I don't want you to worry, Ellie. The boys and I won't sell you to anybody. There ain't that many who can afford you."

Minnie gave her a smile so sweet it gave Ellie a bellyache. "Just tonight Whisky Mansfield offered twenty thousand for you."

"That's a joke." High and strained, Ellie's voice didn't sound like her own. "He wouldn't actually pay that."

Patrick and Paul huddled together and wouldn't look at her.

"You agree with this?" Ellie wanted them to look her in the eye as they betrayed her. Her brothers, her blood, her kin had agreed to this plan.

Patrick puffed a cloud of smoke and glanced at her through

it. "You don't understand, Ellie. There's things you don't know."

"What things?" Dear God, if they were fixing to sell her body for those things, didn't she have the right to know what they were?

"That's not important," Jake said. "But the boys are in agreement with Minnie and me, and that's all you need to know."

The absurdity of the situation almost made her laugh, except nobody in the room thought it was a joke. After she'd been deflowered, she would take her place with the other girls. Was this her punishment for running girls all these years?

That had to be it. She was being punished for her wickedness. It didn't matter she had never wanted to do it. What mattered was that she had sold women for money, and now her family had decided to toss her on the fire with all the rest.

"What makes you think I'll go along with this?" Ellie looked from one to the other of them.

Jake's gaze grew harder than steel. "What makes you think whoever buys you will care if you agree or not?"

Ellie's stomach lurched, and for a horrible moment, she thought she might lose her dinner. There were always men who thought a whore didn't have the right to refuse them. Ellie'd had Caleb throw their fair share of that kind out.

"Now, wait a minute." Paul sat up straighter. "You didn't say nothing about Ellie being forced." He looked at Patrick, who nodded. "Nobody said nothing about rape."

Ellie stared at the twins. Sure, they weren't the sharpest, but how the hell else did they think it was going to happen?

"Now, boys." Minnie fluttered her lashes. "There won't be no forcing about it. Ellie's old enough to need a man's touch." She winked at Ellie. "You have wants, same as anyone, don't you, Sugar? I saw the way you was eyeing Whisky tonight."

Her thoughts dragged themselves into a comprehensible order at last. Her brothers were planning to sell her. Tomorrow night. There was some kind of weird auction already happening.

"Make no mistake, Ellie, this is happening. It's too late to stop it, even were I so inclined." Jake leaned over her. "Whether it goes good or bad is up to you."

Minnie stood and approached her.

If she came much closer, Ellie would rip her throat out.

She must have read the murder in Ellie's eye because Minnie stopped. "It's just your virginity, Ellie. One quick poke and it's gone." She forced a laugh. "You won't even miss it, and you are twenty-five. Most women have had babies and more than one man by your age."

Not a virginal woman who had been running a whorehouse for all these years. A woman like that didn't know where to go to change that situation without it becoming a huge joke. A woman like that didn't meet the sort of man who could help her out with her little problem discreetly.

Except for one.

Cole's face popped into her mind and kept the panic at bay. Cole didn't even like Jake. He would help her.

GETTING to Cole proved more difficult than Ellie had thought. Jake knew her well enough not to trust her to stay put.

Patrick and Paul took her to her room.

"You can't let this happen." Maybe she could get through to them, make them see reason.

The twins looked at each other for a long moment.

Even with Minnie's scheming and prodding, Jake wouldn't

stand against all three of them. If she could just get through to them.

"It's just sex, Ellie," Patrick said. "We all done it except you. This time tomorrow, it'll be all over."

"We don't aim to let Jake turn you into one of the girls," Paul said as he nudged her into her room. "Just go along tomorrow night and then we'll find something else for you to do."

"It's rape," Ellie pleaded. "You are going to take money for someone to rape me. You know you don't want that."

Paul glanced at Patrick and frowned.

"No." Patrick shook his head. "Minnie's right. Besides, it's only rape if you fight. Just go along with it, Ellie. It'll be over in ten minutes and we'll all be richer for it."

"We aim to share the takings with you." Paul closed the door.

The key scraped in the lock, and Ellie was alone.

Later, she would sit down and rage about her brothers and what they'd done. Sure, Minnie had given them the idea and talked them into it, but Minnie was not her kin. One day she was going to rip every hair from that bitch's head.

But first, she needed to escape.

Ellie peeked out her window. If not for a guard on each side, it would have been easy enough to sneak out her ground floor window.

Jake wasn't stupid. She needed a plan.

While she wracked her brain, Ellie changed into a traveling gown and cloak. She swapped her heeled boots for a pair of practical riding boots.

A chink of light still shone through the bottom of the door.

Ellie shoved things into a bag while she waited. When her opportunity came, and it would come only once, she wasn't going to miss it.

Eventually the light under her door went out and deep silence settled around the house. She reckoned it must be close to three in the morning. She needed to be gone before the sun came up, but if she panicked now, she might lose her chance.

A key sounded in the lock, and Ellie's heart jumped into her throat. The door creaked open, and Pearl whispered, "Miss Ellie, Caleb is outside and waiting for you. You get out of here, Miss Ellie, and don't you come back."

CHAPTER
FOUR

Cole hadn't said goodbye to Ellie, not properly anyway. Part of him couldn't admit he wouldn't see her again. He had been finding his way to Rattler's Gulch for the best part of the last eight years, and she had always been part of that trip.

By the time he'd met Ellie, his reputation as a gambler who could back his cards with his Colt had already been made, and he was no longer that wet behind the ears, scared kid trying to stay alive long enough to make his way back home.

He opened the hotel window to get some relief from the hot night. The unrelenting dryness of the air was so different from where he'd been born and raised, and he'd gotten used to it.

Cool night breeze ruffled the dingy pinkish curtains stained with blowing red dust. The hotel had only been built two years ago when the railroad had found Rattler's Gulch, but already it had the same weary air as the rest of the town.

Ugly, bare and sun bleached as it was, he'd miss the town.

He'd miss Ellie too. Too late to figure out now that he could have come around more in the last year.

Damn, she had a brand of pretty that always took him by surprise. Unlike other girls at the Four Kings, Ellie retained a freshness that he'd never seen in a whore, let alone the madam of a whorehouse.

Tugging his shirt from his pants, he pulled it away from his sticky skin. Ripping it over his head he caught a hint of Ellie's perfume from when she'd hugged him as he left.

Roses. A scent so incongruous with a grim town on the edge of the mines. So many of these towns stayed around until the seam was played out and then crumbled back into the baked earth they'd sprung from.

He plunged his hands into his wash basin, and then his face. He came up, dripping cool water over his hot skin. Still wet, he walked to the window and let the breeze cool him further. Twelve years of his life he had carved out in this dusty, dry tough land of even harder men and women scratching out a living in towns like Rattlers Gulch.

With a pack of cards and a quick draw, he had rebuilt himself into a man of means. Somewhere along the way, Colorado had become part of him. In Denver it was easy to forget how far he'd come. In the bustle of that rapidly blooming city, he could almost convince himself these lost pockets of the west didn't exist anymore. Five minutes in Rattler's Gulch would set a man right on that score. Huge tracts of the west remained wild and untamed, and he would always carry a part of that savagery inside him.

Footsteps came up the stairs, scuffing on the uneven fifth step from the top.

Cole waited and listened.

Whoever was out there was light on their feet but didn't know enough to avoid the creaky board in the center of the corridor. The steps stopped outside his door, and Cole palmed his Colt Double Action.

A soft knock on his door got him moving that way.

Pressing his back to the wall to the side of the door, Cole cocked his pistol. "Yeah?"

"Cole?"

That sounded like—

"Cole, it's Ellie. Open the door, please."

He put his Colt away and whipped open the door. "Ellie? What the hell?"

Roses! She pushed past him and into the room, motioning at the door. "Close it."

Now Cole wasn't a man to turn down a lady who wanted him to close his bedroom door. So he did.

Ellie rushed over and locked it.

And Cole got his first good look at her face. Ellie looked upset and like she may even have been crying, but he couldn't be sure because the idea of Ellie crying didn't sit right with him. "Sugar?" He closed the distance between them and took hold of her shoulders. "You doing okay?"

"No." Ellie's jaw tightened. "But I will be."

She wasn't wearing her normal saloon getup but a plain traveling coat over a dark blue dress. Also, and it stopped him, she had a travel bag that she must have dropped inside the door when she came in.

The same gut feel that often made him turn the next card, that had kept him alive more times than he could count, whispered to him now that his life was about to get a lot more exciting. His blood awoke to the challenge, thrumming through his veins in a reminder of how alive he was.

Ellie walked over to the window and peered out. "Can you turn down the lamp?"

In other circumstances, he and Ellie, alone behind a locked

door with the lamp turned low, he might be getting all kinds of interesting ideas.

Not tonight, however. Ellie looked tense enough to explode.

He waited while she watched the street in a loaded silence. Finally, she breathed the smallest sigh of relief and turned to him. "I need your help."

"I figured that much already." He picked up the bottle of whisky he had brought to his room and offered it to her. "No glass I'm afraid."

"I'm not that much for glasses," she said and took the bottle and swigged. She came up coughing and spluttering and wiping her eyes.

Cole took it back from her and took a sip. She also didn't have any of the face paint on she used in the saloon. Whatever her age, it was younger than he had thought.

"I came to make you a deal," she said. "You once offered five hundred dollars for a night in my bed."

"Actually the last offer was twenty thousand." This was getting more and more interesting. Desperation like the sort you saw across the table when a man had lost money he didn't have, clung to Ellie. "And I made it tonight."

She waved a dismissive hand. "You didn't mean that one. I meant the last serious offer was five hundred."

Actually, the twenty thousand might be worth it to satisfy an itch eight years in the making. "You sell yourself short."

"I don't have time to haggle. Let's call if five hundred." The desperation in her eyes and in her voice gave him pause. Ellie was deadly serious and whatever had brought her here tonight had gotten her spooked.

"What do I get for the five hundred?"

"Nothing."

He almost laughed. "Ellie, sugar, that's not how bargaining works."

"I know that." She gave a small chuckle but even that sounded forced. "What I'm saying is I don't want the five hundred."

"But you do want something?"

"Yes." She nodded and went back to staring at the street. "I need you to take me with you."

That caught him with the bottle halfway to his mouth. "Take you with me?"

"When you leave. I need you to take me with you."

Something was not right. "Why not ask one of your brothers to take you?"

"You ask too many questions." She scowled at him. "I'm offering you me, my everything, and all you got to do is get me out of town."

"And then what?" His gambler's sense prickled a warning at him. Ellie's was holding cards on him. "Say I get you out of town, then what?"

"That's my problem. You leave me at the closest train station, and I'll take care of myself from there." she said. "But I've never been anywhere on my own and I would get lost."

"Sugar." This plan made no sense to him and it reeked of trouble. "I can't leave you at a train station and ride away."

"You can." She nodded, but her eyes shone like maybe she was holding back tears. "That's all I want from you."

"And I get you in exchange?"

Her chin came up and she nodded. She looked like she was steeling herself for an ordeal. Now Cole didn't like to think of a night in his bed as a trial. "You get me."

As he considered her, he took another sip of whisky. There was a whole lot about this that made no sense. Ellie wanted to leave town and leave her business behind.

Puzzle pieces slotted into place. The tension between Ellie and Jake tonight at the saloon had to have something to do with why Ellie was knocking on his door in the middle of the night and acting jumpier than a squirrel in a coyote's den.

Cole had always seen the mean streak in Jake, but Theo kept him under control. With Theo out of the way, there might be no controlling Jake. Especially if he was getting his nob polished by that piece of cheap ass Cole had seen him with. A woman like that could play a man with Jake's conceit like a fiddle.

He offered Ellie the bottle and she took it. This time her sip was smaller but her big eyes stayed fixed on his face, her entire petite form tense and alert, waiting for his response.

So, trouble with Jake had brought her running to him. How much trouble was anyone's guess, but as she'd never done anything like this before, he was guessing big.

What the hell! It had been a while since he'd rolled the dice, spat in the eye of fate, and it might very well be his last chance. "Like I said before, Sugar. You undervalue yourself. For a taste of what you got, I'll take you all the way to Denver."

Her shoulders collapsed and she heaved a sigh of relief. "Thank you."

Now that the bargain was made, Cole's cock got behind the idea. Typically, his cock ignored his brain, which was letting it know how they weren't doing this to get laid. They were doing this to see what the game was. Now, if in the discovery of that game their might come a time, a mutually agreed upon time, when he and Ellie scratched that itch, then so be it. He lay back on the bed and patted it beside him. He'd never forced a woman and Ellie didn't have a ready for loving look on her face, but he was shuffling the deck here, seeing what dropped out. "You're going to have to get a lot closer than that to fulfill your side of our bargain."

"Actually." She twisted one of the big brass buttons on her coat. "You're going to have to accept an IOU on the getting me part."

This was getting more and more intriguing. "Why's that?"

"Because we need to leave now," Ellie said. "Right this minute."

CHAPTER

FIVE

Ellie thanked God Cole asked no more questions, because she was running out of the sort of answers she'd like to give. He grabbed his shirt and put it on, which was also a relief. Ellie had seen plenty of bare chests in her time, but Cole's was the only one that made her want to sink her nails into it.

The man was put together fine, and it had gotten harder and harder not to stare.

While he shoved his few belongings into his saddle bags, she checked the street again.

Pearl would cover for her until the saloon woke up, but there was always the chance something would happen, and she would be discovered missing. She also had most of the last three nights' take in her bag, and Jake would be livid about that.

"Ready?" Cole shrugged into his duster. "I don't suppose you have a means of getting your sweet ass out of town."

"Means?" She hadn't gotten that far.

After Pearl had released her, she'd grabbed her bag, the

take from Jake's office, and made tracks. Her plan had been formulated in the five minutes it took her to run over to the hotel.

"Never mind." Cole cracked the door and peered through the gap. "We can get you a horse."

He leaned out and checked the corridor before he motioned her out. "Now, I suggest you stay out of sight while I pay up." He stopped and raised his brow at her. Those gold eyes of his gleamed with humor. "Assuming you don't want to be seen leaving town."

"No, I don't." She grabbed his arm, the female part of her registering the muscle, and pulled his head closer to hers. "This is not a joke. I'm in danger."

"Sugar." He looped his arm around her waist and pulled her flush with his body. "Then you came to the right man."

Son of a bitch was loving every minute of this, but as long as that got her the hell outta town, she could live with it. Also, when he held her close to him, she felt better and better about their bargain.

He motioned her back as he strolled to the front desk and rang the bell. He had to ring it a couple of times before the door to the back opened and Ezra Patterson stumbled out, hair mussed and shirt unfastened. He blinked at Cole. "What is it?"

"I need to pay up and be on my way."

Ezra squinted at the clock. "At this hour?"

"Yep." Cole leaned forward and dropped his voice. "A little matter of a lady and her enraged husband. A man like you, you know what I mean."

Like hell Ezra knew what Cole meant. According to Maisy, Ezra was a once and done kind of man.

Ezra puffed up and blushed, but he tallied Cole's bill and

took the money with a gruff, "You go on now, and watch yourself."

Ellie waited until Ezra went back to his quarters before she crept to the hotel door, staying close to the wall. Nobody was about, but she didn't want to chance somebody spotting her now.

Outside, Cole emerged soundlessly from the shadows and took years off her life.

She got such a fright, her heart leaped into her throat. "What the hell are you doing?"

"Waiting for you." He took her bag and led her down the walkway. For a big man, he moved like a ghost, his boots making no sound on the wooden planks.

Ellie tried to imitate him, all the while checking to see if anything moved around the Four Kings.

Cole ducked into an alley and motioned her after him.

"Stay here," he whispered, his breath stirring wisps of her hair. "I'm going to procure you a means of escape."

"You mean buy a horse?" Even at this hour Cole smelled good. Like leather and whisky and soap.

He chuckled and slipped out of the alley. A bright moon showed him as he crossed the street to Gus's livery, opened the door and disappeared inside.

The alley smelled like somebody had thrown up and she didn't want to risk stepping into anything nasty.

Boots clopped on boards. Heart racing, she flattened herself against the building, praying the deep shadows would keep her hidden.

Deputy Riley strode past, stopped a few feet away and struck a match. He put it to the end of his cheroot and dropped the match almost at her feet. Tobacco scented the air, and then he moved on.

A hand fastened around her waist and mouth. "Hush," Cole whispered in her ear. "It's me."

She was going to have to fix his habit of scaring the life out of her, but later.

Still holding her about the waist, he pulled her deeper into the alley and toward the other side.

Something soft slid beneath her heel and she didn't want to think about what she was stepping on.

The alley came out behind the general store.

Cole motioned two horses standing by a trough. He whipped off his hat and gave her a low bow. "My lady, your steed."

"Thank you." Ellie didn't think it a good time to mention she had only ever ridden a mule, and years ago. It couldn't be too much different. Right?

Horses were a lot further off the ground, as it turned out, and Ellie had to use the edge of the trough to clamber into the saddle.

Cole swung himself up with the sort of easy grace that made her want to kick him. It was not a good idea, however, to give one's rescuer a kick in the britches, so she settled herself as comfortably as she could.

Fortunately, her horse was a follower, and dropped into place behind Cole's horse as if she'd asked him to.

They took a slow walk out of town, that nearly set Ellie to screaming with nerves, but she understood why. Hooves galloping through town in the night would bring every set of eyes to the window to see what was up.

She didn't draw a proper breath until they reached the outskirts of town and Cole kicked his horse into a canter.

～

By the time Cole called a halt for them to rest, Ellie was not sure if she wanted to shoot Cole, her horse, or herself more. Her tailbone and thighs ached from staying in the saddle all night.

Willing her limbs to swing over the saddle so she could dismount, she stared at the ground. It wasn't going to happen.

Cole, the insufferable braggart, had already swung out of the saddle and was unsaddling his horse. He glanced over from loosening the girth. "We'll rest here for a few hours. Give the horses something to eat and drink and move on after the heat of the day has worn off."

The ground was a long, long way down, or she might have thrown herself at it.

Cole stopped and looked at her. "What are you doing?"

"Aching." She was way past pretense.

He flashed her his wicked grin and sauntered to her horse's side. "Need a hand?"

Oh, how she would like to slap his outstretched hands away, but pride came before a fall. In this case, a long fall to the hard-packed red clay ground.

Ellie lurched into his waiting hands.

He gripped her waist and guided her gently to the ground. "You don't spend much time in the saddle, do you?"

"Nope." It would not behoove her to show her annoyance. She had asked him to rescue her, and that's what he was doing. She was tired, hungry and ornery, and none of that was Cole's fault.

He'd been trying to put as much distance between them and town as he could. The very thing she'd bargained with him to do.

"Will they come looking for you?" He half carried, half dragged her to a dead tree trunk and helped her sit.

She wanted to offer to help set up camp, but the torturous

few steps from that bedamned nag to the tree had discouraged that idea. "Pearl will cover for me as long as she can."

"Going to tell me what kind of bother you're in?"

Ellie stretched her legs out in front of her, one careful inch at a time. "Nope."

"That's what I figured." He unsaddled her horse, brushed them both down with dried grass and led them to the small, near dried up riverbed to drink.

The sun peeped over the red rocks and turned the sky rosy.

Cole had chosen a big rock to shelter them while they rested. He dropped their saddles to the ground in a puff of red dust.

"I guess we'll be sharing my blanket," he said as he laid it down in front of their saddles. "Unless you thought to pack one for yourself."

Ellie shook her head. Other than the few belongings in her carpetbag and the money she'd snatched on her way out, she hadn't thought to take anything else.

Cole dipped his bandanna in the stream and wiped his face and neck.

Ellie's gaze refused to move away from the blanket. Although she was untouched, there wasn't much Ellie didn't know about what happened between a man and a woman. Her girls spoke candidly in front of her, and it wasn't like she'd never caught herself an eyeful here and there.

Still, Cole's blanket stretched in front of her, an otherwise innocuous thing that would mean a huge step forward for her.

All things considered, it was amazing she'd gotten this far with her virtue intact. She had Theo to thank for that. No big brother could have been more protective. Even nice women were mostly married and had a few children by the time they reached her age.

She wasn't exactly nervous. Maybe a little nervous, but

more disappointed. Some hidden part of her had been hoping she might get rid of her virginity at a time of her choosing.

Her profession ruled out any hopes of love and marriage, but she could take herself a lover without anyone thinking any worse of her. How much worse could they think of her anyhow?

Finding the right lover had proven tricky. The only man she'd ever met who could be trusted with her secret was, well, Cole. Given that, it was fitting he would get the business done now. Still, she had hoped to have more to it than a quick poke on the hard ground.

Getting comfortable, Cole stretched out on the blanket, his long legs in front of him and his head propped on his saddle. He patted the ground beside him. "Come on, Ellie. Get some rest. We'll be riding hard again tonight."

"Shouldn't one of us stand watch?" Her body protesting every movement, she got up and looked about her.

Dried ground, brush and scrub oak stretched all the way to the lightening sky.

"Nah." Cole tipped his hat over his eyes. "I sleep light enough to hear anyone coming." He yawned and crossed his ankles. "Besides, they will only now be figuring out you're gone and we're hours ahead of them."

With less grace than a punch-drunk cowhand, Ellie lowered herself to the blanket beside Cole.

Her leg muscles protested as she imitated him and stretched them in front of her.

She crossed her hands on her chest and waited. Cole had never struck her as the shy kind.

His chest rose and fell, and the slight huff of his breathing rode the still dawn.

Uncrossing her arms, Ellie placed them by her sides. She had made a deal with him, and she wouldn't be the one welching. Maybe he thought her crossed hands meant she wasn't willing.

She was. Sort of. In the way of having made a deal and sticking to it.

With the rising sun, the first glimmer of the day's heat started up. It looked like it would be a hot one, and Ellie unbuttoned the top three buttons of her fitted jacket.

Cole's breathing lengthened, and he snored softly.

He was asleep. Not laying there waiting for the right time to get his leg over, but fast asleep.

As the sun climbed higher, Ellie lay there prepared to do her part.

Cole slept on.

Finally, she undid the rest of her buttons and wriggled out of her jacket. Laying it between her head and the hard saddle, she settled in to rest. They would be riding hard tonight, God knows where to and toward what, but she wanted to be ready for it regardless.

CHAPTER
SIX

Ellie woke to Cole preparing to move them on. The sun blazed down from a mercilessly blue sky and grit coated her eyelids.

"Here." Cole handed her a water canteen. "Time to get moving."

"What time is it?" The water was cool and fresh in her dry mouth.

Cole looked up. "I would guess a little after midday."

"I thought we were waiting out the heat of the day?" Her bottom ached enough to make walking difficult.

"I've let us rest for as long as I dare." Cole rolled up the bedroll and secured it behind his saddle. "They must know you're gone by now. I haven't seen any sign of anyone, so we're still ahead of them, but I want to keep it that way."

That got her moving. After finding a useful bush, Ellie mounted with Cole's help and they moved into the blazing afternoon.

He kept the horses to a walk, sticking close to the rock face and taking advantage of what shadow he could find.

Beneath her smart jacket, sweat slid down her sides. The sun beat down on her hat, and flies buzzed around her mouth and eyes.

Other than the occasional stop for water, Cole kept them moving steadily forward.

As the hours wore on, the shadows lengthened but the sticky heat remained. Her entire traveling costume felt like a sweat rag. It would be ruined.

Ahead of her, Cole sat his horse like he didn't notice the heat or the flies.

The silence made each hour seem like an eternity. "Cole?"

He half turned his head.

"Are you married?"

He barked a laugh and turned all the way around. "Now you ask me?"

"Just making conversation." She swatted a fly. A man being married was not a topic that came up much in a brothel. Besides, it was nothing to her and her girls if he was.

"I'm not married," he said.

"Ever been married?"

"No."

"Engaged?"

His back stiffened, and Ellie thought he wouldn't answer and then he said, "Once. A long time ago."

"What happened?"

Cole stopped his mount and turned in the saddle. "If you're feeling chatty, why don't we talk about why we're out here in the first place?"

That she wasn't going to risk doing until she could concoct a plausible enough lie, so Ellie kept her mouth shut.

"That's what I thought." He turned and got his horse moving again.

A gust of wind provided a few moment's relief, and then it

disappeared again, chasing dust devils across the empty expanse.

Ellie had not been out of Rattler's Gulch since Pa had brought them from Pikes Peak after the seam there dried up. Then Pa had forced her to walk behind the wagon, so she'd not tire their one ox.

Theo had put her on his shoulders when her legs had gotten too tired to move, but it felt the same as this journey. Long, dry expanses of nothing and with no idea of where they were going or how long it would take to get there.

Pa had not allowed questions from his children. They had done what he said and not talked back.

Of course, there had been times when Theo had gotten mouthy with Pa, but mostly in defense of her or the twins. Theo had also paid for his disobedience.

"Cole?"

"Yep."

"What brought you out here?"

"You." He glanced over her shoulder. "You needed to leave town in a hurry."

If she'd been any less hot and tired, she might have laughed. "No, I meant before. What brought you out west?"

"Ah." Cole fell silent. Their horses' hooves clopped on the hard-packed ground. "Not much different to everyone else. I came to make my fortune."

"Where did you come from?"

"East," he said. "I heard the stories about gold lying around in the streets, waiting for anyone to come along and pick it up."

Ellie suspected there was a good deal more to his story, but she left it there before he got it into his head to start asking those questions of his own.

Nobody really knew where Cole "Whisky" Mansfield hailed from. Some said New York, others Boston, and others Philadelphia. What they knew of him for sure was this: he had the manners of a gentleman until provoked, the cards loved him and turned up sweet for him, and he was as fast with that Colt at his hip as if he'd been a gunfighter and not a gambler.

Another breeze sent a flurry of sand into her face and Ellie ducked. Longer shadows stretched over the parched red soil. A pair of turkey vultures rode the stifling air above them.

Ellie would give anything for a cold glass of Pearl's lemonade. She hoped Pearl didn't get into trouble for hiding her disappearance. Guilt smacked her. She had given no thought to Pearl when she had used her to aid her escape.

Jake had Pa's mean streak. Theo could be tough, and nobody crossed him on purpose, but he was also fair, and one could reason with Theo. Even with his mean streak, Ellie would never have believed Jake could have done what he had threatened to do.

With the twins, nothing would surprise her. They weren't called the Triggers for nothing. Patrick could never keep his mouth shut, and Paul was always there to take on anyone who took offense. Of the two, Paul scared her more. He was just plain mean and a little bit crazy. Get some liquor into either of them, and Ellie stayed well clear.

Still, she had believed her brothers loved her, cared for her at least. When Pa had died, they had taken care of her, bringing her into the business with them as soon as she was old enough to pass for grown.

Once Pa died, it was easy to expand their operation. When the local saloon owner had objected to the competition, Paul and Patrick had paid him a visit.

Ellie's sigh came from her boots. She would never have thought she'd be running from her own brothers. Minnie's influence over Jake was a terrible thing.

She wished for the thousandth time Theo would get back.

He had a way of keeping the other three in line. If Theo knew what they were up to, hell wouldn't be able to hide the other three.

Imagining Theo's reaction kept her mind off the heat long enough for the sun to sink behind the horizon. And Theo would find out because he wasn't dead. Ellie refused to believe her favorite brother was dead.

It took her bruised backside a while to catch on that they weren't on a horse anymore. She followed Cole into the hotel of some dusty town she hadn't caught the name of, her legs so bowed she'd have no trouble catching a pig in a passage.

Full dark had fallen a few hours by the time he led her into town. Curious gazes followed them, but the streets were quiet.

The familiar sounds of laughter, glasses and high-pitched giggles came from the saloon two doors down. Ellie was too darn tired and sticky to care.

Cole got them two rooms, and she dragged herself up the stairs after him.

Two rooms didn't sound like he was going to collect on her debt tonight either. Two rooms also meant a nice hot bath, and a clean bed, and that damn near brought her to her knees.

Ellie felt downright cheerful as Cole handed her a key.

For a small town, it had a decent hotel. Colorful curtains fluttered in the breeze through the open window. A matching comforter made the bed look welcoming.

She dropped her bag, limped over to the one chair in the corner, and sat. It took several goes to get her tired body to bend over and untie her boots. Her toes gave a grateful throb as she wriggled them clear.

A knock on the door got her moving.

A round-faced maid stood on the other side. "Pardon, miss, but your brother said to get a bath ready for you."

Her brother?

It had been so long since Ellie could claim to be any kind of respectable that she nearly burst out laughing. If this girl with the sweet smile had any idea who she really was, she wouldn't be standing in the hallway looking like she wanted to help her.

"That would be greatly appreciated." Ellie managed what she judged to be a respectable woman sort of smile.

The girl bobbed a curtsy. "Then I'll get that sorted for you. Unless you need help with your dress."

"Er...no, thank you." Ellie wouldn't inflict herself on anybody right now. Nobody deserved that kind of grubby.

The girl disappeared down the hallway and Ellie limped back into her room.

Another knock revealed Cole at her door. Already bathed and looking like he'd stepped out for the first time that day, he grinned at her. "I asked them to arrange a bath for you."

"They did." Standing in front of his cool elegance, she felt every grain of dirt she carried and every drop of sweat she'd shed. "Thank you."

"I'm going out." Cole shoved his hands in his pockets. "Thought I might play a hand or two."

Guilt assailed her. Cole must need to plump up his pockets. "I have money, you know." She didn't want him to think she was leeching off him. "Let me pay you back for the horse and the hotel."

"Ellie." His smile stopped her. The man could get a three-day dead mule back on its feet with that smile. It crinkled up the corner of his eyes and softened his features. He almost looked boyish when he smiled. "Save your money for Denver. In the meanwhile, I'm going to see who will let me lighten their pockets."

"You do that." Feeling strangely alone, she stayed in the doorway as he strode away. For years, she had lived in a house with fifteen women and her brothers. There was always someone demanding her time or her attention, always a task that needed doing or a chore to finish. All she had to do tonight was take a bath, eat her dinner and get into bed.

The girl came back with a couple of men. They made short work of filling the tub.

"Put your clothes outside the door." The girl handed her a sack. "And I'll see they get brushed and sponged."

Once she was alone again, Ellie wriggled out of her clothes. She slid them in the sack and placed it outside the door.

Then, she sank into the hot, fragrant water.

And groaned.

It felt so good on her sore muscles that she groaned again. It had been beyond sweet of Cole to think of this for her.

She took the time to wash every inch, including her hair. The night stayed warm, so when she was done, she sat by the window.

They came to take her bath away and the girl brought her dinner.

Ellie sat by the table close to the window and ate her dinner. Some kind of chicken with a thick sauce that could have done with some more whisking smooth. But the biscuits were light, fluffy and hot, and the corn was buttered.

There was even a small jug of wine with her dinner and she felt like a grand lady as she sat by her window, ate her dinner and sipped her wine. Now that she'd put distance between her and her brothers, she could draw breath. This was the biggest adventure of her life, and she aimed to suck up every minute of it.

CHAPTER
SEVEN

As sure as the bastard sitting to Cole's left had nothing in his hand, Ellie was lying to him. Not outright lying but holding back the truth.

Funny thing, he'd always known there was something about her that didn't quite fit. The outside picture was perfect, like that gaudy oil painting above the bar at the Four Kings, but something didn't sit right. He'd made his living and stayed alive out here by his gut, and it had never led him wrong yet.

"Raise." He tossed a couple more chips into the pot.

The bastard to his left raised again. The guy had a tell. He sucked his front teeth when he was bluffing, and he'd suck those teeth right down his gullet before this hand ended.

Enough. Cole saw him and laid down two pairs, ace high.

"Son of a bitch." Tooth Sucker tossed a pile of crap on the table. "I felt sure you had nothing that time."

Cole scraped his winnings to his side of the table. The air in the room was getting chilly, and he didn't mean the weather. The cowboy to his right had lost a week's wages and was already four whiskies down. Cole wanted to tell him to cash in and go home. Find a warm woman for the night and enjoy what was left of it.

But that would add insult to injury.

The most important thing about making your living by cards was judging the right moment to leave the table. Too soon, and they thought they'd scared you off, which got their thirst up for your money. Then they took it personally when you didn't want to give them the chance to take it off you. Too late and you ran into the sore losers, who had seen more money than they could afford head into your pocket and felt it had to be because you'd cheated.

Now Cole couldn't say he'd never cheated at cards. Back when he was young and new out west, he'd had to eat, and a couple of aces had found their way up his sleeves. But cheaters always got caught, and he'd gotten better at cards fast enough not to need to cheat anymore.

Across the table, an older man dealt. He was also starting to look twitchy.

Cole picked up his cards. Three sweet ladies peeked up at him. He sipped his whisky. What could he say? He'd always had luck with the ladies.

"Three." He slid the lovely ladies facedown to the dealer as discards. His dance card was full tonight.

Liar or not, Ellie was in trouble, and trouble so deep she'd followed him on that hellish ride without complaint. She'd even made that ridiculous deal to get his help. It was kind of insulting she thought he was the sort to barter his help for her body.

He glanced at his cards. Of course, he had picked up trash.

The table looked to him for his bet. He checked his cards, fiddled with a couple of chips and then tossed them into the pile. "Raise."

So far his plan for Ellie was to take her to Denver, and it

hadn't progressed much past that. Best he start thinking about what to do with her before he left for New York. Getting her to Denver and then letting her walk into a future of not much planned didn't sit well with him. Somebody needed to make sure Sugar Ellie was taken care of until that same somebody could find Theo. If Theo was dead or remained missing, he couldn't leave for New York not knowing if Sugar would be fine.

"Raise." He let the betting go one more round until the pot started to make eyes gleam around the table, and then tossed his cards down. "Sorry, boys. I'm gonna fold."

Smirks appeared around the table. There was enough money in the pot to get them chipper for a few more rounds.

"Well, hello there." A busty brunette slid her arms around his shoulders. "Fancy some company?"

The cleavage thrust in his face might change another man's mind, but she smelled of stale beer and sweat.

Cole managed a smile. "Not tonight, sweetheart."

"Sure?" She pouted and batted her lashes at him. "I could put a smile on your face."

"I don't doubt it." None of Ellie's whores wore the same air of desperation as this sweetheart. Out west was a tough place for women. Cole admired the sort of grit it took for the women who came west, bad girls and good girls alike. "I'm gonna say no to that." He pushed up from the table. "But why don't I buy you a drink for your trouble."

"You leaving?" Sore Loser glared up at him. "Without giving me a chance to win my money back?"

Cole suppressed a sigh.

His female companion had been at this long enough to read trouble on the wind and she disappeared. He wanted to pick the kid up and shake him. The golden rule to gambling, the one no gambler should ever forget, you never played with money you couldn't afford to lose.

If he backed down now, he'd end up with a bullet in his back, or a knife coming out of the dark. "That depends." He pushed his coat away from his Colt. "On whether you're gonna let me buy the pretty lady a drink, or whether you want to make something of it."

Indecision played across his face as the cowpoke gave it some thought.

Then his buddy leaned over and whispered in his ear.

The guy flushed bright red and swallowed. "Nope. Enjoy your night."

Cole's lady friend had drifted over to a group of filthy miners and seemed to have struck gold there.

At the bar, he ordered himself another whisky. He didn't intend to play anymore tonight. He missed the excitement of playing to keep clothes on his back. Now it was a way to take money off kids like that cowpoke. Money they could ill afford to lose.

"You Whisky Mansfield?" The barkeep slid a bottle his way. "You'll be wanting that."

With the bottle, Cole's night improved. He slid some money and bit extra for the keep and poured himself another glass.

Three or four whores worked the saloon. He studied them, trying to find what it was about Ellie that was so different.

She lacked their sense of bone-deep weary. Despite her life, Ellie kept that light of hope in her eyes. And Ellie was smart as a whip. Smart enough to know the real money didn't come in lying with a man. The real money came in being the one who made that happen.

Shit! He was out here worrying about leaving Ellie in Denver, and maybe it should be Denver he was worried about.

A hazy plan formed in his mind. He could set Ellie up in her own place. Give her enough to make it classy.

Denver didn't stand a chance. He raised his glass in a silent toast to Sugar Ellie.

∿

COLE STAYED for long enough to make sure there were no lingering hard feelings at the poker table. Then he let himself into the cooling, cloudless night.

Back east, summer heat clung to your skin, hot and muggy. Here it cut through harsh and bright, and faded away with the sun.

Whisky left a low feel good singing through his blood. Enough to take the edge off but not enough to forget he was a stranger in town and people tended to try their luck with strangers.

Ellie's hotel room created a warm, yellow rectangle of light. Curtains fluttered at the windows.

Her silhouette crossed the light, a shadow made up of curves and swells.

It occurred to him that he did, in fact, want some company tonight. He was just particular about who that company was to be. Well, Sugar Ellie was the kind who knew the score between a man and woman and with the whisky making him feel kinda mellow and relaxed, he planned to drop by for whatever she had for him.

Nobody was about as he climbed the stairs from the small hotel lobby to the bedrooms. He'd had a hankering for Sugar Ellie for more years than he cared to count. Sure, he joked around with his outrageous offers, but if she'd said yes, he'd have paid the lady and followed her upstairs.

Moving as quietly as he could, he stopped outside her door and knocked softly.

The door opened a crack and Ellie peered through. "Cole?"

The familiar smell of roses crept out the room and beckoned him closer.

"Evening, Ellie." He let her know with his smile what he was doing here. "Fancy some company?"

Ellie blinked at him, blushed and then took a deep breath. Not the reaction he had been expecting, but he got distracted by the way her flimsy red silk robe didn't so much hide her shape as accentuate it.

Red was a good color on Sugar Ellie.

"Come in." She pushed the door open and stood back.

Her room was almost the same as his, except for a different counterpane.

Cole had everything he needed for a good night. A half-decent bottle of whisky, a big old bed and the sweetest armful to share it with him.

Hooking an arm around her waist, he tugged her close to him. Her full breasts flattened against his chest.

Ellie gasped and hid her eyes from him.

He'd been waiting too long for this to let her cheat him. "Look at me, Sugar."

Those brown eyes crept up past his chin, lingered a moment on his lips and found his. She breathed his name in a whisper that went straight to his cock. "Cole."

"I was playing cards, and I got to thinking about you in here all on your own." Damn, she smelled so good and felt like heaven pressed against him. Not able to resist he cupped her round ass and pushed her against his erection. "Denver is a little ways away still, and I thought we might keep each other company."

He dipped his head and gave in to the lure of her silky

shoulder. He trailed his lips from her shoulder to the curve of her neck, and breathed her in.

She took a deep breath. "Have you been drinking?"

"Not that much." He got a bit distracted by the rise and fall of her breasts, but not distracted enough. Ellie didn't seem that into the idea of them putting the night to good use. Pulling back enough to see her face, he dropped a soft kiss on her lips. Some whores didn't like to be kissed, and maybe Ellie was one of them. "May I kiss you?"

"Um...sure." Color spread over her cheeks.

Cole was getting an off notion. "Ellie?"

"Yup." She squared her shoulders and looked at him. "Everything is fine, honey." Draping her arms over his shoulders she pressed against him. "I stand by the deal I offered."

For a small woman, Ellie had the ripest curves. And her mouth! Dear God, it was a dream of pillowy softness that he'd spent many a night fantasizing about.

Kiss her. Take her.

Damn it to fucking hell. Cole put her at arm's length. "Deal? This has nothing to do with that."

"It doesn't?" She looked up at him with those sleepy kitten eyes. "You know I like you Cole."

That was much better. He dipped his head to take the kiss he craved.

But...

"Like me?" Women liked their brothers, their friends and white fluffy kittens. Like didn't mean they wanted to get hot and bothered with a man.

"Cole." She stamped her foot. "Just do it already." She threw herself against him. "Take it. Me."

There were times when a conscience was a definite liability, and this was one of them. Ellie had a look on her face like she was about to swallow a spoonful of castor oil. He forced his reluctant arms away from her and took a step back. "I'm missing something here."

"No, you're not." She rolled her eyes. "I want this. Let's do it."

"Yeah." And therein lay the rub. "I hear the words, Sugar, but I still get the sense I'm missing something."

"Like what?" She eyed him askance.

"Enthusiasm." He shoved his hands in his pockets before he grabbed her again. "Desire. Lust."

"Why do you have to be so contrary?" She actually stamped her foot. "Any other man would be finished by now."

"Um." And he rather thought not! "I'm sure you've seen more than your fair share of that type at the saloon, but I'd just be getting started."

"Cole." Dragging his name out, she flounced over to the bed and plopped onto it. "It's nothing to do with you. It's me. Something about me."

"You have the pox?"

She scowled at him. "I do not!"

"Then what?" His gut whispered that here lay a vital piece to the mystery of Sugar Ellie, and he pushed. "As we're not rolling in the sheets right this minute, you owe me this."

"Oh, all right! I suppose you need to know whatever happens between us." She sighed and blew out a long breath. "First, you have to swear this goes no farther than this room."

He waited.

Ellie twisted her hands in her robe. "I might not be as experienced as you believe me to be."

"As in life, travel, adventure, or are we talking about sex?" He already knew Ellie hardly ever took a client anymore, but she must have before. "How inexperienced?"

"A lot." She swallowed. "Like no experience. None. At all."

"None?" An odd sort of notion crept into his brain. "Like nothing?"

She nodded.

"Ellie." Cole couldn't actually believe he was going to say it, and he must have been a whole lot drunker than he thought, but there he went. "Are you telling me you're a..." The words got stuck, so he cleared his throat and tried again. "Are you trying to tell me you're a virgin?"

Ellie went bright red and dropped her head. "Yes."

"Shit!" Cole got the fuck outta there.

EIGHT

That had not gone how Ellie had imagined it would. Her closed door stared back at her.

The door opened again, and Cole walked in. He threw his arms wide and glared at her.

"I suppose you'd like an explanation?"

He scowled at her and dragged a chair over to the bed and sat in it.

"Right." She had known she would have to have this conversation with someone at some point. Her girls always spoke about first times being awkward and going a lot better if the man you were with knew he was going where none other had before. "It really was Theo's idea."

"Your brother put his virginal sister in charge of a whore house?" Cole gaped at her.

Yeah, it sounded bad when he strung it all together like that.

"It all came about after Pa died," she said. "Theo and Jake had been running a still in the woods for a few years before he died. Only they didn't want to tell him about it because he always took any money they made and pushed it down that played out mine of his."

"How old were you?"

"Fifteen." She tried to keep it light. It didn't need to be a big deal. Minnie was right about that. One poke and she'd be done. Only, this way, she got to choose who did the poking. "Pa and the boys had been keeping me quiet and out of sight as much as possible."

Cole flinched. Everyone knew how rough mining towns could get. Certainly no place for a young girl.

"After Pa died and we didn't have any money, the boys came up with the idea of opening a saloon, and they didn't know what to do with me." She shrugged. "The plan was to send me back to my aunt, but she died about six months after Pa. My brothers are the only family I had."

"I'm still not getting how you ended up running the girls."

Ellie shrugged, because it hadn't been one single decision so much as a series of events. All in all, Cole was taking it rather well. "Jake came up with the idea of having the girls, but none of the boys wanted to run them."

"So they gave you that job?"

"Well, I kind of started doing it one day, and one thing led to another." Then life had rolled on with her. "And everybody assumed I was a whore as well. I never corrected them. People believe what they see."

Cole nodded and leaned his elbows on his knees. "And once you were cast in the role of madam, you had to keep your lack of experience hidden."

"Yup." Now that it was out there, she felt relieved. "But if you want to sweeten your deal, I'm totally willing."

"Ellie." He looked at her. "I was never taking that deal."

"No?" She didn't want him thinking she was welching. "You should you know because I need to get rid of it anyway."

He stood and went to the window. "You may as well tell me all of it. Why are you running from Jake?"

"I'm not—"

"Ellie..." he growled.

Well, she'd come this far. "Jake wants me to start working the saloon. As one of the girls. He came up with the idea to auction off my virginity."

Cole gaped at her. "Son of a bitch. Shit, Ellie!" He winced. "Beg your pardon for my language ma'am, I—"

"Cole!" She wanted to stamp her feet at him. She wanted to hug him for being a big idiot. "I'm the same girl you flirted with all these years. The same girl you tried to buy for twenty thousand dollars."

He blushed. "Well, obviously that's not going to happen anymore."

"Obviously?" She really didn't see any obvious about it. "I want it to be you. I choose you to deal with this little detail for me."

"Hardly a little detail." He stared out the window.

Ellie's sense of humor rose to the fore. "My girls tell me it's a very little detail. One prick and—"

"Ellie." He glared at her. "Could you give a man the chance to get this all straight in his head before you start the thigh slappers?"

"Sorry.' But she wasn't. Not really, and she grinned.

"But if I'd known what the son of a bitch was up to, I might have shot the bastard," he said.

"Yeah. I might have held him still while you did." It still seemed unreal to her, Jake's plan. "I'm not sure it was his idea. I think Minnie has been whispering in his ear."

If anything, Cole looked angrier. "That's no excuse, Ellie. If Minnie had told him to shoot you and bury the body out back, would he have done that too?"

He had her there, and it was a depressing thought. She and Jake had never been close, but this went beyond that. "Of course, the twins sided with him."

"I'm gonna be honest with you here, Ellie." Cole looked at her. "I don't like your brothers."

"Me neither." And for some reason that made her giggle. "But with your help, I've gotten away from them."

He went back to staring out the window.

As there was nothing out there, and he had that look of a man about to confess to something, she waited.

"Actually, Ellie, this complicates matters a bit more than you think."

Here it came. When one ran a brothel, one got to know men real well.

Cole rubbed the back of his neck. "I'm...ah...not staying in Denver."

"Really?" That could mean many things but the way he was hemming and hawing had her thinking he meant something more final.

"No. I never meant to live out west for the rest of my life. I came out...well, that's a long and boring story." He turned to face her. "Suffice to say I'm heading back east. For good."

It surprised her how much that cut. Cole drifted in and out of her life, but he always drifted back again. This last absence had been the longest one yet. Apparently a much longer absence was to come. "Okay." She nodded. Things weren't dire. She had the money she'd taken, and she knew how to fend for herself. "That's fine."

"I don't think you understand, Sugar." He came to sit again, his knees touching hers. "I'm leaving Denver, which means you'll be there on your own."

She almost laughed at him, but she could see by those compelling golden eyes of his, that he was dead serious.

"Which part of me running a cathouse since I was fifteen made you think I couldn't take care of myself."

"Ah." He reared back and studied her as if he was only now seeing her. "I suppose...well, nothing."

Ellie pressed her advantage home. "And as for you getting all honorable about our deal, I may not have lain with a man myself, but I've seen plenty of it done. And other things as well. Things I couldn't unsee if I tried. As far as I'm concerned the deal stands."

"Ellie." He gave a nervous laugh. "I'm not taking your innocence."

"I lost that years ago." Her virginity had been a burden for a long while now. Finally, she had the chance to get rid of it and move on. Besides, doing it this way beat the hell out of what Jake had planned for her. "In a peculiar way, you'd be doing me a favor."

Cole looked horrified. "That's ridiculous."

"No, it isn't. Nobody expects me to be what I am. And I'd much rather you than some stranger who bought me from Jake."

"Thanks." He gave her a sardonic look. "But that part of this is not up for discussion."

Ellie needed to bring some of her experience to bear. She put her hands on his knees and leaned far enough forward for the neckline of her nightgown to gape.

Cole's gaze went right where she thought it would.

She slid her hands higher up the rock-hard muscle of his thighs and dropped her voice into a husky whisper. "Are you trying to tell me you didn't come here tonight for exactly that reason?"

"Ellie." His gaze grew hotter, and he swallowed. "That's before I knew you weren't...experienced."

"Hmm." She slid closer, dropping to her knees between his

spread thighs. "You don't look like a man who's changed his mind." Her fingers stopped shy of his cock and she pressed her breasts to his chest as she whispered in his ear. "You look like a man who's seen something he wants." She sucked his earlobe and nipped it lightly.

Cole hissed in a harsh breath. "Sugar, you are not playing fair."

"Poor Cole." She teased the strong line of his jaw with her lips. This close, her senses woke to him. Her breasts pressed full and swollen against his hard chest. He smelled like leather and sandalwood soap and she wanted to rub against him like a cat and take that scent on to her skin. If she shifted her hand one inch inward, she could touch him intimately.

His erection tented the front of his pants and nudged her belly. She moved against him and he screwed his eyes shut and groaned. "Sugar."

"Mmm?" She stopped with her lips a breath from his. She wanted to kiss him, but the next step had to be his. "What do you want?"

He gripped her face, his fingers spearing into her hair. Pressing one hard kiss on her mouth, he let her go and stood. "You're trouble, Sugar."

Ellie sank back to her bottom.

"Ellie." His heated gaze licked at her exposed legs. "I would have paid twenty thousand dollars to tumble you. You know I want you, but what you told me." He heaved a sigh. "It changes everything."

After Cole left to his own room, sleep was even further from possible. She poured herself a drink, took it to the window and stared into the dark street.

A lone dog sniffed at the shadows and trotted away

She hadn't been fair to Cole. If Jake found them, he might take his anger out on Cole. True, Cole could defend himself— at least that's what she'd always heard. What if that wasn't anything more than gossip and Jake found them? She'd seen Jake fight, and he was mean and quick, and he liked his knives.

When she'd arrived at Cole's hotel room that night, she'd been alone and scared and not really thinking straight. She and Cole might have known each other a long time, but if they collected all the time they had actually spent together, it probably wouldn't even fill up a small pail. They were certainly not the sort of friends who demanded favors from each other. Cole had agreed to help her thinking one thing, and now she'd gone and changed the dang rules on him.

That was not fair play. But she could fix it. In the morning, she would thank him for his trouble, pay him what she owed him and be on her way. She already knew where Theo had gone. It couldn't be too hard to find him. Theo was not the sort who got overlooked either.

And that was the plan, until she stood outside Cole's door the following morning. A woman's giggle from inside stopped her before she could knock.

Well, Cole sure hadn't hung about waiting for her any. Not that she had any right to get jealous about it. Cole and she were...she didn't really know what, but they weren't what was happening inside his room.

Turning about, she grabbed her bag and headed down the stairs.

CHAPTER
NINE

Cole needed coffee, and he needed it before he dealt with his newest screwup. What was his thing with charging in and rescuing the damsel anyway? Somewhere between leaving Ellie's room last night and this morning, he'd picked himself up another damsel. The details were still hazy.

Ellie was one thing. He liked Ellie, more than liked Ellie, last night's unwelcome revelation aside. A virgin posing as a brothel madam was a real head scratcher. Ellie hadn't posed as a madam; she'd been one. When they caught up with fucking Theo, Cole had some hard questions for him.

"I like cakes." Bridget, his latest poor decision, bounced on his bed and giggled. "I was never allowed to have cakes at the saloon because they didn't want me getting fat."

At least Ellie knew when to stop talking, and she didn't have Bridget's high, breathy voice that drilled a hole in your ear. "We can get you cakes."

Right after he found the coffee and tossed it down his gullet.

"Yay!" Bridget clapped and squealed.

It ricocheted through his sore head.

Bridget's smile reminded him of why he'd taken it into his head to rescue her in the first place.

Cole had seen more lovely women than he could rightly remember, but Bridget had them all beat. With wavy, chestnut hair and indigo eyes, she was soft in all the right places and willowy in all the others. Her skin was a delicate pink and white confection that looked too perfect to be real. Pairing her beauty with her sad life story had brought out his knight in tarnished armor.

There was something vulnerable and fresh about Bridget that reminded him of Ellie. Both Ellie and Bridget had these airs of being delicate blooms in a shit heap. He didn't know how Ellie had held on to her freshness all these years, but she had.

When he had refused to take Bridget upstairs at the saloon, the owner had come over and proposed a poker game. Three hands later, and Bridget was his. At the time he'd wondered why the man would part with a treasure like Bridget. He had brought her back to his room and given her the bed while he made do with the floor. An inkling of the reason behind the saloon owner tossing Bridget into the pot was creeping past his hangover.

"I like all cakes." Bridget bounced on the bed, squeaking the springs. "I like the pink ones and the ones with raisins in them. Oh!" Her eyes widened and she bounced faster. "I especially like the ones with little sugar flowers on the top." *Squeak, squeak.* "I like chocolate cake—" *squeak,* "—and lemon cake—" *squeak,* "—and I think marble cake is real pretty. How do you think they do that?" She blinked up at him, mercifully giving the springs and his head a rest. "Make the two different colors sit in the same cake?"

"Magic," he whispered, a drowning man.

"I like pies as well," Bridget told him. "Not as much as I like cakes, but pies are so pretty. They go that lovely golden color when they're baked. Strawberry is my favorite pie because strawberries are pink and that's my favorite color." She frowned and Cole hoped she'd run out of words. "Maybe strawberries are more red than pink. Do you think strawberries are red or pink?"

"Eh."

"You're right." She giggled. "They're red not pink, but when you cut them open, they can be a little pink inside. Mostly white but a little pink."

Coffee! Now! "Let's get Ellie and see if we can find those cakes."

"Yes." She popped to her feet and grinned at him. It was such a ridiculously beautiful smile it made his head reel when Bridget used it. "Let's go find Ellie."

She stood by the door waiting as he shrugged into his coat and strapped on his gun belt.

"Ellie is such a pretty name. Is Ellie pretty like her name?" Bridget followed him into the hallway.

"Yup." Ellie was more than pretty. She had strength to her, substance that made her beautiful.

Bridget stopped and chewed her lip. Pearly white teeth gnawing at her plump, rosy lip, and all Cole could think about was getting Ellie and coffee. "Women don't like me. They're mean to me. The girls at the saloon used to pull my hair and try and push me down the stairs." Her eyes filled with tears. "One of them even tried to cut my hair off when I was sleeping."

Those indigo eyes swimming in tears could bring a hard-ened Comanchero to his knees. Cole patted her shoulder. "Ellie isn't like that. She'll like you fine." Ellie might gag Bridget to stop all the chatter, but she wouldn't be jealous. Come to think on it, he might gag Bridget and end his torment.

He knocked on Ellie's door and waited.

"Blueberry," Bridget said and wrinkled her nose. "I'm not partial to blueberry. They stain your teeth."

If there was a god in heaven, Ellie would open her door. Soon.

"Most people like peach, and I do too, but strawberry is still my favorite. Do you know why?"

What the hell was Ellie doing in there? "Because it's pink?"

He got a glittering smile for that. "Yes. Although strawberries might be more red than pink."

He hammered at Ellie's door.

"She ain't there." A maid came around the corner.

Cole turned his attention on the older woman.

Open-mouthed, the woman was staring at Bridget as if she'd seen an angel.

"Where is she?" He stepped between the maid and Bridget.

"Huh?" The woman blinked him into focus. "Oh, that one?" She jabbed a thumb at the door. "I don't know where she went, but she paid and took her stuff."

Everything in Cole went very still as he grappled with the new information. "She paid and left?"

"That's what I said." The maid lumbered past him and into Ellie's room.

It was empty. The bed neatly made and wash water still in the basin. He threw open the wardrobe, praying the maid had lied to him, and found it empty. No sign of Ellie remained in the room other than the faint scent of roses.

"Where is she?" Bridget peered over his shoulder.

"I don't know." But he felt like he might puke.

Bridget stuck her ass in the air and checked under the bed. "Is she hiding? Is this a game?"

"No and no." Cole fought down the wave of panic and went back to the maid. "Did anybody come for her? Did you see any men around?"

"I didn't see nothing." The maid got squinty-eyed and heaved a breath that lifted her ample bosom. "All I know is that I'm to clean this room because nobody is in here anymore."

"Shit!"

"There ain't no call for that sort of language." The maid looked scandalized.

Bridget gave him an apologetic smile. "I don't mind. Much."

"Hey!" The maid drew herself up. "This is a respectable place here. You said that other woman was your sister. If she's your sister how come you don't know where she is?"

"We don't like to speak of it." Cole thought fast. "She always plowed her own row, our Ellie."

The maid sniffed and eyed Bridget. "I suppose she's your sister too?"

"No." Bridget giggled. "I—"

"My cousin." Cole held the maid's dubious stare. "She's our cousin. On our mother's side." He needed to get Bridget out of here. She was looking like she might speak again. "Now, if you'll excuse us. I need to find my sister before she gets into trouble."

"You don't look nothing alike." The maid followed them into the hall.

"I don't know about that." Thank God for a lifetime of perfecting the bluff. "We have the same mouth and face shape."

The maid eyed him and then Bridget. "I suppose so."

Bridget blinked at him as if trying to piece it all together.

Taking her arm, Cole sidestepped the maid. "Good day to you."

"Yeah, bye." The maid went back into Ellie's room.

Last night when he'd left her, Ellie had seemed fine. Fine for that awkward as hell conversation they'd both had, but still fine.

It still made his head spin. It was a helluva secret to keep all these years. It didn't seem likely Jake had been able to remove her from the hotel with nobody being any wiser. Not likely, but he couldn't ignore the possibility it had happened.

"What about my cakes?" Bridget stopped when he tried to lead her past the dining room.

He counted to ten for patience before turning to her. "We can get you cakes later. Right now, I have to find Ellie."

"But..." Tears spilled down her satin cheek. "I like cakes, and you said we could have cakes."

"Look, Bridget. I need to find Ellie." He used a firm tone to impress on her the seriousness of the situation.

A matron and a younger woman approached the dining hall.

Bridget hiccupped a soft sob. "But you promised I could have cake."

"Dear Lord, man." The matron stared down her nose at him. "The girl has to eat." She stopped suddenly and glared at him. "Why did he promise you cakes? What did he get from you?"

"Oh, nothing." Bridget gave her a sunny smile. "He's been ever so kind to me and not even asked for a thing. Last night he—"

"You're right." Cole steered her into the dining room. "I promised my young cousin cake, and cake I should get her."

"She doesn't look like your cousin." The matron scowled.

"We have the same mouth," Bridget said. "And a slight

resemblance around the eyes." She blinked her sooty lashes over her lovely eyes. "See?"

"Er...yes." The matron gaped at her.

Cole had an inkling the saloon owner had folded a winning hand last night. He would get Bridget her damn cakes and then find Ellie. And they had coffee in the dining room.

To give her due, Bridget ate her cakes quietly and quickly, and he was able to toss down some bills and have her out the door within thirty minutes.

Dust swirled in a dry, baking wind as they made their way down the boardwalk. Not many were out this early, and Cole said a quick prayer of thanks.

A cowboy sauntered past, caught sight of Bridget and gaped. He stood there catching flies as Cole guided Bridget past him.

Another man, dressed like an undertaker, walked right into a horse trough.

Bridget didn't seem to notice, but kept up a steady stream of chatter, which Cole barely paid attention to.

As their morning progressed, Cole's unease grew.

The horses he had gotten for him and Ellie were still at the livery. The stage was not due in until later that day. He marched Bridget to the railway station.

The stationmaster was still on the platform when they got there. "Can I help you?"

"Good morning." Bridget dimpled at the station master.

"I'm looking for a woman." Cole could balance on his head for all the attention the man gave him.

The stationmaster pointed his gnarled old finger at Bridget. "What's wrong with this one?"

"Not like that." Cole grabbed for his dwindling patience. Ellie could be anywhere by now, and he had no idea if she was safe or not. "The one I'm looking for is my sister. We were traveling together."

The stationmaster grunted and stared at Bridget.

Bridget fiddled with the beading on her bodice. He hadn't been paying attention before, but Bridget looked like a whore in that dress.

"She's short, dark hair, brown eyes."

"No, she ain't." The stationmaster stared at Bridget and then seemed to collect himself and scowled. "And if she's your sister, I'm a mule's ass."

Not far from the truth. "I was speaking about my sister. The one who I'm looking for."

"She a whore too?" The stationmaster eyed Bridget like a side of beef.

"No, she most definitely isn't." Cole chose the simple answer to the question. Also, the one closest to the truth in Ellie's case. "And neither is my cousin." He thought fast. "She has an unfortunate tendency to get in with the wrong sort, and this is the result." He indicated Bridget's beaded, low cut evening gown, on which the skirts were so thin they clung to her legs.

He was definitely going to have to do something about that dress.

"Wait!" The stationmaster clicked his fingers. "I did see a woman this morning. She took the first train to Denver."

"Thank you." Cole forgave the man's leering. "When is the next train to Denver?"

"Mornin'" The stationmaster plugged a wad of tobacco in his cheek.

Dammit! He'd already lost so much time. He could ride, but that left him with a problem of Bridget. He turned to her. "Can you ride?"

"What?"

Dear God, what else could he be talking about. "A horse."

"Oh, no." Bridget giggled and smiled.

The stationmaster choked on his tobacco and started heaving and coughing.

"Well, it's easy enough and I always say the quickest way to learn something new is to do it." He liked the sound of that. He might use it again.

Tears sprang into Bridget's eyes. "I'm sorry to be a bother, but I'm scared of horses."

"You can't make her ride." The stationmaster glared at Cole. "You'd be the worst sort of monster to make this pretty, little thang get on a horse when she's so scared."

"I can't help it." Bridget shrugged and looked like a woebegone angel. "I've been scared of them ever since I was a girl."

Which reminded Cole, he didn't know how old she was. Only that she'd been sold into prostitution at thirteen. That's what had gotten him entangled in Bridget's story in the first place. That and the way she had told it to him as if it were the most normal thing in the world.

"I tell you what." He could travel a lot faster without her. "I can leave you in the hotel with enough money for a few days and ride to Denver."

Bridget gasped. "You're going to leave me here?"

"Just overnight. You can catch the train to Denver in the morning."

The stationmaster muttered something dark sounding and scowled.

"I'll ride to Denver and find Ellie. Ellie and I will meet you at Denver station."

"No, you won't." Bridget shook her head sending shiny curls cascading down her back. "You'll say that and then you'll leave me there. And I'll be back to having to do what the men want when they pay me."

"No, I won't—"

"My pa said he'd be back, and he never came." Bridget sobbed into her hands.

The stationmaster straightened his shoulders and faced Cole down. "You can't—"

"Gimme two tickets to Denver on the morning train." He almost snarled at the man. Ellie was out there, maybe alone. For the first time he hoped Jake was with her. Jake wouldn't let anything happen to her. Not unless he had orchestrated it at least.

"Are you taking me to Denver?" Bridget's tears dissolved into a huge smile. "With you."

"Yup." If he said anything more, he would cuss a blue streak.

"That's lovely." Bridget bounced along beside him. "And I can have more cakes in the morning."

CHAPTER
TEN

Ellie stared out her window as the train carved a straight line through the parched land. From Denver, she could catch the train to Cheyenne and from there, she could take the train to San Francisco the next day.

Why, in three days she could be with Theo. Not that she expected him to be hanging around the train station and waiting, but she might get lucky and pick up his trail quickly.

She didn't know how long it would take to find Theo, so she bought the cheapest train ticket. Sandwiched between the window and a young cowhand whose boots still smelled sharply of manure, she was almost regretting her decision to be careful with her money.

This was her adventure, her first and only grand adventure. She had money hidden in a special pocket in her drawers, she had a small knife tucked into her boot for protection, and by now, she had seen the worst men had to offer.

The young cowhand glanced at her and smiled.

Ellie nodded back, polite but not encouraging.

Across from her, a rough sort with unkempt hair and a beard looked and smelled like he was sleeping off the night before.

Next to the rough, a young mother dealt with her fussy little one, and a slightly older child who refused to sit still. She managed her children while trying to maintain the scant inch of space between her and the tough.

The rest of the carriage was full and the press of so many bodies made her hope some folks would be getting out along the way.

The conductor came around and took their tickets. A young man with a dapper mustache and a neatly pressed uniform, he stared at Ellie and then her ticket. "You traveling alone, miss?"

"Missus." She hadn't thought of that. Being a whore meant nobody expected you to be respectable. "Mrs. Ephram Pierce."

The conductor gave her a hard stare but handed her clipped ticket back to her.

The cowhand took his hat off and perched it on his knee. He cleared his throat. "Mister Pierce back in Denver then, is he?"

"Er...no." Jake always said when you were going with a lie keep it simple. "He's in San Francisco. I'm meeting him there."

"He must miss you." The cowhand blushed. "I mean... pretty wife like you. Man wouldn't..." He cleared his throat and nearly mangled the brim of his hat.

Ellie took pity on him. She knew men like this. He was a harmless sort with a sweet heart. "He does. But I'm not sure when he's expecting me. We were not entirely sure which train I would come in on."

Across the aisle, the baby started to wail, and his mama rocked him against her shoulder.

The tough guy grunted and shifted. A waft of stale whisky

and beer crossed the aisle, and Ellie gave the mother a sympathetic smile. His smell must be even worse being that close.

"My ma will be meeting me at Bitter Root." The cowhand gave a shy grin. "She's bringing Miss Rebecca with her."

"Miss Rebecca?" Ellie warmed to him as his blush deepened. "Is that your sweetheart?"

The cowhand's face flamed. "Not yet, but I'm aiming to fix that. Ma and me got a sweet spread north of town. It ain't much yet, but I been working on larger ranches, figuring the rights and the whatnots of ranching." His chest puffed with pride. "I'm about ready, I reckon."

"You a cowboy?" The little boy from across the aisle stared at the cowhand.

"I was." He held out his hand to the boy. "Name's Matthias Groenwald, former cowboy and now rancher."

"You stink of cow shit." The rough spoke from beneath the lowered brim of his hat.

The young matron gasped and tried to get another half inch away from him.

"That's as may be." Matthias straightened. "But that's not the kind of language for when ladies are present."

The rough grunted and folded his arms. "Sorry."

Like Ellie believed that for a second, but she didn't want Matthias strapping into his armor and taking on the rough. Ellie recognized his type too, and he was not someone she wanted herself or Matthias messing with. The gun butt was worn smooth from frequent handling and his gun belt looked well worn.

"Tell me about your Miss Rebecca." She wanted Matthias to turn his attention to something else.

It worked a charm as Matthias colored up. "She's perfect." He beamed. "She's so pretty and sweet and Ma says she knows her place and how to keep a man fed and his house clean as he could like it."

In another time, she might have been a Miss Rebecca. If she hadn't had the papa she'd had, or the brothers she'd had. Or spent years trailing her father from strike to strike.

Perhaps she could never have been Miss Rebecca. But it did make her wonder if there would have been a Matthias out there somewhere for her. A young man who blushed when he said her name and thought she was perfect.

Cole didn't think she was perfect, and now he knew more about her than anybody outside of her family. It rankled that he had barely waited for her to go to sleep before he must have gone back out hunting for company.

Some men had that thing. They could do what they liked with a whore, but a virgin was untouchable. Well, she'd like to know how they thought a girl went from virgin to whore.

"Pardon, Miz Pierce." Matthias looked at her.

"What?"

"It sounded like you said something."

"Er...no." Ellie fanned herself with her hand. "Just hot, that's all."

The rough stretched his boots out in front of him, which meant Ellie had to tuck her feet under her bench or risk one of those enormous things landing on her foot.

Matthias tutted and shook his head. He leaned forward in the aisle. "Excuse me, mister."

The rough breathed in and out.

"Mister!" Matthias nudged one of his boots. "I'm speaking to you."

Ellie's nape prickled a warning. Matthias had a look on his face that meant he was fixing to interfere.

"It's fine." Ellie gave him a big smile. "I'm perfectly comfortable and he has much longer legs than me.

The rough pushed back his hat and stared at her. "Sugar Ellie!"

Her heart hit her boots and she forced herself not to look at him but to keep staring out the window. Dressed like this, she might be able to get away with pretending she wasn't Sugar Ellie.

"Hey!" He nudged her knee with his boot, leaving a mud smear behind. "I been trying to figure out where I know you from." He chuckled and leered at her. "You're Sugar Ellie."

"Is he talking to you?" Matthias looked at her with concern. "Didn't you say your name was Pierce, Mrs. Pierce?"

That would get her for not using another name.

"She's a Pierce all right." The rough rubbed his palms on his thighs and leered at her bosom. "But she ain't no Missus. Not unless somebody done married her since I was last in the Four Kings."

The matron eyed her like she might strike at any second. She tucked her little boy close to her knees. "Is that a saloon? Is the Four Kings a saloon?"

"Saloon and the best cathouse in these parts." The tough's voice carried through the carriage.

Heads swung their way, gazes alight with interest.

Heat crept over Ellie's cheeks. Beneath her corset a trickle of sweat slid down her ribs. "I'm sorry." She met the rough's eyes and any hope of bluffing disappeared. She knew him and she knew him well enough not to be able to pretend. "Hi, Snake."

Snake Cromer, and a regular visitor to the Kings. At least once a month and some months more. "What the hell are you doin' on this train, Sugar?"

"Sugar Ellie?" Matthias shifted away from her. "Even I've heard of Sugar Ellie."

The situation was rapidly sliding from bad to worse. "I

don't want any trouble." She glanced at Matthias, then the matron and finally looked back at Snake. "I'm on my way to join Theo in San Francisco. He's waiting for me."

"I thought you said your husband's name was Ephram?"

Snake scoffed. "You ain't too quick, are you? Theo is her brother, and she don't have no husband on account of she's a whore."

The word dropped like a filled boot in the silence.

The little boy tugged at his mother's skirts. "Mama! What's a whore?"

"A bad woman." The matron's lips narrowed into a vicious snarl and her eyes bored into Ellie. "A woman of the worst moral character. A godless woman."

The boy started to cry and pressed closer to his mother. "I don't want to be near the godless woman."

"Now, ma'am." Matthias twisted his hat in his hands. "I don't know that I'd go that far. Our Lord thought mighty highly of a certain lady of loose morals."

Ellie's face burned with humiliation. All eyes were now on her. Most were hostile, but others were openly ogling.

"I don't righty know about ungodly." Snake sat back, smirking. "They say a night with Sugar Ellie will cost you twenty thousand dollars, and make you see Jesus."

Gasps rang out across the carriage.

"Trollop." The matron hissed at her. "Hussy."

Snake eyed Ellie from toe to top. "You don't look like there's enough of you to be worth that much money."

Even Matthias was looking uncertain. "Is that true? About the twenty thousand dollars?"

If she looked at the matron again, there was a good chance she'd be turned into a pillar of salt. "It's more a joke. It's not really a thing."

Snake sat forward. "If that's not real, then I got a powerful hankering to know how much you would be, Sugar?"

"God protect us." The matron threw up her hands. "You." She scowled at Snake and then Ellie. "And...her. My children shouldn't be exposed to this."

Ellie heartily agreed. Nobody should have been exposed to this. All she wanted was to get on a train and find Theo. She didn't want any trouble or to bother anyone.

She glared at Snake.

Chuckling, he dug in his pocket and brought out two bits and some twine. "Will this do it, Sugar?"

"No!" The matron surged to her feet. "I should not have to witness such moral reprehensibility. He's offering her money, for..." She gestured Ellie.

"Quite right!" A man with a tremendous bristly mustache stood from further down the carriage. "This is a respectable carriage filled with respectable people. It's not for the likes of them."

"I ain't a whore." Snake looked about him all innocence. "Can't blame a man for taking advantage of what's before him."

"Ah!" The matron clutched her baby and looked about her. "We need to leave this train. At once."

"Now, Madam. Calm yourself." Mustache reddened and squared his shoulders. "It is not you who should leave the train, but her."

And all at once, Snake was not the problem, but she was.

Assenting mutters and snippets of conversation rose from the carriage.

"The audacity of her..."

"Riding this train like she had a right to."

"You'd think she had the decency to stick to her own kind."

I am your kind, Ellie wanted to yell. And how did they think whores got out west in the first place? They didn't crawl out of hell riding a demon. Next time she was buying a hat with a veil, and dressing as a widow. Nobody bothered a grieving widow. In fact, people gave widows a wide miss as if they feared she might spread death.

"I just want to get to San Francisco," Ellie said. "I can sit somewhere else if it makes you feel better." The last to the matron, but the woman wasn't listening. Her cheeks were flushed and her eyes bright with the fervor of her conviction.

"She is selling herself in front of my children."

Louder condemnation came from the other passengers. Some were turning downright nasty.

"She must be removed." Mustache should get into politics, with the way he postured and posed for the other passengers. He had his hands tucked into the placket of his coat and he sneered down his nose at her. "Woman! Get thee to a nunnery."

"I dunno about no nunnery." Matthias shook his head. "And it pains me to say it, Miz Pierce, but you might consider leaving this train at the next stop."

From the building anger around them, Ellie was inclined to agree. She stood and grabbed her bag from beneath the seat.

The matron shrank back as Ellie slid past. "Good riddance!" She spat and hit the hem of Ellie's dress.

"Stop it!" Ellie had had about enough of the uppity bitch. She was Sugar Ellie, and she ran a cathouse of fifteen girls. She kept them and their customers in line on a daily basis. Pinning the woman with a deadly stare, she dropped her voice for the woman only, "I'm leaving the train at the next stop, but if you spit at me again, I'll show you how I deal with unruly whores."

Which was the last thing she said until she was standing

underneath the lean to and shack that served as the train depot for Silver Creek. Despite the fancy name, Silver Creek consisted of one dusty street fronted by some ramshackle buildings interspersed with large, mining town tents. Ellie watched the train until it disappeared over the horizon. "Well, hell!"

CHAPTER

ELEVEN

Ellie ducked the broom aimed at her head and staggered back. She missed the top step, stumbled, and almost fell into the dusty street.

The stout matron wielding the boom raised it again. "You get out of here. I'm not going to tell you again. I don't want your type here."

"I'm not—" But what was the point. News of who she was had gotten off the train with her. Silver Creek only had one boarding house and it was run by the same woman who owned the broom and was glaring at her, arms crossed over her gleaming white apron bib.

Ellie grabbed her stuff and tromped back down the pretty walkway edged with purple flowering bushes. The door slammed behind her.

The dry, dusty main street of Silver Creek shimmered in the noonday heat. Her dark blue traveling dress made it hotter than ever. She trudged down the street and back to the station. At least the heat was bearable beneath the depot. A handful of wooden sheds skirted the tracks, all of them worn but sturdy.

The saloon was doing a good trade for such a small town, and she sat on a crate and tried to come up with what next. No hotel, and the boarding house was out. She could see if the saloon would rent her a room, but it would likely come with a lusty cowpoke attached.

"Hey, Sugar!" Snake yelled from the saloon. He had a group of friends with him and they were all staring at her. "You changed your mind yet? Got a warm bed here for ya."

His friends laughed uproariously and thumped him on the back.

There went her nice quiet rest at the depot, and she stood and walked in the opposite direction from the saloon.

After she'd been dropped from the train, Snake had jumped down after her. He'd gone straight to the saloon, and she'd tried to find somewhere to sleep for the night.

What she needed was a plan, and getting back on the train didn't look possible. The conductor might remember her, and she'd be right back where she started. Silver Creek's livery stable looked as ramshackle as the rest of the town and she didn't fancy her chances on horseback, but she had spotted a sign for the stage.

"Aww, don't be like that, Sugar." Snake trotted after her, his boots making tiny puffs of orange dust. "I'm only trying to be friendly."

"I don't need a friend." Ellie quickened her pace. She particularly didn't need a friend like Snake. Snake liked to play rough with her girls, and Ellie didn't tolerate that. She had almost banned him from the Four Kings several times.

Stopping, she crouched and pulled her knife from her boot. Theo had taught her how to use it. He wanted to be sure if none of her brothers were around Ellie could look after herself.

Snake drew level with her. "You keep this up, Sugar, and I might get to thinking you don't like me."

The rotgut on his breath could bring a cow to its knees. Ellie kept walking.

"Hey." Snake caught her arm and tugged her back. "You're getting me mad, Sugar and you don't—"

"Get your hands off me." Ellie pressed the knife into his throat, right over his pulse.

Snake stilled and dropped her arm.

"I'm gonna drop this knife, and you're going to step back." Ellie pressed the tip into his skin and drew a trickle of blood. "Because if you don't, I'm gonna cut your pecker off. You get me here, Snake?"

Snake nodded but his eyes filled with impotent rage. She needed to make sure he never caught her without her knife.

"Hey!" Boots pounded the sidewalk. "What's going on here?"

A middle-aged man, balding and wearing a deputy's badge drew closer to them. "Is this man bothering you, ma'am?"

"She ain't no ma'am." Snake barely moved his mouth, his gaze transfixed on her knife at his throat. "She's a whore."

Men sure did like to toss that word around, acting like it was dirty when they were quick enough to find one of those dirty whores when they had an itch needed scratching. "He's bothering me all right."

The deputy hitched his gun belt. "Looks to me like she don't wanna be your whore."

"I don't." Ellie took her knife away and stepped back. "I don't want any trouble. I just want to be on my way."

"Get on then." The deputy jerked his head at her. "Me and Snake will have a little chat about some friends of his."

Ellie quick footed it out of there. As soon as she could, she ducked between the livery and the undertaker and got out of Snake's line of sight. It said all she cared to know about Silver Creek that the undertaker was as big as the livery. At the general store, she peered around the corner at the main street.

The road was clear. Snake was either with the deputy or back to drinking with his buddies, and she didn't plan on finding out which. The schedule for the stage was pinned to the outside of the general store. Right in Snake's line of sight.

"You hidin'?" A man spoke from right behind her.

Startled, Ellie turned. A ragged older man with a huge beard and a mane of tangled hair stood behind her. He peered around the corner of the general store. "You hidin' from Snake?"

"You know him?" Ellie slid away from the man. He didn't seem harmful, but she was learning caution the hard way.

The man hawked and spat. "I know you had to draw that little pig sticker to get rid of him." He hauled his threadbare pants up by the rough rope belt holding them. "You'd a been in a whole heap of trouble iffen Shorty didn't come up then." He sniffed. "Problem with them little pig stickers is when you gotta take them away from your man. See, you draw a pig sticker and you either gotta be prepared to stick the pig with it or run real fast."

He had a point. He could also be the solution to her predicament. "Do you know anything about the stage?"

"I know it comes around noon every day," he said. Blue eyes twinkled at her from between his shaggy hair and his beard. "That the kinda thing you looking for?"

"That'll do." Ellie slipped back behind the buildings. Now she needed to stay out of sight until noon tomorrow.

～

ELLIE DIDN'T REMEMBER FALLING asleep, but she woke up in a nightmare. Her head hurt and her belly threatened to revolt any second. Everything was swaying, and she couldn't make it stop.

She must have dropped off again because when she woke a second time her head hurt as much as ever, but her tummy had calmed some. She wouldn't say she was ready for a banquet, but at least her boots were safe.

Where were her boots? Her parts didn't seem to be where they ought.

Hair curtained her face and swished with the ongoing swaying sensation. All she could see was dry dirt beneath her, and it was moving.

No, that was her. She was moving. All except her hands which she couldn't seem to get to obey her. They remained stubbornly behind her back. Something was digging into her wrists—

Her hands were tied behind her back.

And she was moving, because she was on the back of a mule judging by her proximity to the ground and the smell, and she was slung over the beast's back.

She tried to sit up.

A hand pressed between her shoulder blades and kept her where she was. "You settle yourself down there, missy, and everything will be fine."

No, everything damn well wouldn't be fine. Her brain clicked the pieces into place and spat out the conclusion that someone had tied her and flung her over the back of a mule.

Putting the missing pieces together took longer than it should have. It was hard to think with the thumping in her head and the churning in her gut. She'd risked the general store for a loaf of bread and some dried-up apples last nig— she didn't know what time it was, or even what day. Not wanting to be seen again, she'd slipped into one of the storage sheds beside the rail tracks. She'd been tired and the shed warm and quiet. She must have fallen asleep, which is where her recollection ended.

Wriggling her ankles, she found them constricted like her hands were. She was hogtied to a mule with no idea how she'd gotten there.

Her stomach roiled, and her mouth flooded with bitter saliva. She was going to be sick. The constant jostling of her belly was making it so much worse.

She needed to stop or sit up before she vomited. "Please—"

"Now, I told you to bide," the man said. "I don't wanna wallop you again, but I will iffen you give me reason to."

Ellie knew that voice but with her sick belly and her aching head she couldn't think where she knew it from. "Did you wallop me before?" That would explain the nausea and the sore head.

He grunted.

"I'm going to be sick." She forced the words through her gritted jaw. "I need to sit up."

"Whoa!"

Her mule jolted to a halt and sidestepped.

A hand fisted in her hair and yanked her head up. Blue eyes peered out at her from beneath straggly, tangled gray hair. His entire chin was covered in a beard that went down to the middle of his chest. "Don't be getting no ideas about that pig sticker of yorn. I done left it behind."

At least it wasn't Snake abducting her, but then again, maybe she would have been better off with Snake. Better the devil you knew. "Who are you?"

"Are you being smart with me?" He peered into her face. "Saying you're feeling poorly and lying."

Faced with more time slung over the mule, she almost yelled, "No. I really am going to be sick. I need to sit up."

Also if he would let go of her hair, that would be lovely. The yanking on her hair roots was cranking her headache up.

"Huh." He dropped her so suddenly she almost slammed her face into the mule's side.

He walked around to the other side of the mule, grabbed her by the waistband and hauled her off the mule.

Ellie's tied ankles gave, and she fell, the hard earth bruising her bottom, but at least she was upright again. And sitting in the middle of nowhere. The only signs of life were her abductor and two mules. No, three mules, there was another animal laden down with packs behind hers. The air was still fresh and the shadows long, so it must be morning. She had no notion of where the night before had disappeared.

"You gonna puke?" He pushed his hairy face in front of hers.

Was she? Her stomach felt much better now. "Could I have a sip of water, please?"

"Only water I got is for the animals. They need it coz they're working."

"Please?" She'd get on her knees if she had to.

Huffing, he stomped over to his mule and grabbed a water skin that didn't look like it was for the animals. He yanked out the top and handed it to her.

Ellie stared at the water skin helplessly and shrugged.

With a growl, he stomped behind her and tugged at her wrists. Her hands came free in a rush of blood and tingling. When she could feel her fingertips, she took the waterskin from him and wiped the mouth.

Mindful of her belly, Ellie took a careful sip and then another.

"That's enough." He yanked the water skin away from her and jerked his chin at her mule. "You gonna git up there and gimme no trouble?"

"I am." Anything beat her former mode of transport. Ellie struggled to her feet. "Can you untie my feet?"

He looked at her feet and the mule and screwed up his face. "I reckon I can at that."

Unsheathing a massive knife from his belt, he hacked through the rope at her ankles.

Tears popped into Ellie's eyes as sensation prickled back into her legs. She staggered to the mule and hauled herself up. Not giving him a chance to change his mind or bind any part of her again. "I won't give you any trouble," she said. "I don't even know where I am. So even if I did run, I wouldn't know where."

Grunting, he scowled at her for a minute before stomping back to his mule and mounting. "You run, I'll kill ya." He wheezed out a laugh. "Wouldn't be nobody to see it but me and the buzzards."

"I won't run." For now. Ellie got the mule moving. She guessed they were moving south east, which didn't really help her because she had no idea if they had come straight from Silver Creek or whether they'd been moving in circles. She also had no idea how long they'd been traveling. Still, she tried to take careful note of the landscape around her.

She cursed her stupidity for setting out on her own, and as the afternoon wore into evening, and her bottom ached more, she cursed Jake for being the reason she'd run in the first place.

Cole would be in Denver by now, getting on with his life. At least she could rest easy in the knowledge she wouldn't cause him any more trouble.

TWELVE

Cole had never seen a woman who could draw stupid out of near enough everyone. They had a couple of hours to kill before their train this morning and he'd taken Bridget to the general store to get her a couple of readymade dresses.

The pink floral thing Bridget had on now delighted her. Standing in front of the mirror, she beamed at her reflection and swished it this way and that. He already knew, sweet as she was, Bridget was not the sharpest knife in the drawer, but as for the rest of them...he shook his head.

The general store owner sat behind the serving counter and stared like he'd seen God. His wife was no better, giving Bridget free candy and a bonnet. Even the morning's customers had stopped their shopping and stared at the beautiful girl admiring her dress.

Because that was the damnedest thing about Bridget. As breathtaking as she was, she wasn't even looking at herself. It was the dress she was loving on.

"We'll take that one and anything else you have in her

size." Cole had to rap his knuckles on the counter to get the storekeeper to look at him.

Beneath his unkempt iron brows, the man stared at him. "What did you say you was to her?"

"Cousin." He dropped a handful of eagles on the counter and Bridget was momentarily forgotten. "Add whatever else she'll need for the journey into that valise you have behind you."

The shopkeeper's wife was tenderly placing a bonnet on Bridget's head.

"Give me a bag of those candies as well." Cole pointed to a jar of brightly colored sweets. Bridget, he was learning, would do almost anything for sugar. The thought made him shudder.

The shopkeeper bundled up everything Bridget would need for a journey, and Cole pried her away from her loving audience.

"You take care now." The shopkeeper's wife got teary eyed. "You're a good girl and you remember that."

"I will." Bridget twinkled at the woman. "Thank you ever so much for helping me. I've never had such a pretty dress before."

"And I've never dressed anyone so pretty before." The woman patted Bridget's cheeks. "That skin." She snatched her hands back. "Like silk."

Cole gripped Bridget's elbow and hustled her toward the door. "Come along, cuz. We've a train to catch."

He kept them to a brisk pace on the walk to the train station. The candies were a savior and she marched by his side contentedly munching and looking about her, wide eyed as if she was seeing everything for the first time.

The station was busier than it had been yesterday, and Cole swore. Already heads had turned their way and gazes were locked on Bridget. He should have gotten her a bonnet with a veil on it or something.

For her part, Bridget was happily sorting through her candies and eating all the red ones first.

The train was already in, and Cole led her to their first-class cabin and sat her down. He wanted to find the conductor and confirm Ellie had been on this train yesterday. Last night he'd lain awake thinking about where she might have gone, and the only conclusion he could reach was that she'd gone to San Francisco to find Theo on her own. When Cole caught up with her, he intended to ask her what the hell she thought she was doing, but he had to catch her first.

He put Bridget in her seat. "You need to stay here."

"All right." Bridget beamed at him. Eyes that blue really didn't belong on this earth. "I won't move."

"Not even if you see something you really want to look closer at." An unfortunate incident the night before with a three-legged dog and some drunk cowboys had nearly ended in his first gunfight in years. "And especially don't go anywhere with anyone who offers to give you something."

She blinked at him. "Like what?"

"Like anything." Dear Lord, the mind went all kinds of places.

Bridget chewed on her puffy bottom lip. "But what if it's something I really, really want."

"Then you make a note of it, and you tell me, and I'll buy it for you."

"Make a note?" Bridget frowned, and Cole swore the sun must have dipped below the horizon. "I can't write."

"Then you take a picture with your mind so you can tell me when you next see me."

A young man dressed in a stiff suit with his hair slicked

back stepped into their carriage. He caught sight of Bridget and stopped moving. Owlishly he blinked at her.

"Get on with you." A tiny woman dressed all in black poked the smitten man in the back. "Stopping in the middle of the way like a fool."

The man jumped and stepped aside. "Sorry, Nana."

"What has you all—" The woman's beady black eyes locked on Bridget. "Ah. Now I see."

And Cole saw an opportunity.

"Excuse me, madam" Older women loved him. He threw her his most charming smile. The sort of smile that said he had a problem and she was the only woman on earth to help him. "Might I have a word?"

"Who are you?" She locked her harsh gaze on him and swept him from head to toe.

"Cole." He bowed. "Cole Mansfield."

"Cole Whisky Mansfield." The young man turned his big eyes to Cole.

Nana sniffed. "Sounds like a no-good gunslinger name to me."

"I don't go by that anymore." He did his best to look repentant. "I had a colorful youth."

"Huh." She waved her parasol at him. "We don't have time for your kind. Out my way."

"For certain." He stepped aside. "Only I have an urgent question for the conductor and I'm reluctant to leave my young niece without a chaperon." He leaned closer and whispered, "She's very young and easily influenced."

"Light skirt, is she?" Nana glared at Bridget.

"Nothing like that." Cole added a touch of admonishment to his tone. "But you can see how it is."

Nana looked at her grandson, who was staring at Bridget, who was staring out the window and eating candy.

"Would you keep an eye on her until I get back?" He threw in all the charm he could muster. "I hate to impose, but I am in a dreadful bind here."

"She doesn't look like your niece." Nana was not going to give over easily.

Bridget turned their way. "Not so much." She smiled. "But a little around the mouth and shape of our faces." She batted her lashes at Nana. "I look like my mother."

"Where is your mother?" Even Nana couldn't hold out against a full frontal Bridget assault.

Bridget's lips trembled. "She died. But I was very young, so I don't really remember her."

"My sister." Cole dropped his gaze to his boots and gave a manly throat clearing. "A little older than I. Really more of a mother to me than a sister."

Nana melted like fall mist. "I'll keep my eye on her. My grandson can keep her company."

"Thank you." Cole bowed over her hand and hurried out of the carriage before grandson got himself smitten enough to annoy Nana.

He found the conductor enjoying a cup of coffee with the stationmaster from yesterday.

"You again." The stationmaster grunted. "What you done with your cousin?"

"She's on the train." He dropped a half eagle on the table. "But I'm still looking for my sister."

"Told you I ain't seen her since she boarded the train for Denver." The stationmaster locked on the coin.

Cole pushed it toward him and put another on the table. "The same train I'm now on. I wanted to make sure she was on the train."

"Are you calling me a liar?" The stationmaster bristled.

SARAH EDWARDS

Cole tucked his jacket behind his gun. "I'm not calling anyone anything, but I need to find my sister."

"I told you, she bought a ticket to Denver, where else would she go?"

"I don't know." Cole switched his attention to the conductor. "That's what I'd like to know."

"There were a lot of people on the train." The conductor eyed the coin and grimaced. "How would I remember one in particular?"

"You'd remember this one." Cole added a second half eagle. "Small, black hair, brown eyes. A smile that goes on for days."

The conductor started. "The whore?"

Damn! It looked like he'd found Ellie.

"You said she weren't no whore, and she was your sister." The stationmaster glared at him. "What about that sweet thing you got with you now, fella?"

"My cousin is on the train." Cole pushed the coins at the conductor. "And what I said to you yesterday is true. The woman I'm looking for is my sister."

"That's not what I heard." The conductor snatched up the coins. "She caused such a disturbance I had to put her off the train." He glared at Cole. "If you're fixin' to create a ruckus like she did, I'm gonna put you off the train right here."

"My sister is not a whore." Cole gave the man a frigid stare. He wasn't Joy Mansfield, society grand dame's son for nothing. He'd grown up watching that stare, even been on the receiving end of it a time or two. "And I am quite certain any ruckus created was not done by her."

He palmed an eagle.

The conductor frowned. "Now that I think on it. It weren't none of her doing. She was sitting there and some range tough starts asking her how much."

A cold, hard rage tightened his belly. "What happened?"

He flipped the eagle through his fingers.

"Had to put her off the train." The conductor watched the coin. "Not that I wanted to, mind, but the other lady on the train was getting herself all bothered."

"Where?"

"Where what?" The conductor's gaze bounced with the coin.

Cole suppressed the urge to hit the man. "Where did you put her off the train?"

"Small town about halfway to Denver called Silver Creek."

"Are we going to Silver Creek now?"

"We go past it." The conductor leaned forward. "But we don't stop."

"We'll stop there today." Cole set the coin spinning on the table. "Won't we?"

The conductor slapped his palm over the spinning coin. "We sure will."

THIRTEEN

Women were trouble, and Cole was rapidly reaching the point where he needed to punch something.

"When we find Ellie, do you think we could buy a cow?" Bridget giggled. "Or a goat. I really like goats."

He'd buy her the moon if she'd shut the hell up.

"We had a goat when I was little. I was scared of him, because he could eat—"

Cole refused to listen to any more of the stream of drivel coming out of Bridget's mouth. The girl was sweet enough, but nothing happened between her brain and her mouth. She thought it, she said it, and that was that.

Trudging through Silver Creek with Bridget on his heels, chattering away like she never took a breath, he was seriously evaluating the impulsive decisions that had landed him here.

It all started with Sugar Ellie and her big eyes and wicked smile. If it hadn't been for Ellie arriving at his hotel room door with her story—had it really only been a handful of days since Rattler's Gulch?—he would already be in Denver right now, sitting with a huge whisky in his hand as he divested the last of his properties and businesses this side of the country.

He'd only planned to visit Rattler's Gulch for a day or two, say his goodbyes to that part of his sorry life, and then it was back to New York City for him. He hadn't set foot in the place in over twelve years. Twelve years in which he'd had plenty of time to regret the stupidity that had gotten his ass on a train and sent out west.

He stopped at the one boarding house in town.

Bridget almost ran into his heels. "Is Ellie here?"

She'd taken to speaking about Ellie like they were best friends.

"Maybe." Cole opened the neat wooden gate. "I want to go in and see if they've seen her."

He didn't want to jinx it by saying, but he would dearly love to open that door and find Ellie sitting in the front parlor sipping a cup of tea. Although she didn't strike him as the tea drinking type. Then again, she hadn't struck him as the virginal type either.

"Can I help you?" A stout middle-aged woman wearing a bright white starched apron opened the door to their knock. She took him in and then Bridget. "This is a respectable house."

"And my niece and I are respectable folk." Cole gave her his most winning smile.

She eyed him askance.

Yeah, it wasn't much in the way of a winning smile. "Actually, we're looking for a relative of ours."

"Your sister, I presume." The matron pursed her lips.

"Actually, yes." Bridget stepped forward. "Well, she's my aunt and not my sister." She gave a tremulous sigh. "She couldn't be my sister, could she? Not with Cole being my uncle and Ellie being his sister." She took a breath and peered around the matron into the house. "You have pretty flowers on your walkway. I hope you don't have a goat because it would eat them."

"Eh?" The woman threw him a desperate glance. "No, that is, I don't think so."

"There was a misunderstanding on the train my sister was traveling on." Cole took the gap while the woman was still reeling from the combination of Bridget's beauty and her unintelligible statements. "She was put off the train here, and I'm desperately trying to find her. It's not safe for a lady all—"

"The whore!" The woman puffed up like a gobbler. "You're talking about that whore, and she isn't your sister." Her scathing glance swept over Bridget. "And I'll eat my best bonnet before I believe this one is your niece."

Bridget's eyes filled with tears. "Ellie is not a whore."

"That's the one." The woman flapped her hands at them. "Now you get before I call Shorty to deal with you." She eased the door closed. "I don't want none of you here. Not that fancy whore standing here bold as brass yesterday and not you either."

Cole stared at the shut door and breathed deep. The desire to get out his gun and shoot the fucking thing open again almost got the better of him. He'd had a gut load of rude, judgmental people and he'd like to teach them a bit of Christian charity by sending them to meet Jesus face to face.

"Oh, dear." Bridget sighed and touched his arm. "Never mind. She's probably angry because she doesn't have a goat, and at least we know Ellie was here now."

"We do?" God, he'd been so mad he'd almost missed the most important detail. "We do." He turned and made it halfway down the path before he couldn't resist any longer.

He strode back to the door and hammered on it. "Lady! You open this door, or I'll shoot it open."

"No." The woman squealed and cracked the door an inch. "I've got a rifle."

"And I've got this." Cole palmed his Colt. "And you better pray I find Ellie in one piece, or Colt and I are gonna be back and we're gonna get really well acquainted."

"I don't—"

Cole tapped the barrel on the door. "You hear me, lady?"

"Yes." She closed the door and the lock tumbled.

Cole already felt better. He straightened his hat and headed into the road.

"Which way do you think she went?" Bridget stood with her hands on her hips and looked this way and then that.

And *snap* his moment of triumph vanished.

There wasn't much of Silver Creek. A saloon, the boarding house, a general stone and sheriff's office on this side of the road and a bank, two churches, an undertaker beside the livery, and a huddle of houses on the other.

He could rule out the churches, not because Ellie wouldn't go there, but because he'd bet she'd had a gut now of being called a whore and tossed out of places.

She would never go near the sheriff and knew better than to enter a saloon. Cole headed for the general store. A notice pinned to the board outside stopped him.

Of course, she wouldn't want to risk getting back on the train, so she must have taken the stage, which meant she'd bought a ticket inside.

Telling Bridget to wait, he went in to enquire, and was back sooner than he'd thought he'd be. Ellie hadn't been seen in the general store.

Bridget, of course, had made a friend. An earnest faced farmer's son was trying to press a bunch of carrots into her hands. "They're the sweetest we ever had."

Cole gave him points for creativity.

Bridget went bright red. "I'm sorry, I don't like carrots."

The kid's heartbreak almost slayed him, and Cole hurried to the rescue.

"Those are some fine carrots, son." Not a thing he'd ever thought he'd say. "But best you keep them for selling. I bet you could get a pretty penny out of those."

"I could." Bridget's bucolic swain wavered, gaze on the carrots. "But I have a whole cartload out back."

With visions of a cart of carrots following him for the rest of his days, Cole tugged Bridget away. "Best you get to selling then."

"I don't like carrots," Bridget whispered. "They make my teeth orange."

Cole nearly asked how she came by that knowledge, but the idea she might tell him stopped him short. "Come on. Ellie didn't get on the stage."

"Oh, I know." Bridget beamed at him. "She was seen behind this very store." She pointed at it. "She was talking to Pigeon."

"She was talking to a Pigeon?"

Bridget giggled. "Not a pigeon, Pigeon. It's a person, and he's very dirty." She looked at him.

Cole hadn't a clue. Not a one.

Bridget sighed. "He's a trapper that lives around here. They call him Pigeon because he's always picking up scraps."

"Who told you this?"

"Zeke." She blinked at him.

He could swear he'd been inside the store less than five minutes. "Who is Zeke?"

She rolled her eyes at him. "Zeke works for the railroad. He saw a pretty girl with dark hair, like you said Ellie looked, creeping around the store." She leaned in closer and whispered, "He wouldn't have noticed, only she was behaving strangely, and he stopped to have a look."

There were times when you had to bow to the inevitable and Cole motioned her to continue.

"Well, first he sees Ellie and he was about to go and ask her if she was all right, when Pigeon got there and started talking to her."

"Did Zeke see where she went?"

Bridget shook her head. "No." Then she brightened. "But Abel did."

Five minutes in the store, five and a half, at the most.

"Where did Abel say she went?"

"Down there." Bridget pointed to a line of shacks beside the railroad. "He saw her creep into one of them."

The way this search was going, Cole knew he wouldn't find Ellie still there, but he went anyway.

This time he left Bridget outside on purpose. Who knew what more she could pick up?

The inside of the hut was dark and hot. Sacks were stacked up against the back wall. The top sacks were sunken as if somebody had lain there. A boy or a small woman.

Cole examined the shack. Not knowing what he was looking for but desperate enough to hope for something. A flash of color caught his eye and he bent. A green apple lay in the dust beside an already eaten apple core.

He kept looking. "Yes," he whispered. Finally, a solid clue.

Half hidden beneath the sacks was a purse and one he'd seen in Ellie's hands. Opening it he found a stash of bills and a handful of double eagles. He tucked it in his coat pocket. Ellie was too smart to have left without her money.

Outside a young man with a round, scrubbed face and a fuzz of yellow hair stared at Bridget with adoration.

They both turned when he left the shack.

Bridget smiled and pointed. "This is Zeke."

Cole shook the man's hand and instantly regretted it. Zeke had a wet, limp handshake.

"I was asking the lady what to do about the bag." Zeke colored to his receding hairline.

If Ellie had left her bag, it meant she had intended to come back for it. His gut got to tingling with that bad feeling. "You mean Ellie left her baggage with you?"

"Sure did." Zeke nodded. "But she only left two bits for me to keep it for the rest of the day. Then she didn't come back for it."

His first real connection with his illusive, small runaway. "We'll take the bag."

"Only. There's money owing on it. Because like I said, she only paid me—"

Cole was going to grind his teeth to stubs at this rate. "I'll pay you the money owed and take the bag."

Relief flooded Zeke's face.

He followed Bridget and Zeke to the small railroad office and waited while Zeke went into the back and brought Ellie's carpetbag out.

Outside again, with the entirety of Silver Creek stretched in front of him, and Ellie's bag at his feet, Cole was flummoxed.

Ellie had been in the shack, but he had no idea where to start looking now.

Footsteps scuffed behind him and he spun, hand on his gun.

A wizened old man in a buckskin shirt with long dark hair stood gazing at Bridget. He jabbed his thumb at her. "This one yours?"

Bridget looked at the man and then Cole. "This is Abel."

"She's my niece," Cole said.

"How much do you want for her?" Abel eased closer to Bridget.

So tempting, but even he wasn't that much of an ass. "She's not for sale."

"For anything." Abel got a crafty look in his dark eyes.

Cole let this play itself out. The gambler in him recognized in Abel a man who thought the deck stacked in his favor. "What are you offering?"

"Information." Abel grinned showing the gums where his front teeth should have been.

"What makes you think I need information?"

"That." Abel pointed at Ellie's bag. "And you been asking about the other gal what got off the train yesterday."

So much for bluffing. "You know where she is?"

"Know where she might be?" Abel peered out the corner of his eye at Cole and wheezed a chuckle through his tooth gap. "Iffen the price was right."

"She's not for sale." Cole shifted his coat away from his gun butt. It had been years since his last gun battle, but he wouldn't back down. At the slightest sign of fear, Abel would take him on. "But how about you tell me what you know, and I'll decide what it's worth."

Abel eyed his gun and licked his lips. "What's in it for me?"

"Your neck." Cole smiled. "You get to keep your head decorating it."

"I think Pigeon has your woman." He glanced at Bridget, and then said sullenly, "Your other woman that is. What do you need two for anyways?"

"What makes you think Pigeon has her?" Cole hardly dared hope.

Abel scratched his head. "Saw Pigeon light out first thing." He shrugged. "Had himself something flung over his mule what might have been a woman."

Cole had to take a minute to breathe deep. "Was she...is she..."

"Dead?" Bridget's eyes went huge as she gaped at Abel. "Did he kill her?"

"Why would he bother to tote her on his mule if she were dead?" Abel gave them a look loaded with scorn. "Only reason to give up room on your mule would be for a live woman."

The relief made his vision swim and Cole drew in two deep breaths before he could speak. "What makes you sure it was a woman and not some supplies?"

"I don't know me any supplies what got long black hair and wears them dainty little button up boots."

FOURTEEN

E ven though riding astride the mule beat the hell out of being carted over its back, Ellie was ready to do anything if she could only stop moving.

Last night, he'd tied her to a tree, and she'd gotten as much sleep as she could. Between her fear of the trapper, the wild animals, and her back aching from the tree bark, she can't have managed much more than an hour total. They had traveled all day. The trapper led her in circles, and as she got more and more tired, Ellie gave up on trying to remember landmarks and concentrated on not collapsing in a puddle of tears.

Every bone in her body ached from the ride, and her head still hammered. The only water she got was the occasional sips the trapper allowed her, and that only after she begged.

As the afternoon waned, they climbed the arid hills to the tree line. Air got trapped amongst the big trees rising on either side of them, and Ellie felt like she was being baked. There was no trail, but the trapper wound them around and through the trees as if he knew where they were going.

With sunset, the heat dropped, and by the time a small cabin appeared in a clearing between the trees, she was shivering so hard her teeth chattered.

The cabin door opened, and a man stepped out. He drew closer, eyes on Ellie. "What you got there, Pa?"

He looked like the trapper, only less hairy, a lot younger and cleaner. Actually, he looked nothing like the trapper, and if she hadn't heard him call the trapper Pa, she would never have mistaken them for relatives.

Pa came to stand beside her mule and beamed up at her. He flashed a smile of surprisingly sparkling white teeth. "I brought you a wife."

It must have been her exhaustion because it sounded like the trapper said—

"A wife." The younger man drew closer to her and stared up at her. "She don't speak much."

"She's tired." Pa sniffed. "She may look like a little bit of thing, but she's got gumption." He grunted and went to the other mule. "Once she got over her complaining."

"What complaining?" Ellie had kept her woes to herself all day.

The son eyed her askance. "What if she don't like me, Pa?"

"I reckon she won't like you." Pa started undoing the ropes binding the supplies to the third mule. "Not at first at any rate."

"Why won't she like me?" He looked crestfallen.

"She's new to the idea of marrying you, is all." He hauled a sack off the mule. "Now get her down from there and come and help with these supplies."

The younger man reached for her.

Ellie stiffened and jerked back.

"She don't want me to touch her." He looked to his father.

"Isaac, I swear to the good Lord, you was dropped on your head as a baby." Pa strode over and grabbed Ellie by the waist.

Before she could get a good scream gathered, she was on her feet and he was striding away again.

"If she's to be my wife, I'm gonna need to touch her," Isaac said.

He had a point, and suddenly Ellie found that so hilarious she started to laugh. Her laughter built to the point where her shaky legs wouldn't hold her up and she dropped to the ground.

Isaac stepped back. "She's not right. Why did you bring me one that's not right in the head?"

"Ungrateful whelp." Pa smacked Isaac over the back of the head. "She's in shock, is all. I didn't exactly ask if she wanted to come with us."

Ellie got herself together and glared up at him. "What your father means is that he abducted me."

"Of course he did," Isaac said. "No women want to come up here any other ways."

So much for any help from that quarter.

"She's pretty, and she speaks nice." Pa went back to unloading his mule. "She'll get used to the idea of being here after a time. Best you use that time to woo her right." He glared at his son. "There'll be no forcing a woman under my roof."

Isaac flushed and shook his head. "I wasn't gonna anyhow."

"See that you don't." The trapper jabbed a finger in Isaac's face. "Until the preacher comes round and gets you hitched right. Man's got a right to do what he likes with his wife."

ELLIE WOKE with the sun in her eyes. Sheer exhaustion had gotten her to sleep last night. After they'd finished unloading, Isaac and Pa had led her into the cabin and showed her where she could sleep. The men had bedded down by the fire in the main room and she'd slept in the only bed, in a loft above the kitchen.

The cabin was solid. She'd caught a glimpse of it before she stumbled up the ladder and fell across the bed.

If ever a girl needed a plan, it was her, and she needed one right smart. She had no idea where she was or what direction town, any town for that matter, was in.

Also, she should find out the name of her abductor. His statement that he didn't tolerate forcing a woman had gone no small way to letting her sleep. Until she was safely married to Isaac, and then she was her husband's property. As she saw it, she needed to make sure she was long gone before the pastor headed this way. Whichever way they were.

She stretched and winced as all her aches and pains from traveling reacquainted themselves. As quietly as she could, she crawled to the edge of the bed and peered below. The cabin was empty with two bedrolls still laid out by the fire.

She'd fallen asleep in her clothes, but Pa hadn't seen fit to abduct her with her luggage, so this was all she had. She climbed down into the kitchen.

Outside the windows, chickens pecked their way across a bare yard. To the right, a stand of aspens guarded a small creek. A couple ducks argued their way along the creek bank. To the left, the land had been cleared for planting and Isaac and Pa were swinging picks together.

She didn't know how much time she had, so she put a pot of water on to boil for a wash. She also did the best she could with the stains to her traveling dress. Her coat had taken most of the abuse and would need a wash. A check out the window reassured her that the men were still working, now even a bit farther from the cabin.

A coffee pot sat on the table, and she emptied the dregs, refilled it and put it back on. Needing to keep her hands busy and her brain working, she tidied away the two bedrolls and put them in a nearby chest. Then she swept the floor and cleaned the tabletop. A plan blossomed as she worked. Her best chance of escape was to lull them into trusting her.

When her water was warm enough, she peeked out at her abductors before washing. It was an awkward process involving keeping as much clothing in place as possible and still getting cleaner.

But she did feel better once she was done, and she took the water outside. Behind the cabin, they had staked out and fenced a small vegetable garden and she tossed her water there.

A handful of tomatoes were ripe, and she picked them and went back into the cabin.

She poured herself some coffee, and even knowing it was probably pointless went searching for some milk or cream. Finding nothing, she settled for a dollop of honey and took her coffee to the porch.

Despite being her jailor, Pa had settled on a pretty spot. The cabin rested on a plateau, tucked in the lee of a large mountain. Behind the creek, she could make out where the land dropped into a rocky gorge.

Wildflowers grew in clumps around the cabin, and venturing off the porch, she picked a handful as she sipped her coffee. She walked into the aspen stand. Split pole fences housed three mules and a couple of cows. A herd of goats were roaming free, and she guessed they belonged to Pa and Isaac as well.

They were set up well. Between the livestock and the

garden, they had most of what they needed to survive. Which meant Pa wouldn't need to go into town all that often.

In her experience, men were driven by their balls and their bellies. As she'd stick a knife in herself or one of them before she went the balls route; she would work on their bellies.

Returning to the cabin, she dusted off her rusty house-keeping skills. At the Four Kings, she had sometimes given Pearl a hand, but it had been a long time since her pa had died, and she had kept house and cooked for him and her brothers. She'd done so in a lot rougher places than Pa's cabin as well. She found what she needed to make bread. Someone had a yeast starter going, so either Pa or Isaac baked. Unless they made a habit of kidnapping women and getting rid of them when they had served their purpose.

No good would come of getting into a dither, as Pearl liked to say, so Ellie shoved any lurking scary thoughts deep.

Further exploration unearthed some sort of meat that she popped in a pot with some carrots and onions from a sack hanging behind the door and added her newly picked toma-toes. She put her stew on the stove to simmer. Next, she attacked the cabin. It wasn't dirty, so much as neglected, and cleaning it gave her an outlet for her energy and a way to stave off the looming dither.

She tossed her dirty coat and two grubby shirts she found hanging behind the door in a pail to wash down by the creek.

Trying to escape one situation, she'd landed herself right in the middle of another. Cole would be back in Denver, doing whatever it was he did. He didn't speak much about his busi-ness, but she got the sense he'd moved on from gambling to something steadier.

If she'd taken his offer all those years ago, the first one he'd made to buy her for a night, things might have been very different right now. Cole wasn't the marrying kind, and she wasn't the kind anyone married, but she wouldn't have minded being Cole's woman for however long it might have lasted. She definitely had the right sort of feelings for him, and it would have been a much better outcome than the one Jake had planned or being Isaac's wife.

Then again, she'd never heard of Cole taking his own woman. Maybe all they would have had would have been one night, which still might have been better than her current future promised.

She was taking the bread out the oven when the cabin door opened, and Pa stood in the doorway, braced like he was expecting trouble. Behind him stood Isaac with his pick raised.

Summoning her best Sugar Ellie smile she waved them in. "Come on in. You're in time to get washed up and ready to eat."

Isaac gaped at her, his pick drooping. "What smells so good?"

"Well, I didn't have much." Ellie batted her lashes and simpered. "But I did the best I could with what I had. I hope y'all dig in now."

Not as easily won over as Isaac, Pa scowled at her. "What are you about?"

"Well, it's like my ma said, you can't uncrack an egg." If she remembered her mother, she might have said something similar. Pearl was as close as Ellie'd come to having a mother, and Pearl wasn't one to calmly accept her lot in life, but she was one to plot her way out of a situation she didn't like. Ellie lifted the heavy cast iron pot off the stove. "You must be hungry." She beamed at Pa. "And that I can fix."

Isaac hurried over and took the pot from her. "Let me take that, Miss."

"Why thank you." She dimpled at him.

Isaac blinked.

"Put that on the table before you spill it." Pa yanked out a chair and sat. He jabbed his finger at her. "I'm watching you, missy."

Ellie batted her lashes and dimpled. And she was watching him, and the minute he turned his back she was mist.

CHAPTER
FIFTEEN

Pa was a stubborn old coot; Ellie would give him that. Two days later, and he still kept a hawk eye on her. At night, she would drop into bed exhausted with keeping up the pretense all day. Happy, cheery Ellie, buzzing around and making herself useful was like wearing a badly fitting corset, but one slip and Pa would be onto her. One question out of place, and he would pick up on it.

Tonight, she'd fed them rabbit Isaac had caught, some early corn and mashed potatoes she'd near wore her arm out pounding smooth.

Pa gobbled it all down without a word. Then he held his plate up for more, and Ellie twinkled and simpered and gave it to him.

She was making progress with Isaac, however.

After he'd finished eating, he stood and helped her clear the table. As Pa lit a fire and sat beside it, she washed the dishes and Isaac dried. After, he took the heavy pail outside and emptied it for her.

He was a sweet young man, and any girl would be lucky to

have him. She was not that girl, however, and her conscience did twinge about the way she was leading him on. Isaac wasn't the one who had abducted her, and he was bending every way to make her feel welcome and not threatened.

The oddly comforting smell of Pa's pipe tobacco filled the cabin and Ellie finished putting the dishes and pots from dinner away and wiped the table. She gave the floor a quick sweep and got a basin of water to wash up before bed. If life had worked out differently, this might have been her life: a house of her own, a husband, and maybe his crotchety old father staying with them. It wouldn't have been a bad life, just not the one she had.

Pa grunted. "Girl!"

"Yes."

"You read?"

Ellie untied her apron. The damage to her dress was irrevocable, and if she didn't escape soon, she might need to ask Pa to get her a new one. "Yes."

"Get it." He pointed to an old battered bible on the mantle. "Read us something."

Isaac came back in. He'd filled the pail up for her again and put it by the door. He eyed the book in Ellie's hands. "That's my ma's bible."

"It looks well loved." Ellie stroked the broken and cracked cover.

"And she's gonna read us some." Pa leaned back and puffed a cloud around his head. "Read."

And she did until bedtime. Her captivity could have been a lot worse, but she was still being held against her will. She would only have to try to run out the door to remind herself of that.

Ellie sat at the table and read. She read until Pa started to nod off and then she put the bible away and went to bed.

As had been the way on previous mornings, she woke to an empty cabin. The men got up with the sun and went out to work.

Ellie got on with her chores. First, she prepared the bread to rise. Then she tidied and cleaned the cabin. After that, she collected eggs from the hens. She needed to ask Pa if they could be fenced in. As it was, they laid their eggs all over the yard. After that she milked the two cows and the goat and got lunch ready.

Once Pa and Isaac had gone back to work, she grabbed the pail of clothes and went to the creek to wash them.

She stopped in sight of Pa working in the field. Testing his vigilance, she moved slightly downstream to see how long it would take him to notice he couldn't—

"Girl!"

She popped into his view again. "Yes?"

"What you doing?" He must have sprinted from the field to be close enough to yell at her.

Ellie smiled and held up her pail. "Washing."

"Huh!" He backed off a few steps. "Just see that's all you're doing."

As she washed the clothes, Ellie ventured a little further downstream. She'd count to ten, then twenty, then thirty, and come back into sight again. The coming back was the key. Eventually Pa would stop watching to see if she did, and then she would be gone.

After hanging the clothes on some bushes, she went back to the house to get supper ready. She'd been so young when her father had died, and the boys had expanded their back-woods still into a bar tent. They'd kept her out of sight, and she'd done the kinds of things she did now. There was a comfort in the old routine.

In a world where she could choose, she would have liked

being somebody's wife. She didn't need a rich man, just a hard working one and a good one, a man to work side by side with her and raise a few children. Instead, she had been molded into Sugar Ellie, and she'd gotten used to it. Out here, however, doing the simple life things most women did, she felt more like herself than she had in a long time.

With nobody to talk to, she also had plenty of time to think. When she got away from Pa and Isaac, she would be truly on her own for the first time. Not that being alone scared her. This time she would be smart and become a widow. Nobody looked at widows, and they steered clear of them too. Like they had some dumb notion that the same thing that happened to her last husband would happen to her new one.

Sugar Ellie would die, and the respectable widow Pierce would rise in her stead. And what would widow Pierce do to keep the wolf from the door? The possibilities were endless and exciting, and for the first time in her life, Ellie could do what she wanted. She didn't have to please anyone.

First, though, she had to get away, and Pa and Isaac were stamping the mud off their boots on the porch. There was dinner and bible reading to be got through before she could go to bed and keep planning.

As she was clearing the dinner dishes away, Pa cleared his throat. "Isaac."

"Yes, sir." Isaac put down his stack of dirty dishes.

"Nice night out." Pa jabbed his pipe to the outside. "Take the girl out there and court her."

Damn, but she almost pitied Isaac.

Blushing, he placed the dishes beside the washing tub and cleared his throat. "We could..." He jerked his head at the door. "Walk, or something."

"We could do that." Despite their situation, Isaac was a

sweet man. He'd been shoehorned into this same as her. She took off her apron and laid it beside the washing tub.

Pa grunted and stretched his bare feet to the small fire. "Do it right, boy."

Whatever that meant, Ellie followed Isaac into the night.

A full moon floated in a cloudless night sky, painting the trees and grass silver and blue. Pa was right about it being a beautiful night out.

Ellie drew the fresh, sharp air into her lungs. Maybe the rain they all needed so badly was on its way.

She followed Isaac off the porch and into the yard.

Jamming his hands in his pockets he rocked on his feet. "Where do you wanna walk?"

"Down by the creek?" With the moon so full she could see clearly.

Isaac grunted and ambled along beside her.

Ellie let Isaac lead as they strolled beside the creek.

He cleared his throat. "I'm not much for this woo—"

"Argh!" A figure leaped out from behind a tree. It slammed into Isaac and took him to the ground.

Ellie leaped back.

Cole had Isaac on the ground with his hand at Isaac's throat.

For a moment she stood there and let it sink in that Cole had found her. And he was choking Isaac to death.

"Cole." She tugged on his shoulder. "Stop! You'll kill him."

Cole glanced at her, back at Isaac and punched him.

Isaac's head whipped to the side and he went limp.

Peering over Cole's shoulder, Ellie didn't like the look of Isaac. "Is he dead?"

"Do you care?" Cole put his fingers to Isaac's neck. "And no, but he's out cold."

He climbed to his feet and stood before her. "Ellie."

"Cole." Her was there and real and the relief made her knees sag.

"I'm so glad—" Cole's eyes widened, and he grunted. He gave a shout of pain and crumpled.

Knife raised to strike again, Pa stood behind Cole.

Cole was struggling to regain his feet.

Leaping forward, Ellie snatched Cole's gun from his holster and stuck it in Pa's face. "You touch him, and I'll blow your brains across this yard."

Pa gaped at her.

Cole gaped at her.

"Ellie?" Isaac moaned.

"Not one step closer." Ellie's finger itched on the trigger. Pa would pay in blood for every drop of Cole's he'd spilled. "And you can drop that knife."

"Now, Girl—"

Ellie cocked the gun.

Raising his hands, Pa dropped the knife and stepped away from it. "He was trying to kill my boy."

"I was rescuing my..."

"Sister," a woman said as she stepped out from the tree screen. "Cole was rescuing his sister."

It must be the moonlight because the woman was a goddamn goddess. Ellie had never seen anyone like her. Not even close. Hair turned silvery in the moonlight framed a perfect face. Her skin looked like it glowed from within.

Isaac sat up, shook his head and gaped at the woman.

"Who are you?" Pa stared even more than Isaac.

The woman smiled and got even more beautiful. "I'm Bridget. I'm Cole's niece." Bridget shrugged. "From he and Ellie's much older sister...Patty."

"Ellie." Cole tugged on her skirt. "I can explain, but first I need to stop bleeding."

Pa had stabbed him. Rage quivered through Ellie and she raised the gun again. She'd shoot his dirty trapper head right off his shoulders.

"I dropped the knife," Pa yelped and shoved his hands up again.

Ellie wasn't feeling forgiving. "You stabbed my...Cole."

"I didn't know he was your brother," Pa said.

To be fair, neither had she.

"Miss Bridget?" Isaac hadn't moved his stare from Bridget. "Can I help you get your uncle into the cabin? So as you and she can tend to him."

Bridget looked at Ellie as if asking permission.

"Of course." Ellie motioned Isaac forward with the gun. "Let's get him inside, but if he dies, I'm gonna shoot both of you and enjoy doing it."

"As much as I appreciate the thought, Sugar"—Cole gave her his jaunty half smile, a little strained but still there—"I'd rather stay alive and avoid all the death."

Ellie choked back a laugh that shifted into more sob than anything else. Cole was there, but he'd gotten hurt. "Get him inside."

"You won't be needing that." Pa pointed at her gun.

Like she would take his word for anything. "Who says I won't?"

"Me." Pa jabbed his thumb at his chest. "I give you my word."

"How do I know I can trust your word?" The man must be mad. He'd abducted her.

Pa sniffed. "I never lied to you yet."

Ellie opened her mouth to argue, but he hadn't. He'd knocked her out, slung her over the back of a mule and abducted her. He'd brought her to his backwoods cabin and given her to his son without a by your leave and had her cook and clean for them. He hadn't, however, lied to her. Yet.

"If I put this gun down, how do I know you won't crack me on the head again?"

Pa scoffed. "'Twas nothing but a small tap. Hardly even worth mentioning, and I thought you had no kin."

"What difference does that make?" Dealing with Pa would drive her batty for sure.

"If you had kin, I wouldn't have taken you." Pa sniffed. "I thought you had nobody in the world, like me and Isaac. Didn't seem no harm in all of us having nobody together."

It made an odd sort of sense. Ellie motioned Pa to go first. "Let's get him inside so I can see the damage. Then I'll decide if I want to put the gun down or use it."

SIXTEEN

Ellie had no clue who Bridget was or where Cole had come across her, but she thanked God for the distraction she provided.

Once they'd gotten Cole inside, she'd forced Pa and Isaac out of the cabin. Looking happy as a lark, Bridget had gone with them, which went a long way to making sure Ellie didn't need to use the gun.

She bolted the cabin door behind them and hurried back to Cole.

Wincing, sweating and swearing, he was trying to get his coat off.

While helping him out of his coat, she still couldn't quite believe he was there.

The sight of his blood-soaked shirt brought reality crashing down. Forcing back her fear, she kept her voice even. "Looks like he got you good."

"Uh-huh." Sweat poured down Cole's face, and he'd gone alarmingly pale. "But I don't think he hit anything vital."

Ellie moved to the front of him and got to work on his shirt. "This is going to hurt to get off."

"You'll be fine." He flashed her a parody of a smile.

"Wait here." Ellie marched to the door and yanked it open.

Pa sat on a bench to the side of the door and looked up when she came out. "He dead?"

"No, and you better pray he doesn't get that way." Ellie patted the gun at her waist. "You got anything for doctoring?"

"Behind the dresser." Pa jerked his head inside. "And you can use that liniment. Got it from that half-breed in town. Don't know what's in it but it works."

Like Ellie had any choice. "You have any whisky or anything I can give him for the pain?"

"Nope." Pa folded his arms. "Don't believe in drinking."

"Really." The relief at not having to pretend made her slightly reckless. "But you're good with kidnapping innocent women."

"You ain't innocent." Pa snorted. "I heard what Hattie at the boarding house said to you. You's a whore."

"No. I am not." Ellie relished saying so for the first time in her life. "Hattie had it wrong." And speaking of innocent girls. "Where's Bridget?"

"Down by the creek with Isaac." Pa smirked.

"He better not hurt her." Ellie patted her gun again.

Pa shook his head. "He won't hurt her. He's a good boy. I raised him right."

"Ellie?" Cole's voice sounded weaker. "Can we get this bleeding stopped?"

After shutting and bolting the door, she hurried back to him. "Sorry, I was trying to get you something for the pain."

Cole had managed to get his shirt off. From the front, he looked fine. He looked more than fine with the firelight gilding the dips and swells of his muscular torso and shoulders.

Beneath his fine tailoring, Cole was built like a man who worked with his muscle for a living.

He turned and straddled a kitchen chair, presenting his back to her and all other thoughts fled.

Pa had put two holes in Cole, and Ellie's hand shook as she put the gun on the table. She wanted to march out there and shoot the miserable bastard for touching Cole.

She got some hot water from the stove and poured it into a basin. She added some of Pa's liniment to the water.

Standing behind Cole, her courage faltered. The bleeding had slowed to a trickle, but the wounds needed sewing. "This is going to hurt."

"Do it."

As she wiped away the blood, he tensed, the muscles in his back moving. She drew closer to a wound and he jerked.

"Sorry." Ellie pressed as lightly as she could.

"Talk to me." Cole sounded hoarse. "Distract me."

"Okay." She cleaned away all the excess blood. The wounds were not as bad as she'd initially thought. "I was real glad to see you."

"Yeah?" He hissed in a breath as she cleaned his second wound. "Why did you run, Ellie?"

A question she'd asked herself only a million times. "You were mad after you found out what you found out."

"That you were a virgin?" He looked over his shoulder at her. "And I was shocked, not mad."

"Either way, it meant I'd broken our deal." Ellie dropped a needle into the kettle and let it boil. "I didn't want to cause you any trouble." She located some rough thread and added that to the needle. She'd patched up her brothers a time or two and plenty of saloon brawlers. "I mean, cause you any more trouble. Jake could be looking for me."

"I'm sure Jake is looking for you." He winced as she caught

the edges of his wound together. "But I knew what I was taking on when I agreed to help you."

She should have spoken to him that morning. As she pushed the needle through his flesh, she winced. "I came to your room that morning to tell you I was going, but you were busy."

"Busy?" He grunted and gripped the chairback until his knuckles whitened.

"I heard a woman in your room, and I didn't want to intrude."

Cole cocked his head. "Woman?" And then he nodded. "That must have been Bridget."

Pure, green jealousy gripped her, and Ellie took the next few stitches with it heating her blood. "I see."

Cole snorted. "I can tell by that tone that you don't see."

"Then tell me." She eased up on the last stitch, snipped off the thread and went to work on the second wound. Neat stitches now held one wound together and she took a moment to admire her work.

"I won Bridget in a poker game." He yelled as she jabbed the needle a tad too hard.

"What?" Ellie glared at the back of his head.

"Jesus, Ellie, take it easy back there. It wasn't my idea." He took a deep breath. "I kind of ended up being responsible for her." He tensed. "But not in the way you're thinking. I haven't touched her, and neither will I."

Ellie found that hard to believe. "She's the most beautiful girl I've ever seen."

"Yeah, she is." Cole chuckled. "And in a couple of days, you'll understand exactly why I'll never touch her."

Ellie finished the last wound in silence. She cleaned away any additional blood and smeared more liniment over the sewn wounds. In the doctoring trunk, she found some cloth and tore it into strips.

"Lift your arms." She nudged Cole's arm up and he complied. Getting him all wrapped up meant putting her arms all the way round him and getting close enough to Cole to feel the heat of his skin. Trying to keep her mind on the job, she wrapped the bandages all the way around his middle. Moving to his front, she tied the ends of the bandages and snipped off the excess. Not a bad job, all things considered.

Cole dropped his arms and caged her to him. "Ellie?"

"Yeah."

He searched her face. "Are you really okay? Nothing...terrible...happened to you?"

"No." And then she caught his full meaning. "No. Nothing like that. Pa's good with abduction, but he don't hold with forcing a woman."

Cole let out a breath. "Okay. I still want to kill him, but a bit less now."

His strange whisky colored eyes gleamed at her. Eyes that Ellie had doubted she'd see again. Without thinking any further, she rolled to her toes and kissed him. A gentle touch of her lips to his, an affirmation of them both here and alive.

Cole made a soft sound of approval and his arms tightened around her. He brought his mouth back to hers for a longer press of their lips.

Relief, joy, longing, fear and about two hundred other emotions coming and going so fast she couldn't name them roared through Ellie, and she deepened the kiss.

Cole opened his mouth over hers and touched his tongue to her bottom lip.

Opening for him, Ellie abandoned herself to the taste and feel of him. She'd made up her mind she would never see him again, let alone touch and kiss him. Giving in to the craving for him, she wrapped her arms around his neck and kissed him back with everything she had.

Cole winced and broke the kiss. "Sugar, your timing is truly horrible."

∼

HIS TIMING NEEDED some work as well. He had no business kissing Ellie and letting her get ideas. Cole let her help him into a shirt of Isaac's.

Holding his shirt up, she winced. "I can see what I can do, but I don't think I can get those blood stains out."

"Not to worry." Isaac's shirt was soft from frequent washing and smelled of sun and earth. "I didn't even know you could wash shirts."

"Anyone can wash a shirt." She snorted and laughed. "When he was still alive, I used to wash for Pa and the boys."

And her pecker-head brothers had repaid her by trying to sell her virginity to the highest bidder, which was another reason his timing was off.

As tempted as he was, Ellie was not for him. He needed to get her back to Denver and set her up in a business of her own. At first, he'd thought to help her open a brothel, but now he'd make sure she didn't.

Ellie put a fresh pot of coffee on the stove. She wrinkled her nose at him. "I don't suppose you brought clean clothes."

"Actually, I did." He eased back to his feet. His back felt stiff and bruised and he thanked God Pa had not gotten a better angle on his knife thrust. "I left our horses about a mile down the mountain."

"I'll send Isaac to pick them up." She took a lump of sickly white dough out of a covered basin and slapped it on the table.

"I brought your carpetbag as well."

She looked up and blinked at him and for a horrible second, he thought she would cry. "You did?"

"Of course I did." And he felt ridiculously proud of himself for toting a bag. "I wouldn't leave it behind."

"Did it cost you money to get it?" Her face creased into a worried frown. "You need to let me know how much it set you back, and also for the hotels and trains and horses." She sighed and looked at him with those big, big eyes. "I'm sorry, Cole. I never meant to cause you so much trouble."

"I'm glad you did." And he meant it. As a last trip out west, this one was perfect. He could have done without the two holes in his back, but this adventure had him feeling alive again, like he had all those years ago when he'd first stumbled off the stage in Montana City with a gut load of bitter regret and a pack of cards.

Back then he'd been fighting to survive, learning as he went. This adventure with Ellie felt the same. It would be the perfect memory for when he was back in New York, maybe settled next to the fire with Victoria.

Which brought him to reason three, and the clincher, for why he shouldn't be kissing Ellie. His heart was not available and hadn't been since he'd left New York under a massive cloud all those years ago. He'd been engaged to Victoria and counting the days to marrying her. Of course she'd broken the engagement after his father had thrown him out, and he really couldn't blame her, but in his heart, he was still engaged.

Ellie pounded her dough into the table. "I'm so glad you brought my clothes, to be honest." She grinned at him. "It's a bit drafty on the days I wash my drawers."

Cole laughed but it sounded strained because it was. His imagination had flown under Ellie's skirts, hoping to find this a drafty day. That also needed to stop. He liked Ellie too much to trifle with her.

Away from the Four Kings, she looked different too. Without powder and paint and her hair in a simple braid down her back, she looked like the innocent she was. He'd liked Sugar Ellie in the Four Kings just fine, but he liked this version of her too.

"Ellie? Cole?" Bridget knocked on the door.

Ellie went and opened it. "Come in."

"Hello, Ellie." Bridget beamed at her. "I'm awful glad we found you."

Ellie smiled back, and beautiful as Bridget was, it was Ellie's smile that held the magic for him. "I'm awful glad you found me too."

Hat brim clenched in his hands, Isaac stood behind Bridget and cleared his throat. "How's your...um...back?"

"Ellie fixed me right up." Cole resisted the urge to mess with him.

"Isaac says he can help me bring the horses from down the hill," Bridget said.

Isaac stared at Bridget as if afraid she would vanish if he took his eyes off her. Cole sure hoped Ellie hadn't formed any sort of attachment to Isaac because it looked like she'd lost her swain.

Ellie smiled at them. "I was about to come and ask you about that."

"I can show you the way." Bridget smiled up at Isaac.

Isaac grinned back. "Okay."

And they stood there, grinning and staring.

"Now would be a good time," Ellie said, but laughter lurked in her eyes. After the door shut behind them, she turned to him. "Does that happen often with her?"

"Oh, yeah." He had to laugh.

Her expression turned wistful. "She's very lovely."

"That she is." Cole flexed his arm to see how much movement he had. "It wears off fast."

"I don't see how." Ellie punched her dough.

Cole would let her find out for herself. Like their guide who had abandoned them after their first day, swearing he'd shoot her if he had to hear her say one more thing. They would have been here earlier if he hadn't abandoned them with some questionable instructions.

"Ellie." He stood on the other side of the table. "When we get you to Denver, what would you like to do?"

"Do?" She tilted her head. "I can tell you what I don't want to do."

She was so emphatic it made him smile. "Run a cathouse?"

"You got it." Then she sighed and put her dough back in the basin. "I miss my girls, though. I worry about them. Minnie and Jake see them only for the money they can make. They're people, though, and they need caring for more than most." She covered the basin with a cloth. "I don't miss their fights, however. It's high noon any time of the day in a cathouse."

She put the dough on a shelf above the stove. Even in her worn and dirty dress, she made that movement elegant and graceful. Maybe in a different world she could have been a dancer or an actress.

"You have the chance to start again." He eased his leg back over the chair and straddled it. "This is your new beginning."

The smile she gave him was like sun on a cloudy day. "I've been thinking about that."

"Yeah?" He'd pay good money to keep that look on her face.

"I want to open a dress shop," she said. "Not for rich women, there are enough of those, but for girls like me and Bridget. Ordinary women who would like something nice to wear."

That surprised him. "You know how to make dresses."

"I do." She laughed and pointed at him. "You don't believe me but who do you think made all the dresses in the Four Kings."

Cole shrugged. "I never gave it much thought."

"Nobody did." She shrugged. "Pearl used to help me, but I loved doing it. Dreaming them up and planning how to sew them. What fabrics to use to keep the cost down." Dropping her head, she looked endearingly young and vulnerable. "I'd like to do that again. And Sugar Ellie is going to disappear forever, and in her place will be the respectable Widow Pierce."

Cole had to laugh. She had gumption. A whore to a widow and all without once having man in her bed.

SEVENTEEN

C ole didn't care how much his back hurt, he was leaving and taking Bridget and Ellie with him. Pete, all things considered, wasn't a bad sort, and Cole rather liked Isaac. In his early days he'd shot men like Pete for doing a whole helluva lot less, but with age came the sort of maturity that meant you didn't need to leave the undertaker with a new client every time someone crossed you.

Pigeon Pete, or plain old Pete as he insisted on being called —and who could blame him—gave up Ellie without a fight. Bridget was another matter altogether.

They were both outside, Cole perched on a log, still feeling beat up and laid to waste.

"My boy's powerful taken with her." Pete tested his axe edge with his thumb. "And seeing as you're all set on taking his first bride away, stands to reason you leave the other one here."

Behind Pete's back, Ellie hung washing on a makeshift line Isaac had tied between two trees. Over his shirt, she stared at him and shook her head. In the couple of days they'd been there, Ellie had gotten to know Bridget better, and was dead set against her being left behind. Bridget, according to Ellie, didn't always know her own mind, and tended to make impulsive decisions. Ellie didn't want one more man taking advantage of Bridget. For good reason, Ellie did not trust Pete further than she could toss him.

It wasn't like Cole intended to leave Bridget behind, but he hadn't given it that much thought. Bridget did seem happy with the cabin, and Isaac was about as smitten as a man could get. Then again, Bridget had giggled and followed him out of that saloon she'd being working in without asking a single question, and Isaac was a young man in dire need of a woman.

"Can't do that." Cole shook his head. "Bridget is my niece, and my sister would never forgive me for leaving her behind."

Pete snorted. Not a total believer in their familial connection. "Woulda thought you'd like her off your hands. Another mouth to feed and all."

"Now, Pete." Cole rolled a double eagle over his knuckles. Pete had his axe, but money trumped blade every time. "Look at the girl. It's not going to be difficult to find someone to take her off my hands."

"Until she opens her mouth." Pete snorted, but his gaze stayed on the double eagle. "I never did hear something talk quite that much, and about nothing and all."

Pete had a point, so Cole offered him something he might want more than a wife for Isaac. "How about a mule?"

Ellie shot Cole a startled glance.

"A mule is even more use than a woman." Cole added some extra incentive for Pete.

The glance Ellie shot him that time could see him buried six feet under. She snapped a pair of pants and Cole feared for his neck. For a tiny thing, she had some power packed into that arm.

At the mention of mules, a crafty look slid over Pete's face.

"But you got two women." He propped a log and split it in two. "Don't see how's that's fair."

"Mule works twice as hard as a woman." Cole didn't have the balls to see how Ellie took that one. "Mule's at least twice as strong as well."

Pete sneered. "But I got both women here, and you don't got no mule."

"I've got money for a mule." Cole didn't like to threaten, but his back hurt like hell and he didn't want to drag negotiations out. "And I'm leaving here with Ellie and Bridget. Only thing you get to decide is if you're going to stand in my way or not."

"You threatenin' me, Whiskey?"

Good, Pete had heard of him. "Do I need to?"

Pete scratched his beard, and Cole didn't want to think what he had stashed away in all those whiskers. "You give me enough to buy me four mules, and we part as friends."

"Enough for two mules, and your son gets to keep his knees."

Anger and fear flashed through Pete's eyes. "Three mules, and I don't bash your brains in."

"Two mules, and I don't gut shoot you and then your boy."

Clean laundry hanging limp in her hand, Ellie gaped at him. But Cole knew a bully when he saw one, and he'd handled tougher customers and better bluffers than Pigeon Pete.

"I'm gonna have to stick on three." Pete went mining in his beard again with his dirty, cracked fingernails. He propped another log for splitting.

"I could decrease the offer to one mule." Cole snapped his fingers. "Or better yet, none, considering you abducted one woman, stabbed me in the back and are threatening to try to keep us here."

"Nobody's stopping you from going." Pete huffed but he

was folding and they both knew it. "Alls I want is them gals. My boy got a hankering for the pretty one. Got me thinking I might like to keep the little 'un. She's mighty handy to have around."

Ellie squeaked and went back to her laundry, furiously pegging things to her line.

"Now we both know two things, Pete." Cole eased to his feet and stretched the sore muscles of his back. "Ellie isn't my sister, and I sure as hell didn't come all this way to leave without her."

"Ha!" Pete jabbed a finger at him. "I knew she weren't no sister of yorn. Don't look nothing like each other."

"Ellie is my woman." A primal surge shot through him as he spoke. Cole tucked it in his sack of crap he didn't want to think about now. "And I'm leaving with her. Bridget is...my responsibility, and I'm leaving with her too. That's the way my woman wants it, and that's how it's gonna be. You getting this, Pete?"

Pete growled and kicked at the splitting stump. "All right, two mules but it ain't right."

Cole handed him half the money. "You get the rest tomorrow."

"Why not now?" Pete glared at him.

"Because I don't trust you." Cole made his way back to the cabin. His injuries slowed his pace. It was going to be hell sitting a horse with his back, but he'd done worse. He had once ridden two days with a bullet in his thigh from a sore loser with bad aim.

"Your woman, am I?" Ellie fell into step with him.

He barely stopped his grin in time. "Yup."

"Well, then it's only right I tell you that your woman might not be able to work as hard as a mule, but she sure as shit can kick your ass even harder."

Two days later, he and Bridget and Ellie were packed and their horses waiting. When they'd come looking for Ellie, he'd had the foresight to bring a horse for Ellie.

The same Ellie who had stubbornly—like a mule—insisted he rest his back two more days before he traveled. Ellie packed a ton of determination in that tiny frame.

Pete, once their price was agreed, turned into an almost congenial host. It didn't cost him any trouble with Ellie and Bridget doing the work. If Ellie's domestic skills had surprised him, Bridget was a revelation. She took to it right away, happy to let Ellie teach her everything she knew.

They learned over those two days that Bridget's mother had died when she was little, and her father had sold her to a brothel when she was thirteen. There were some men in this world Cole would like to rip apart with his bare hands. Jake was one of them, and Bridget's father ran a close second place. Men like that didn't deserve the women entrusted to their care, and Cole didn't believe they deserved to use up any more space and air.

Mounted, he and Ellie waited for Bridget to say her good-byes, which were taking some time. She and Isaac stood on the porch and stared at each other, misery carved into both their faces.

They made a weirdly sweet pair. He leaned closer to Ellie and whispered, "We could leave her here."

"I will not hesitate to shoot you." She didn't even glance his way.

So much for that, then. Sass and vinegar were part of the deal when you liked your women feisty, and he most definitely did. "Bridget." If he didn't break it up, they would be here come sundown. "We've got to get going."

"And we've got work to do." Pete had been particularly gruff this morning, almost as if he would miss the company. With a sniff, he stomped out to the field.

Isaac followed reluctantly, keeping his gaze on Bridget, only stopping when he tripped over a feed trough and nearly ended up ass over end.

They finally got Bridget on her horse, and Cole led the women out of Pete's yard and into the trees. Pete had drawn him a crude map of how to get to Denver. It might mean sleeping rough tonight, but it beat going back to Silver Creek. Cole didn't trust himself not to start shooting at all the folks who had led Ellie into Pete's clutches. Maybe he should find Snake, and the two of them could have a nice chat, over his peacemaker.

ELLIE HAD BARELY KNOWN Bridget a handful of days, and even she could tell Bridget's current silence was unusual. She'd been so sure leaving Bridget at the cabin was the wrong thing to do. Bridget had loved the goats, spoken for hours about the pretty cows, and Ellie had taken her talk of Isaac with a pinch of salt.

Doing the typically man thing, Cole ignored the silence and Bridget's lingering glances behind them. The longing in those looks made Ellie feel guilty as hell.

Maybe she should have let Bridget stay.

Then again, Isaac was a nice enough young man, but no girl deserved to be stuck in the back of nowhere with Pete. As Pete ruled Isaac, Ellie couldn't leave Bridget in Pete's clutches. If Isaac had shown some gumption, she might have changed her mind, but in Bridget's short life, she'd already been handed around like a parcel too many times for Ellie's liking. The next move in Bridget's life would be one Bridget had some say in.

Cole looked strong in the saddle, and Ellie had her eye on him, looking for any signs of weakness or pain. The stupid man would push himself and risk her neat stitches if left to himself.

As much as she'd come to know Cole as the well-dressed, smooth gambler who fit right in at a saloon, out here he looked at peace. A gentle breeze ruffled his dark hair beneath his hat, and he rode with ease that spoke of hours in the saddle.

She'd been stupid to leave Cole and run off on her own. She doubted she could ever repay his kindness, but she would try. Part of that also meant no more running off on her own. Cole's pledge to help her was his bond, and he stood by it.

He sure was a handsome devil with the strong lines of his face. Ellie had never met anybody highborn, but Cole looked like he came from good breeding stock. He spoke like an educated man as well.

Bridget sighed and glanced over her shoulder. What that girl needed was some distraction, and Ellie nudged her horse closer. "I like your dress. It's pretty."

"Thank you." Bridget looked at Ellie like she might bite. At Pete's cabin, it had been less notable, but Bridget sure was wary around her. Girls who looked like Bridget wouldn't make any friends in a cathouse. She was too much competition for the other girls.

The men in Bridget's life had certainly not been any better. It made her sad for the girl. A girl that beautiful could bring the world to its knees. She shouldn't be cowering and flinching when another woman spoke to her. "Did Cole buy it for you?"

Bridget looked nervously at Cole and then nodded.

"He's kind like that." Ellie already owed him more than she could ever repay. "He took me away when my brothers wanted to turn me into an auction."

"He won a game of cards and got me." Bridget warmed slightly. She took a deep breath, as if daring to go further and

145

said, "Men like the way I look, but they soon get tired of my talking."

Except Isaac. Isaac had appeared to be happy to listen to Bridget chatter all day long. If Bridget didn't change her mind, Ellie might need to reconsider her stance on Bridget and Isaac. In the meantime, when they got to Denver, they would have to find something to do with Bridget. Ellie had an idea, and it was such a good one it made her smile. "I'm going to set up my own dress shop when we get to Denver."

"You are?" Bridget gaped at her. "You must be very good at sewing."

"I'm passable." Some of her finest stitchery was Cole's back. "But I'm better at dreaming up the dress and making the pattern to sew it. I plan on getting a couple of women to sew for me."

Bridget sighed. "I like pretty dresses."

"I think most of us girls do." Ellie's shop was taking place in her mind. "But sometimes they can be really expensive. I want to make dresses for girls like us."

"Whores?" Bridget frowned at her.

Ellie hated that word more and more. "We don't have to be whores anymore, Bridget." She had gotten away from that life, and so had Bridget. "We can be what we want this time. A fresh start."

Bridget brightened considerably. "Then I'd like to be a wife."

"A wife?" A girl as beautiful as Bridget could go far. "That's what you want?"

Bridget flushed and looked more beautiful than ever in her shyness. "It's all I ever really wanted. A good man, a house of my own." She went pinker. "Some children."

"How many children?"

"Eight is a good number," Bridget said with a definite nod.

"That way, the older ones can help you look after the young ones."

As farm families went, eight wasn't an unusual number. It just seemed like more children than Ellie wanted to have.

If her future was now wide open and full of choices, then children could be part of that future. Ellie liked children. It struck her that a widow might marry again and have children. A widow with her virginity, however, would have as much explaining to do as a virgin whore.

Her gaze tracked Cole. He certainly liked kissing her, and if she hadn't told him the truth that night, they'd have been lovers.

He glanced at her and smiled.

Cole had everything she needed to fix her problem.

EIGHTEEN

Fountain Colony was a much bigger town than Silver Creek, and they reached it late the next day, about the time Ellie's bottom had gone numb from riding and her concern over Cole had reached screaming point.

The stubborn man didn't say a word, but she could see by this pallor that the ride had cost him.

They found a hotel and got two rooms, one for Cole and she and Bridget would share the other.

Ellie stopped Cole at his door. "You need to rest."

"I'm fine." His jaw was set in a stubborn line.

"You're not fine." Ellie lowered her voice and stepped closer. "Now you go in there and rest, or I'll send Bridget to chatter to you until you do."

He smiled but even that looked like an effort. "You could never be that cruel."

"Really?" Ellie pinned him with a look. He would injure himself further if he kept it up. "Don't underestimate my determination to get to Denver. If something happens to you, I don't get there."

"You can't bluff me, Sugar." His face softened. "You're not that mean and thank you for caring."

Ellie was saved from responding when he opened his door and stepped inside. Before he shut it, he flashed her a quick smile. "But I will rest."

"Good."

He hesitated. "See you later, Sugar."

"See you later." She waited until his door shut, and then led Bridget down the hall to their room. The hotel wasn't grand, but its wooden floors were clean, and the rooms were large and airy. The one she shared with Bridget had two beds. And a brass tub behind a screen.

First things first, Ellie called for some water.

Bridget sat in a heap on her bed, staring out the window and sighing.

"Bridget." Ellie perched next to her and took her hand. "We couldn't leave you there."

"I know," she said in a tone that suggested she knew anything but.

Ellie patted her hand. "I'm going to take a bath; would you like a bath?"

Bridget shrugged.

Dealing with female issues had been a part of her life for so long, and Ellie stood and left Bridget to herself. Bridget would talk when she was ready, or she'd think her way out of her funk.

When her bathwater arrived, Ellie perked up. She took great delight in peeling her dirty dress off and kicking it aside. There might not be enough water and soap in the world to get that dress clean, and a part of her never wanted to see it again.

The water was lovely and hot, and Ellie leaned back in it and let it soothe her sore muscles. As the water started to chill, she washed her hair and stepped out.

Bridget was still sitting where Ellie had left her.

This might be a long funk to find her way out of.

Ellie wriggled into clean underthings and a dress that buttoned up the front. "I thought we might visit a dressmaker."

"A dressmaker?" Bridget finally looked at her. "I have three dresses. Cole bought them for me."

"All my dresses announce what I used to be." Ellie toed her carpetbag. "I need to look more like a regular woman."

Bridget gave her a misty smile. "You'll never be a regular woman, Ellie. You're not a regular sort of woman."

Ellie wasn't sure what to make of that, but at least Bridget was speaking again. "Do you want to change, or are you ready to go?"

Standing, Bridget patted her skirts. Clouds of dust rose from her skirts and she sneezed. "I think I should change, don't you?"

"I definitely think you should change." As she had a little time, she could check on Cole. To make sure he was resting. "I'll be back shortly."

She walked down the short hallway to Cole's door and tapped on it. "Cole." She kept it low, not wanting to wake him on the off chance he'd taken her advice and was resting.

The door opened to Cole dressed only in his pants.

Ellie forced her eyes to stay on his face. "I thought I'd check on your back, make sure you haven't opened anything up."

"Nope." He shook his head. "You stitched me up good."

Opening the door wider, he stepped out the way.

Ellie walked into his room. It was smaller than hers and Bridget's. A full tub near the window meant Cole had spent his time like she had.

She motioned him to turn. "I hope you didn't get your stitches wet."

"I was careful." But he turned and let her look.

The smooth, tanned skin of his back covered a fascinating play of muscle. Now that she had decided Cole would be the one to cure her inconvenience, her mind kept drifting to all the bawdy stories she'd heard from her girls at the Four Kings.

Would Cole please her enough for her to dig her nails into the smooth expanse of his back?

Heat prickled beneath her skin, and she forced herself to look at his wounds and keep her mind on her task.

Cole's arms bulged with muscle that begged her to touch and see if it was as hard as it looked. She would never have counted herself as one of those women who liked her men big. She was learning new things about herself nearly every day.

"This looks fine." Her stitches had held, and Cole's wounds looked none the worse for wear.

He turned and gave her a roguish smile. "Thanks, Mother."

"I'm not your mother." The words snapped out of her before she could stop them.

Cole cocked his head. Those lion eyes swept her from top to toe. "I'm aware of that, Sugar." He checked himself and stepped away from her. Clearing his throat, he motioned her dress. "Are you going out?"

"I thought I might find a dressmaker and introduce the widow Pierce to the world."

Cole chuckled and reached for his shirt. "Let me go with you."

"No, that's fine." She caught the edge of his shirt and held fast. "You need to rest, and I'll be fine. Bridget is coming with me."

"Ellie." Cole pulled his shirt from her grasp and shrugged it on. "Last time I lost sight of you, I almost lost you to a trapper's son."

Even knowing he didn't mean that like it sounded didn't

stop a small thrill from coursing through her. "I'm only going one street over."

"Then we're only going one street over." Cole buttoned his shirt.

Part of her wanted to stop him. It seemed a pity to cover all that beautiful man up. "It's not necessary."

"I think it is." He winced as he tucked his shirt into his pants. "Let's go."

Ellie suppressed a sigh. He wore his stubborn expression and Cole, she was learning, didn't shift when he'd made up his mind.

"You're being stubborn," she said, as he followed her into the hallway and locked his room behind him.

He motioned her forward. "Let's get Bridget before she enslaves someone else."

"She genuinely seems to be sad about Isaac."

Cole gave her a surprised look. "I would have thought she had forgotten about him already."

"Apparently not." Ellie knocked before opening their bedroom door.

Bridget was dressed and back to sitting on the bed and staring out the window.

Ellie sent Cole a speaking glance. "You ready?" She put a dose of chipper into her voice. "Cole is being a stubborn mule and insisting on coming with us."

"All right." Bridget stood and left the room, hands folded in front of her. "Isaac had mules." She sighed. "I liked Isaac's mules."

Cole pulled a face at Ellie behind Bridget's back. Yeah, Ellie was having trouble believing it too, but Bridget seemed to be fond of Isaac. She still had trouble justifying leaving Bridget with Isaac and Pete, but her doubts were starting to nag at her.

Bridget might not be the brightest candle on the cake, but

she was an adult woman and entitled to make her own decisions.

Ellie's conscience whispered to her. The very reason she was on this journey with Cole was because people had taken her right to make decisions about her life from her. In their desire to protect Bridget, had she and Cole done the same thing to her?

Outside, the sun was winding down through a sky tinged red by the ever-present dust.

Three doors down, they found a dressmaker.

A small salon invited them to take a seat amongst the two women already there. Both women looked at her and Bridget and then Cole.

Cole backed out. "I'll see you once you're done."

"You can go back to the hotel."

He actually growled at her. "I'll wait."

The two women stared at Cole.

"My brother." Ellie forced a light laugh. "He's so protective since my man passed."

One of the women, the taller and younger one, softened immediately. "You lost your man?"

Ellie nodded and motioned Bridget to sit before she did. "A month ago, now."

"You poor dear." She shook her head. "And still so young."

"How did you lose him?" The older woman leaned forward. "Mines?"

"Yes." Ellie heaved a sigh. "I told him that claim would be the death of him."

Both women shook their heads.

"Men." The younger sighed. "Can't tell them a thing."

Bridget sniffed, then a fat tear dribbled down her silky cheek.

"Oh dear." The younger woman scooted to the edge of her seat. "Does she miss your man?"

"I miss my man." Bridget sobbed into her hands.

"Good afternoon." The dressmaker chose that moment to come through from the back. She looked at Ellie and then Bridget. "Is something amiss?"

"It's my sister." Ellie put her arm over Bridget's shoulder. "I'll take her back to the hotel."

"No, you won't." The older woman bustled over. "Ruth and I will take care of your sister." She gave Ellie's dress a pointed look. "I imagine you need something more...appropriate to wear. People do talk so, don't they?"

And gosh darn did they. Ellie nodded and wondered what the woman would think if she'd seen one of the getups Sugar Ellie used to sport. "I should stay with my sister."

"Myrtle is right." Ruth took the seat next to Bridget and took her hand. "You go and do what you need. We'll look after her." Ruth patted Bridget's hand. "What's your name, sweetheart?"

"B-Bridget." Bridget gazed at her with huge, waterlogged eyes. It would take a harder heart than either Ruth or Myrtle had to withstand such a heartbreaking sight.

The dressmaker looked like she wanted to ask a bucket of questions.

Despite Ellie's misgivings, Ruth and Myrtle did seem to be having a calming effect on Bridget, and she was tired of being tossed out of respectable places. She stood and approached the dressmaker. "I need something for a widow."

The dressmaker's eyes gleamed and she puffed up. "You're a widow."

"The mines." Myrtle clucked her tongue. "And she told him that mine would be the death of him."

The dressmaker melted. "Oh, you poor dear. And so young."

"So young." Ruth sniffed and looked like she might burst into tears herself. "Such a pretty young woman to be a widow."

"But she has a brother." Myrtle pointed outside the window, where Cole was leaning against a post near the door. "He watches out for her."

"That's nice, dear." The dressmaker took her hand. "It's good to have a man looking out for you. This town is no place for a young woman without a protector."

"Thank you." Ellie hated lying to these genuinely nice women. She followed the dressmaker into the back.

"Now I have a few things that I keep for...these situations." The dressmaker winced.

Ellie was relieved. "That would be fine."

The dressmaker nodded and walked through a curtained area to the back.

As much as lying to these women made her feel bad, these same women wouldn't share space with her if they knew who she really was. And if Ruth and Myrtle had any idea of who Bridget was, they would not be so happy to comfort her.

Ellie stood still while the dressmaker helped her into a dress and got pinning.

Widows were invisible and nobody paid much mind what they got up to. She didn't want to be anyone's wife. Growing up like she had, she'd seen whores and she'd seen wives, both of them treated like property, and only one of them getting paid.

"That's done." The dressmaker stood and helped Ellie ease out of the pinned dress. "I have another one like it..." Her eyes gleamed

Ellie looked at the dress the woman showed her. This one

had some beading on the bodice and was cut for evening. Being a widow didn't have to mean dowdy. "I'll take it."

No, she'd much rather have her own business, maybe even have a discreet lover on the side. For that, she needed to proceed with Cole's help. She wasn't asking him to do anything he hadn't offered a lot of money to do. Her dang head however, kept getting stuck on the idea of Cole being the discreet lover she kept in her life for a good long time, which was plain dumb because she knew better than to build castles in the air. The other thing running a cathouse had taught her, don't go hanging your dreams on a man. If you've got a dream, you're the one who has to make that happen.

"Oh my." Ruth gasped from the other side of the curtain. "That's terrible."

Ellie's nape prickled. Bridget had been on the quiet side for a while now.

"Well!" Myrtle huffed. "We'll see about that." She ripped the curtain aside and glared at Ellie. "I am shocked, Mrs. Pierce, shocked!"

On the sofa, Bridget huddled next to Ruth, managing to look enchanting even with her red nose and blotchy eyes.

"Shocked?" Ellie crept closer to the hovering storm on Myrtle's face.

Myrtle pointed her arm at Bridget and puffed up like a rooster. "That poor child. She's told us everything, and I can't credit my own ears."

Somehow Ellie doubted Bridget had told her new friends everything. The girl might not be the brightest star in the sky, but she had a healthy enough streak of self-preservation to work the truth her way.

Bridget kept her eyes on the floor as she cowered next to Ruth.

"Is this about Isaac?" Ellie played her hunch.

"What else?" Myrtle galloped into her stride, the bow on her bonnet quivering with outrage. "To keep such wonderful young people apart, and for no good reason other than you have a grudge against his father."

Now, Ellie wasn't one to begrudge a girl doing what needed doing to get along, but she drew the line at Bridget shoving her in front of the stampede. Best she head this off before she and Bridget ended up with their butts in the dust. "Bridget is so young." Myrtle struck her as a sensible woman. "And so very lovely. Her brother and I are concerned for her safety." She leaned in toward Myrtle. "She's such a trusting soul as well, and that can lead her into trouble faster than you can say jack rabbit."

Myrtle sniffed and simmered down. "Young girls are not always sensible."

"But she's in love." Ruth ruffled up.

"I know she thinks she's in love." Ellie smoothed down a wrinkle in her skirts and tried to get her thoughts in order. "But she barely even knows the young man in question." Ellie appealed to Myrtle, Ruth and the dressmaker and got knowing looks and nods in response. "So she's not thinking straight." She nodded to Cole standing outside. "That's why her brother and I are doing her thinking for her."

Myrtle was on her side. The dressmaker looked about ready to run Bridget out of her store.

Ruth's soft heart kept her teetering to Bridget's side. "To find a man you love and who loves you and wants to marry you is so rare."

"It's marriage we're speaking of, Ruth." Myrtle straightened her bonnet. "No reason to bring love into that."

"Right you are." The dressmaker stabbed Ellie's hem with a pin. "You don't marry a man to sigh over. You marry one who provides for you, keeps your children's bellies full. A man who treats you with respect and attends services every Sunday."

Ruth bit her lip and glanced at Bridget. "Only she looks like a princess. I want her to have her prince."

"Never mind a prince." Myrtle snorted. "A farmer is what that girl needs, or a storekeeper like Jeremiah Barnes."

"I don't want to marry a farmer, or Mr. Barnes." Bridget wailed, tears streaming down her face. "I want to marry Isaac."

She looked so exquisitely pitiful, Myrtle and the dressmaker wavered.

"I thought you needed to think on it a bit before you made up your mind," Ellie said, but she had to admit she'd made an awful lot of assumptions about what was good for Bridget. If anybody needed to think more on the matter of Bridget and Isaac, it was her. "And nobody said you couldn't."

CHAPTER

NINETEEN

Both new dresses tucked under her arm, Ellie chewed the scene with Bridget and the other women over in her mind as they left the dressmaker. If Bridget really did love Isaac, then she'd done her a huge disservice. She'd just wanted to protect Bridget from tumbling into another bad situation. If she had left Bridget at the cabin, and she'd been unhappy, there would have been nobody she could turn to.

"What's up?" Cole lengthened his stride to keep up with her.

Ellie sighed. "I'll tell you back at the hotel."

A cowboy staggered out the saloon, looked at her with a sloppy grin then gaped at Bridget. "Hey, honey," he slurred. "You're mighty pretty."

"Thank you." Bridget giggled.

Ellie tucked her arm through Bridget's and glared at the cowboy.

He flattened himself against the wall of the saloon as she led Bridget past.

Bridget was so blindly trusting that Ellie had gone right

ahead and made the girl's decision for her. She'd run girls like Bridget at the Four Kings, the sort of girls who needed a firm hand at the reins.

The hotel clerk looked up. "Good Eve—"

"Good evening," she said.

"Will you be joining us for dinner, Miss...um..."

"Missus." Ellie fixed him with the sort of look she imagined a respectable woman would use. "That's Mrs. Pierce." She managed a sniff. "I lost my husband recently."

Cole snorted softly.

The clerk's face nearly touched his desk he inclined his head so low. "I'm terribly sorry Mrs. Pierce. I didn't know."

"Mrs. Pierce's bereavement is such a recent occurrence, it hardly seems real," Cole said.

That man was too cute for his own good sometimes. She held her parcel up to the clerk. "Which is why I needed to get myself some mourning dresses right away."

"I see." He glanced at the stairs as if willing her to take them at a run and straightened his lapels. "Will your...family be joining us for dinner? Only, the chef likes to know."

"No, thank you." Ellie motioned Bridget up the stairs. They needed to talk.

Adoring gaze locked on Bridget, the clerk said, "I could have dinner sent up to your rooms. It's not something we normally do, but given—" He flushed deep red and dragged his gaze back to Ellie. "Given your recent bereavement, I feel sure we can make an exception."

"Could you?" Ellie was not above using Bridget's ability to render people smitten. "And for my brother as well, if you would."

Cole leaned closer to the clerk and lowered his voice. "That would be wonderful. Between us men, I don't like leaving my sister alone. She's inclined to become overcome by her emotions."

"Ah...oh, certainly. Most understandable." The clerk swallowed and watched Bridget climb the stairs.

Inside their room, Bridget stopped and turned to her. "You're mad at me." Bridget was eyeing her warily, probably thinking she was going to be mean to her like almost every other woman in Bridget's life.

"No. No, I'm not mad at you. I didn't understand how you felt about Isaac."

"I love him." Bridget's eyes filled with tears.

"Are you sure?" If she was mad at anyone, it was herself. "I mean, the cabin is a long way from anywhere, and there is Pete."

"Pete's funny." Bridget took her hat off and put it on the dresser. "He makes out like he's so mean and ornery, but he's got a kind heart."

Ellie took a seat on the bed. She should have had this conversation with Bridget at the cabin. "How can you be sure of that? He kidnapped me."

"But he didn't hurt you, Ellie." Bridget sat next to her and took her hand. "Not really, and if he was a really mean person, he could have done anything to you at any time."

She might have done the worst thing possible to Bridget. "He stabbed Cole."

"He thought Cole was going to kill Isaac." Bridget sighed. "I'm not clever like you, Ellie. I don't need big things in my life. I wouldn't be very good at big things anyway. I'd just get confused and that would make me unhappy."

Then Ellie asked what she should have before deciding for Bridget. "You said you wanted a man of your own, and a house?"

"That's what I want." Bridget's expression grew wistful,

and she looked heart stoppingly beautiful with the waning sunlight kissing her face with pink. "A place where I can be me and people don't stare at me all the time. I don't feel silly or like I talk too much when I'm with Isaac. And Pete doesn't yell at me when I get things wrong."

Ellie had made a big mistake. Huge. "In the morning, we'll take you back."

"No, Ellie." Bridget shook her head. "Cole is hurt, and we need to get him to Denver. And this way, if I still miss Isaac when we get to Denver, I'll know for sure." She patted Ellie's hand. "And you'll know for sure as well, and then you won't feel so bad about me going there."

Ellie wanted to cry, and then kick herself. If she'd been Bridget, she was damn sure she wouldn't be trying to make the woman who had made a bad decision for her feel better about that decision. She needed to talk it through with Cole. "I'll be right back. I want to make sure Cole is all right."

"He's doesn't like anyone to know when he's not all right." Bridget brightened all of a sudden. "Do you think they'll bring me cake with my dinner?"

"I'm sure they will." Cake didn't make up for the wrong she'd done Bridget, but if it made Bridget's evening even a touch brighter, Ellie would shoot up the town for that cake. "I'll ask him before I see Cole."

"Okay." Bridget took the package with Ellie's two dresses in it. "But don't get any for Cole, because he doesn't really like cake."

Cole opened his door, took one look at her face and motioned her inside. "What happened?"

"I think I made the wrong decision with Bridget." She went on to tell him about the dressmaker and her recent conversation with Bridget. "I think she really does love him."

Cole grimaced. "I agree we should have asked her, but

we've both seen how she is. I wasn't going to leave her there either."

"We should get to Denver, and then we can send someone to Pete." And hope Pete didn't shoot a strange rider on sight.

Cole nodded. "You want to leave in the morning?"

"Maybe." The idea of being back on a horse didn't fill her with joy.

"We can make this right, Ellie." Cole smiled. "And maybe a day or two will give all of us some perspective."

"Do you really think so?" Ellie was grasping at straws.

Cole shrugged. "I really don't know, Sugar. But I know you, and I know you were acting out of what you thought were her best interests."

"Thank you." Ellie was now out of reasons to stay in his room. The air grew thicker and harder to breathe. "How's your back?"

"Right now it feels just fine." His eyes glowed like liquid gold. It was like being trapped in a mountain lion's stare, only she wanted to run toward him not away from him. "Ellie?"

"Yeah, I'll see you in the morning." Her feet rooted to his floor and wouldn't move.

Cole shifted closer to her. "In the morning."

"I should get back to Bridget."

"Yes, you should." His shoes nudged hers. He loomed over her, his face in shadow. He must have shaved while they were out because his cheeks were smooth and he smelled of sandalwood. His gaze drifted to her mouth. He whispered her name like a hoarse promise, "Ellie."

A knock on the door made her jump.

"Mr. Mansfield." The clerk spoke through the door. "I have your dinner here. The one your sister ordered for you."

"Thank you," Cole called and lowered his voice so only she could hear. "But she's really not my sister. Not in any way."

As it turned out, over breakfast the next morning they decided that even though it wouldn't leave until the next day, they would take the train to Denver. It was far more comfortable, and Bridget was even unhappier than Ellie about getting back on a horse. True to his word, Cole provided distraction. Shortly after breakfast, he pulled up to the hotel in a hired buggy.

Ellie blinked in the bright morning sun. "What are we doing with that?"

"Picnic." Cole grinned as if he'd turned water into wine. "Maybe some fishing."

"Fishing." Bridget squealed and jumped up and down. "I love fishing and I'm really good at it." She clapped her hands like a little girl. "I bet I can catch more fish than any of us."

Cole must have been a genius or the luckiest man alive to have gotten it so right. "Let's go and get our bonnets then." She herded an obedient and smiling Bridget back to their room and they fetched their bonnets.

Riding out, even jammed between Cole and Bridget on the buggy seat, Ellie approved more and more of his idea. The day was beautiful, and a series of streams made the land greener than she was used to.

She'd never been on a picnic, and never been fishing either. Another part to her adventure was unfolding and she planned to enjoy it.

"You're smiling." Cole looked down at her with a warm expression.

A blush heated her cheeks. "I plan to have a good day."

His smile broadened into a grin. "And I plan to see that you do."

They found a shady spot outside of town and Cole

unloaded a hamper, a blanket and fishing poles from the buggy.

Bridget immediately went about baiting a hook with the sort of efficiency that meant she really did know how to fish. It was the first time she'd smiled since they'd left Isaac, and Ellie felt relieved.

Taking off her shoes and stockings, Bridget tucked her skirts into her waistband and armed with her pole, waded knee-deep into the clear mountain water.

With Cole's help, Ellie spread the blanket and opened the hamper. She took a seat and pulled her bag of sewing closer to her. The dressmaker had done a good job, but she wanted to make alterations. If things went her way, her next dress, she'd be making for herself.

Cole stretched out on the blanket, wincing a little as he got comfortable.

"How's your back?" She watched him as she threaded her needle.

He shrugged and then winced. "Getting better every day."

"Uh-huh." For a poker player, he was a bad liar. "So, Denver tomorrow?"

"Denver tomorrow." He nodded. "And we can get you all set."

"I'll pay you back." She met his gaze and held it. "For everything you've paid for, and for getting me set up in my store."

He lay down on his side and propped his head on his hand. "We'll talk about that when it comes to that." Cole could be a slippery fish when he chose.

"We're talking about it now. And I don't want to take your money."

"Ellie." Face serious, he stared at her. "I don't need the money. In fact, you'll be doing me a favor."

Eyes on her sewing, she chuckled. "This, I have to hear."

"I'm leaving Denver," he said. "Forever and going to New York."

Denver would be their goodbye, and the idea felt like a rusty blade in her chest. Once Cole went to New York, she wouldn't see him again. She kept her expression blank and bent over her sewing. "That's where your people are, isn't it?"

"My mother." He sat up and dug through the hamper. "And my brother. My father died a couple of years ago."

"I'm sorry."

"Don't be." His face hardened. "He was a mean son of a bitch, and the world is a better place without him."

Cole didn't talk about himself much, especially not that time before he came west. The bright morning light etched the clean, handsome lines of his face. "Are you going back to see your mother?"

"In part." He plucked a long strand of grass and chewed on it. "My brother, if he'll see me, but he was always my father's son."

Ellie sensed there was more and waited.

Then, so quietly she almost didn't hear him, Cole said, "And Victoria."

"Victoria?" She didn't even know who Victoria was, but the reverent way Cole said her name told her much more than words might have. "She's waiting for you?"

"No." He shook his head. "She got married. She's not waiting for me."

Ellie trod carefully. "But you wish she was?"

"Yeah." He breathed soft and slow. "I don't talk about her much."

"I'd like to hear about her. If you had a mind to talk about her now."

Cole stared at the river.

Intent on her fishing, Bridget was still in the water.

"I loved her," Cole said. "She was the woman I was going to marry."

There was no good reason for the pain his words caused. Cole was not, nor had he ever been, hers. Just because she'd gotten used to thinking of him in an intimate capacity, it didn't make him any more hers now either. Really, she ought to be glad he loved this Victoria. It would make matters so much easier between them.

"You didn't marry her?"

"No." He shook his head. "I was a wild one, kicking out against the world, my father, whatever felt like it was tying me down."

Ellie could see that. She still remembered the first day he'd wandered into the Four Kings, so handsome and devil-may-care, wearing his capacity for violence and danger like a cape swirling behind him. Their eyes had met over the length of the bar, and for once, Ellie had considered taking the money and the man to her bed.

She edged closer to him. "What happened?"

"I did some stupid stuff, got myself into a stupid situation, wasn't accepted in polite society." His smile was rueful as he stared out at nothing. "My father was furious and threatened to disown me. Of course, I had to push that to its conclusion."

"He disowned you."

Cole turned to her. "Yep. Tossed me out with the clothes on my back and the money I had in my pocket."

"How did you end up out here?"

"I went to the train station and bought a ticket for as far as my money would take me." He smiled at her. "And it brought me here."

"And Victoria?"

His smile faded. "She married somebody else."

"I'm sorry." It must have broken his heart for him to still be wanting her back after all these years. "And that's why you're going back to New York."

"I'm going back because it's where I belong." Cole shrugged. "I've lived here and done well for myself, but it's not home. I'm reaching that point in my life where I want home. I want to settle."

That wasn't the Cole she knew, but she kept her thoughts off her face.

"Victoria's free now," he said. "Her husband died six months ago. The time is right."

Ellie had no words, so she nodded. Lucky Victoria to have a man like Cole pining for her.

"To be honest, I'm not sure Victoria is the reason I'm going back." Cole cleared his throat. "It's been a long time, and people change. It's more like everything is pointing me that way."

"I'll miss you," Ellie said. So much more than she dared express. "We've been good friends over the years."

"Yeah, friends." He pushed a hand through his hair. "Of a sort."

Yeah, and it was that *of a sort* part she wanted to talk to him about, but another time.

CHAPTER

TWENTY

Cole left Ellie and an exhausted Bridget, still happily clutching her catch, at the hotel and went out. His conversation with Ellie had left him feeling antsy.

All these years he'd lived in Colorado, he'd never told anyone about Victoria until today. When he'd first arrived, keeping to himself had been a life prolonging strategy. Staying to himself had become a habit, broken only by his trips to the Four Kings.

He had never put the pieces together before, but he went to the Kings for Ellie. She was the closest thing he had to a friend out there, and he would miss her too.

Like any other time he was troubled, his path took him into a saloon. He didn't bother to get the name. They were pretty much all the same, some rougher than others. This one sat squarely between blink-and-somebody-will-shoot-you and don't-want-no-trouble.

He bellied up to the bar and tapped it for the keep's attention. "Whisky."

"Comin' up." The barkeep stopped and stared at him. "You ain't Whisky Mansfield, is ya?"

Cole nodded.

The cowpoke next to him sidled a few steps away from him. A young tough at the far end eyed him with interest. Jesus, Cole wasn't up for one of those glory seekers tonight. They had a nasty habit of crawling out of the shadows when you least wanted them.

There was no Whisky Mansfield in New York, just plain old Cole Justin Mansfield. And how his parents' set would stare at the six-shooter strapped to his hip.

Cole met the glory seeker's stare and held it. "I'm gonna give you some free advice, son."

"Yeah?" The kid sneered. He couldn't be older than nineteen. Way too young to die.

Cole downed his whisky and motioned for another. "Don't do it."

While watching the interchange between Cole and the kid, the barkeep filled his glass.

The kid scoffed. "I don't know—"

"Right now, you're thinking you've heard the name Whisky Mansfield," Cole said and downed his whisky. He held up his hand to stop the keep from pouring another. If this went the wrong way, he needed a clear head. "You're thinking that being the one to shoot Whisky Mansfield dead would make a name for you."

The kid coughed. "I—"

"But that's not how this is going to go."

The saloon had fallen dead still around them. A fly buzzed against a glass, loudly, as all attention was now focused on their conversation.

Cole kept talking. "You're going to pick a fight with me. At first, I'm going to try not to react because you're a kid."

"I ain't a kid." The tough puffed out his chest. "I'm twenty-six."

"Nineteen." Cole shook his head.

The kid blushed. "Twenty."

"Close enough," Cole said. "And still too young to die."

"Who said I'm gonna die?" He got his swagger back.

"I do." Cole let that sink in. "You're going to start something with me, and I'm going to finish it." He eased his coat away from his gun. "And when I shoot, my bullet's going to take your life. A man only has so much luck, the way I see it. If I don't kill you today, you might like your chances another day, and that might be the day my luck runs out."

The kid swallowed but kept coming. "Who's to say you ain't the one who gets dead?"

"It could happen." Cole shrugged. "But that's not likely. I earned the reputation you seem so intent on trying to end."

"You ain't so tough." But the kid was on the back foot now, and Cole motioned the keep to pour that third whisky.

"Now." He sipped his drink. "We can either start fighting and let the bullets fly, or we could get ourselves a bottle of this fine whiskey, play a few games of cards and enjoy our evening."

The kid flushed. "You'd drink with me."

"Rather do that than kill you."

"Well, hot damn!" The kid laughed. The tension in the saloon eased, and a few chuckles joined his. "If I can't kill you, I can at least tell the story of the day I drank you under the table."

"You can try." Cole grabbed his bottle and headed for a table. "You can certainly try."

Cole chose a table that gave him a full view of the room and kept his back to the wall. His habit of a lifetime served him well as the saloon doors opened and Patrick and Paul walked in. Seeing Ellie's twin brothers got his blood pumping.

They hadn't seen him yet. Shoulder to shoulder, they strode to the bar, cocks of the walk and sure nobody would take the pair of them on. They were right about that. Nobody but a fool took on the Triggers. A fool and the young and stupid. Cole glanced at his new, young friend.

Damn, the kid had already noticed the brothers and looked ready to start up where he and Cole had left off. Pushing back his chair for room to move, he hollered, "Well, look who found their way here."

"Mansfield." Patrick barely paused as he changed direction and charged for him. As always Paul flanked him, the quieter and more dangerous of the two.

Cole got to his feet.

Patrick got toe to toe with him. "Where is she?"

"Who?" Cole would be damned before he backed down. "You want to know where Ellie is?"

"You took her, and we want her back."

"I didn't take her anywhere." Where had these two assholes been when Jake hatched his sick plan? "She came to me, and she didn't like your little plan for her."

Patrick flushed. "Weren't our plan."

"But you didn't oppose it either." Cole let them see his derision. "Which in my book makes you partly responsible."

Paul's dead-eyed stare made Cole even angrier. These were her brothers, and they showed less emotion than they would have for a poker hand.

"We didn't do nothing." Patrick crowded into his space.

"Yeah, you did nothing." Cole wasn't inclined to back down. They wanted to take him on, fine. He was going to carve a piece out of both of them for their trouble. "And that's my biggest problem with you."

"You got a lot of opinions about our sister." Patrick shoved his shoulder. "That, and the fact you were seen leaving town with her, tells me you know where she is."

Cole stared at Patrick. "You put your hands on me again and you'd better be ready to take this outside."

Patrick shoved him again.

Cole breathed deep, hauled back and punched the son of a bitch in his smirking mouth.

Staggering back, Patrick lost his balance and crashed into a table behind him. The table held but the men sitting at it scattered. Cards, glasses and the whores trying to ply their trade went flying.

Paul moved, and Cole locked eyes on him. "You gonna keep this fair?"

"He's my brother." Paul shrugged and threw a punch.

Cole ducked the first, but Paul's meat hammer fist landed in his gut. He breathed deep past the need to puke.

Patrick was back on his feet, wiping a thin trickle of blood from his chin. "You're gonna regret that."

Yeah, Cole didn't think so. What kind of dumb, cruel fucker auctioned their sister off to the highest bidder? Who did that to any woman, for that matter?

The metallic cock of a hammer sounded from the bar. The keep shouldered his rifle. "Take it outside, boys, or the next punch gets answered with a bullet."

The kid tucked himself behind Cole's shoulder. "Two against one ain't fair. Let's even those odds some."

Dear God, befriending the kid could get him hurt more than facing him down on the street.

"This isn't your fight." Cole trailed the Pierce twins to the street. "This has got nothing to do with you."

The kid grinned. "I aim to make it so."

With a whoop, he launched himself on Paul's back,

surprising the bigger man into dropping to his knees on the street.

Patrick turned, swinging and Cole saw stars as he landed his punch.

A red haze dropped over Cole's vision and he lost track of the kid, Paul, the street—anything but the need to make these fuckers pay for what they'd done to his Ellie.

He felt no pain as he rained down vengeance on the Pierce twins. Every shot he landed came with a visceral thrill. He craved violence, and the fight thrummed in his blood and clouded his mind.

"Cole! Whisky!" The kid shaking him brought him back. He was astride Patrick in the dusty street, turning the bastard's face into a meaty pulp.

The kid shook him again. "It's over, Whisky. You gonna kill him if you carry on."

The temptation hovered on the outskirts of Cole's awareness. If he finished him, Ellie would be safe from at least one of her bastard brothers.

"Stop." Paul staggered toward them and threw himself down beside his brother. "Stop, Mansfield. It's done."

Around them, spectators had gathered, their fascination ranging from delight to horror. The crowd parted and the sheriff crouched beside him.

The sheriff eyed his fist. "A fight is one thing, and don't got no problem with a bit of reckoning between folks, but this is heading someplace else."

Cole lowered his fist. It took every vestige of civilization to force himself to stand and step back from Patrick. "I haven't seen your sister."

Paul helped Patrick to his feet. "You were seen with her."

"I helped her get out of town." He wiped his chin and his fingers came away bloodied. Now that the blood lust was subsiding, aches and pains made themselves known. Patrick must have gotten a few good licks in to his ribs. Something wet trickled down his spine and Ellie was going to take up where her brothers had let off if he'd split his stitches. As satisfying as the fight had been, he needed to make sure they stayed away from him. "And I'd do it again to get her away from what Jake had planned for her."

Paul flinched. "Yeah, that weren't good."

"Really?" Cole loaded as much sarcasm as he could into that one word. He had the sudden desire to start the fight up again. "But I left her with a trapper who took a shine to her."

"What?" Paul scowled at him. "Why would you do that?"

"He liked her." Cole shrugged and regretted it as his ribs squealed at him. "He liked her, and she wanted to stay." He got one more verbal punch in. "And even a dirt-poor trapper is doing better by her than you assholes."

He was done with them, and Cole turned and managed to contain his limp all the way back to the hotel.

The clerk stared at him as he got inside the doors. Cole's knees almost gave in and he leaned on the wall for support. Jesus, he hurt in places he didn't even know it was possible to hurt. And he still had to make it up those stairs.

The kid pushed through the hotel doors and eyed him. "Need some help?"

"What do you think?"

The kid laughed and shook his head. "I think I'm glad you stopped me from picking a fight with you."

Pounding on her door ripped Ellie out of sleep and had her staggering to the door. She stubbed her toe on the bed leg on her way. "Ow, dammit!" She yanked the door open. "What?"

"Ma'am?" A handsome young stranger stood outside her door blinking at her. He had Cole hanging off his arm.

"Is he drunk?" Ellie couldn't remember ever seeing Cole the worse for whisky.

"Nah." The stranger grinned at her. "This is what's left after he handed out the best beatdown I've ever seen."

Cole looked up then. He sported a developing black eye, his lip was split, and his nose looked like it might be broken. "Hey, Ellie."

"Ellie?" The stranger blinked at her and then looked at Cole. "Goddamn crazy man. All the time you knew where she was?"

"Wasn't going to let those assholes know," Cole said.

And Ellie recovered from her shock of seeing Cole looking so beat up for long enough to listen. "Who was looking for me?"

"The twins." Cole winced and eased in a short breath. "I threw them off your trail, but I could sure do with your help right now, Sugar."

"My brothers are here?" Ellie's heart jumped into her throat. Even knowing Cole wouldn't be standing in the hall if her brothers were there, she still had to look left and right down the corridor.

"I wouldn't be worrying about them, ma'am." The stranger winked at her. "If you think Whisky looks bad, you should see what we handed out."

Ellie struggled to clear the fear from her thoughts. "We?"

The stranger looked bashful and shrugged. "I helped a mite."

If he'd survived her twin brothers, he'd helped more than a mite. Ellie needed to get her head together.

Bridget sat up in bed. "Ellie?"

"It's okay." Bridget needed to stay where she was. They

didn't need another smitten admirer on their hands. "You stay there. I'll be back in a bit."

"Okay." Bridget snuggled into her blankets and rolled over.

"Right." Ellie grabbed a shawl and motioned the stranger. "Let's get him taken care of."

The stranger gave her a slow perusal and his smile got rakish. "You sure are pretty enough to get a man's fighting blood up."

"Kid?" Cole scowled at his friend. "What's your name anyway?"

"Will. William."

"Let me give it to you straight, William." Cole grimaced. "I'm obliged for your help with Ellie's brothers, but that gratitude don't extend to watching you flirt with my girl."

Ellie almost tripped over her feet as Cole called her his girl. Part of her really wanted that to be true. That part wanted it to be true so bad that Ellie needed to remind herself Cole wasn't hers and she wasn't his. Their paths would cross for as long as it took to get her to Denver. After that happened, Cole was getting himself on a train to New York and going back to the woman he'd loved from afar all these years.

But did he still love her? She must have changed.

Not her business. Ellie followed Will and Cole into Cole's room.

First she looked at Will. "Do you need fixing up?"

"Nah." Will winked and chuckled. "Whisky will hand me my ass if I ask you to take care of me." He grinned. "Might be worth it though."

Cole sat hard on his bed. He was looking pale and she needed to look at his back. If he'd been in a fight, she was willing to bet he'd opened those wounds up again. "Thanks for helping him."

"Kid? Will?" Cole stared at him through his functioning

eye. "You didn't see anybody when you brought me back to the hotel, you follow?"

"Whisky, I didn't see nothing but the whore who's going to make my hurting go away as soon as I get myself back to the saloon." He let himself out the room with a wave. "Pleasure making your acquaintance, Whisky."

Ellie shut the door behind him and helped Cole ease his coat and then his shirt off. "What were the twins doing here?"

"Looking for you." Cole hissed in a breath.

Like she'd suspected, Cole had reopened his stitches. "I'm going to have to restitch you and it's going to hurt."

"Hand me that." Cole motioned the whisky bottle by his bed.

Ellie handed it to him. "How did they know I was with you?"

"Someone saw us leaving town."

"Damn." Ellie fetched a cloth and wiped away the blood so she could see what she was doing. If the twins had found her, Jake might not be far behind.

"I told them I left you with a trapper." Cole chuckled and took a big swig of whisky. "Wasn't too far from the truth in any case."

"Except you didn't leave me with that trapper." Cole had ridden to her rescue then as he had today. "Looks like I owe you for another rescue."

"Nah, Ellie." He caught her chin in his hand. "You don't owe me a damn thing. It's about time somebody stood by your side."

TWENTY-ONE

T he next morning, Ellie watched from Cole's hotel room window as her brothers dragged their sorry asses onto their horses and left town. Not taking any chance of them staying longer, the sheriff stood by and watched as they did.

On the bed, Cole slept deeply, his light snoring from his busted nose the only sound in the room. She hadn't had the heart to wake him in time to catch the train, but she couldn't risk letting him rest any longer. He needed more time to heal, but they dared not wait around town. She wouldn't put it past the twins to sneak back and make Cole pay for besting them.

The hotel clerk had brought her bandages and liniment and all the gossip from the fight. On one point everyone was clear, Cole had won.

The twins wouldn't like that. It had been some time since they'd been beaten. Patrick had the more explosive temper and was always leading the pair into trouble. However, Paul was the one you didn't want to rile, and he always got riled in defense of Patrick.

It looked as if the widow Pierce would be making an appearance this morning.

She pinned her hat in place and drew the thick, black veil over her face.

"Sit with Cole while I go out." She motioned Bridget into a chair near the window. "Don't open the door to anyone, and don't let Cole out of that bed."

"Okay, Ellie." With a heart wrenching sigh, Bridget took a seat by Cole's bed. "He gets hurt a lot, doesn't he?"

Ellie opened her mouth to deny Bridget's statement, but she couldn't. Cole had gotten hurt a lot lately, and all of it in defense of her. She had no right to ask any more of him. Despite what he said, she owed it to him to get him on the train to New York, hale and hearty, and ready to claim his sweetheart. Even if the idea hurt her heart more than she cared to think on.

Cole opened his eyes and looked at her. "I don't need a nursemaid."

"I think you do." Ellie nearly fetched a looking glass so he could see what she saw. "I need to run some errands and Bridget can stay with you."

"No." Wincing and hissing in pain, Cole sat up.

Ellie rushed to his side and pushed against his shoulder. There was no way he could get out of his bed. "What are you doing?"

"Coming with you." Cole nudged her hand off his shoulder.

"You can't."

"Beg to differ, Ellie." He rocked to his feet and stood there swaying. "But either you take Bridget or me with you." His earnest face said he meant every word.

Ellie wouldn't put it past him to stagger along behind her every step of the way. "Fine, I'll take Bridget."

One of these days, she might even win an argument

with him.

~

EVEN HER WIDOW'S weeds didn't stop Toothless Sam at the livery stable trying to cheat her on the price of a carriage and four with driver and outrider.

The threat of the twins made her add the outrider to their transportation.

But even Toothless Sam's sharp negotiating powers died before Bridget's sweet smile, and Ellie arranged for the carriage to fetch them all from the hotel within the hour.

Feeling rather proud of herself, she walked with Bridget back to the hotel. Rounding the corner to the hotel, she stopped dead.

Paul and Patrick slouched against the smartly painted pillars outside the hotel. Like she'd suspected, they had turned around as soon as the sheriff took his eye off them. Will was also right about who had taken the most punishment. Patrick had one arm in a sling and his face was riddled with bruises. Paul looked marginally better, but only just, with one side of his face hugely swollen.

"What is it?" Bridget blinked at her.

Her voice carried to the twins who looked over.

Patrick's gaze snared on Bridget and stuck.

Paul's gaze slid past Bridget, came back and then slid past again and landed on her.

If she didn't keep walking, she would draw attention to herself. Dressed from head to toe in black, with a large veil covering her from head to waist, there might be a chance the twins didn't recognize her.

After all, they were used to seeing Sugar Ellie in her short skirts and shiny silk corsets.

With both twins focused on them, she dare not tell Bridget who they were. Keeping her voice low and making it higher than normal, she said, "A pebble in my boot."

"A pebble?" Bridget frowned down at her feet. "Does it hurt?"

Ellie regretted her pebble ruse. She didn't want to stand in front of the twins, the risk of being recognized huge, and discuss dirt. Shaking her head, she marched forward.

Patrick lounged directly in her path, his outstretched legs blocking the walkway.

Heart pounding hard enough to drown out all sound, Ellie stared at the feet and then the man. Perspiration slid down her sides. Between her and the hotel door were about twenty steps, and they would carry her past first one brother and then the other. Her chances of slipping inside looked bad. And when she was there, she still had to make it to her room without one of them stopping her.

Ah, well. She raised her chin and stared at Patrick legs and then up at him.

With a sneer, Patrick looked her up and down.

Ellie held her breath, waiting for discovery.

Patrick looked right past her at Bridget. His expression grew lascivious. "Hey, sweetheart. Where did you come from?"

"Shame on you." Bridget bent her huge blue eyes on him, brimming with reproach. "Accosting a poor widow and her husband not yet cold in his grave."

Jerking upright, Patrick yanked his feet out of her way. "Begging your pardon, Ma'am."

Not quite believing it, Ellie hurried past him and into the hotel.

"Excuse me, Ma'am?" Paul had a huskier voice than Patrick. He strolled toward Ellie. "Real sorry to hear about your husband, but maybe I knew him."

Bridget appeared at her side, eyes snapping wrathfully. "Are you trying to upset her?"

"No." Paul took a long slow look at Bridget but came back to Ellie. "Only there's something familiar about the widow lady."

"She's a widow dressed in black." Bridget looked at Paul as if he'd taken leave of his senses. "It's not her fault they all must wear the same thing."

"Right." Paul backed away from them, but his gaze strayed back to Ellie. "I'm sorry," he said. "Real sorry."

How Ellie made it up the stairs without falling on her face, she'd never know. Her legs shook so badly they threatened to drop her to the floor with every step she took.

Finally, they turned the corner and out of sight.

Still, Ellie kept walking and she didn't stop until she was safely in her room. Once there, she slammed the door shut and locked it. Her legs gave out and she dropped to the bed.

Bridget collapsed on her bed beside her. "Your brothers look like you."

She couldn't recall telling Bridget anything about her family or what she was running from, but underestimating Bridget was something she'd never do again. "You saved me."

"Not really." Bridget shrugged but looked pleased. "But I knew who they were the moment we saw them."

"They want to take me back home."

"Do you want to go?" Bridget's eyes held a piercing intensity.

"No."

Bridget shrugged. "Then that's all I need to know."

They got all packed, and Ellie went to Cole's room to get him ready to travel. As soon as the twins moved away from the hotel door, they were heading out.

Cole was fast asleep when she let herself in.

He lay on his side, bare chested with the sheet around his waist. Deep, heavy breathing told her he was sleeping the good healing kind of sleep. She wished she could give him longer to sleep, but they needed out of town.

Cole was beautifully put together. The marks he'd earned in defense of her were the only flaw on him. Her chest ached near her heart. He'd done all this for her. Nobody, not even Theo, had showed her that much caring. It must be why she was getting all soppy and maudlin over him, standing there staring at him sleeping like a moonstruck heifer.

When she peeked out the window, her heart sank. Paul and Patrick were still keeping vigil outside the hotel. They might have been waiting for another chance at Cole. Well, she'd give herself up to them before she allowed that to happen.

"What's up?" Cole's voice sounded rusty from sleep.

Ellie turned and tried to brazen her way through. Cole's weird gold eyes stared at her and demanded the truth. "Patrick and Paul are waiting outside the hotel."

"Damn." Cole rolled to his back and winced. He rolled back to his side with a groan. "I keep forgetting to stay off my back."

"We need to get out of town."

Cole nodded. "Yup. We need a way to do that."

"Already arranged." It gave her an inordinate amount of pleasure to tell him as much. "I hired us a coach and four with a driver and outrider." She hoped he didn't cut up nasty about the next part. "I had to take some of your money to do it."

He eased to sitting. "It's okay, Ellie. You take what you need."

"I'll pay you back." She wasn't his charity case, and she really didn't want to keep costing him in every part of his life.

"Ellie." Cole patted the bed beside him. "Come and sit."

"No." Sitting that close to an almost bare Cole was a bad idea. "I need to pack."

"Ellie." He used a preemptory tone that got her hackles right up. He needed to rethink if that tone was aimed at making her mind him.

She folded a shirt of his and packed it. "I said no."

"Please, Ellie." That and the soft entreaty from his strange, beautiful eyes got her over to him and perching gingerly on the edge of the bed. She was right where she'd plotted to be from the start of this adventure, in Cole's bed. The thought nearly made her giggle, and she bit the inside of her cheek to stop herself.

Cole chuckled and turned her face his way. His fingers were warm beneath her chin, warm and strong and making her skin sensitive. "I'd dearly like to know what's going on in that head of yours right now."

"No, you wouldn't." Her dumb imaginings and even dumber heart fluttering were nothing Cole needed to know about. She steeled herself and met his gaze. "What did you want?"

"You did well, Sugar." He slipped his hand beneath her chignon and cupped her nape.

The touch shot through Ellie like a bolt of lightning, and she wanted to purr and rub against his hand. It took her a minute to find a voice that she hoped came out normal. "I didn't do anything."

"You kept your head." His long fingers stroked the column of her neck. "You kept your head and got us a way out of here."

"You would have done the same."

"Maybe, but you still did well." He shrugged. Slumberous warmth crept into his eyes and he stared at his fingers on her neck. "Your skin is soft."

"Oh." Nothing else came into her mind, and she dropped her gaze before he saw how much he affected her.

"Smooth and silky." His voice grew deeper, huskier, and it

rasped against her senses like his touch. Her girls had spoken of men who could melt your bones with a touch. Unaware of her innocence, they had shared all their bawdy stories in her hearing.

Ellie knew what was happening. She was in lust. Her woman's body craved Cole. It had nothing to do with deeper feelings. "Cole?"

"Hmm?" He trailed his fingers to the button at her neck. "It makes me wonder all sorts of things."

God help her, but she couldn't stop herself. "What sort of things?"

"Like, is it as soft all over?" He popped her top button open and slid his fingers into the opening. Leaning closer to her, he popped a second button. "Will it taste as good as it looks?" Another button slipped open, and his hand slid beneath her chemise and found her skin. He growled and spread his fingers. "Still soft here."

He wove enchantment around her in the brush of his long, clever fingers and the rich burr of his voice.

Ellie's breath caught as a fourth button popped open. Her corset top peeked out.

"I've always wondered." He brushed her open bodice to the side and spread his hand over the swell of her breast. "So many times." He pressed closer, his lips skimming her cheek. "More times than you know, I've watched you, Sugar, and thought about putting my hands on you." He dragged his hot mouth down her cheek and to her neck. "Putting my mouth on you."

Ellie felt like she might go up in flame any moment. Her befuddled brain barely clung to the knowledge that he wanted her as well. Her response whispered out of her on a soft moan. "Me too."

"No, Ellie." He groaned against her shoulder. "You're not

supposed to say that. Tell me to get off you. Tell me to keep my hands to myself."

"I don't want to." For once, could she not have what she wanted? Heart thudding, she said the words that had been hovering on her lips for days now. "I want you to touch me. I want you to do those things to me and more."

Cole stilled and straightened away from her. He removed his hand from her bodice and cupped her cheek. "You don't know what you're saying, Ellie, what you're asking for."

"Yes, I do." He needed to see her for who she really was. Not some sheltered princess to be left untouched on the shelf. "I might still be a virgin, but I ran a cathouse, and I know more than most about what happens between a man and a woman." With him looking at her like he wanted to consume her, and her own senses screaming for more of the same, Ellie took her chance. "I want you to show me all of it. I don't want to spend my life hiding my secret."

Cole frowned. "Be straight here, Ellie. I don't want any room for misunderstanding."

"If you were so inclined." Ellie had to stop to catch her breath and summon her last ounce of courage. "I'd like you to be the one who takes my virginity."

Cole blinked at her. "Shit! That was honest all right."

"Yes, Cole." She stood and buttoned her dress "Now you need to decide if that's shit yes or shit no." She walked on rubbery legs to the door. "But it's going to happen whether it's you or the next man I meet who I think will do."

"Ellie." Cole spoke her name like a harsh demand. His gold eyes blazed at her. "There won't be any other man. Got it?"

There was that bossy tone again, and she aimed to cure him of that. Summoning her sassiest version of Sugar Ellie, she met his gaze with all the boldness she could muster. "Maybe. I'll let you know."

TWENTY-TWO

T hree days of hard traveling later, Ellie stood in the hallway of Cole's Denver house wanting to commit murder. The only thing stopping her was she couldn't decide who to kill first, Bridget or Cole.

Getting past Patrick and Paul had been ridiculously easy. They'd stayed in the hotel until boredom and the lure of liquor pulled the twins into the saloon. Once they were all three safely in the carriage and Cole settled as comfortably as possible, Bridget started talking.

Bridget hadn't stopped talking for all three of those traveling days. To get away from her, Ellie had tried to bribe the outrider into riding in the carriage. Until she'd spent three days in a carriage with Bridget, she would have thought it impossible that one person could have so much to say about nothing.

Ellie had all but thrown herself out of the carriage when Cole had announced their arrival at his home. Soon after that point, Cole had moved into first place on her murder list.

Standing before the gleaming wooden stairway, on a rug so fine it made her want to apologize to it for brushing it with the unworthy skirts of her widow's dress, she straight up gawped.

"Do you think Cole is rich?" Bridget whispered, loud enough for the poker-faced butler to hear, not that he showed an indication of having heard. He directed a couple male servants with the baggage.

Ellie didn't bother to reply to the flaming, blasted, bedamned obvious. Cole was rich. Not, a nice house with some pretty horses rich, but a goddamn castle-like mansion with more rooms than she'd had cups of tea rich. From the sheen of it, she'd bet that pale gold wallpaper above the gleaming wainscoting was silk.

Cole, who should now be known as a dirty, low down, deceiving snake, had disappeared shortly after their arrival with a mousey, earnest looking younger man who called himself Cole's secretary.

"Oooh. Pretty." Bridget reached out to touch the shimmering crystal of a wall sconce. "How do you think they make them so shiny?" She turned to the butler.

Ellie almost told her not to touch, but then Cole could go out and buy himself a million more crystal wall sconces to match the exquisite chandelier above their heads.

"Do you polish these every day?"

"Yes, miss. Our housekeeper, Mrs. Fuller, is most particular." The butler bowed and motioned the staircase. "If you would follow me, I am sure your rooms are ready."

"Our rooms?" Bridget scampered to catch up with the butler. "Are Ellie and I sharing a room?"

"No, miss."

"I don't mind sharing a room with Ellie. She doesn't snore or anything, and she's real careful not to wake me if I'm still sleeping." She threw a smile over her shoulder. "Ellie likes to wake up early."

"I'm sure." The butler kept climbing stairs.

Ellie followed in their wake and gave up trying not to stare. Cole had the temerity to not only have lied about his wealth but to have built the sort of house she would have fallen in love with. Despite its opulence, everything had the subtle elegance that screamed old money.

In light of this, she started revisiting all she knew of Cole. He came from New York and she would eat her hat if he didn't come from a house like this one.

Bridget carried on peppering the butler with questions. Did they have to sweep every day—yes, they did. Was that real glass in the windows—yes. How did they make it so sparkly— vinegar and water. He handled the barrage with grace and politeness.

They reached the first floor and he turned left, motioning her to follow. He opened a tall, carved wooden door and looked at Ellie. "Mrs. Pierce, we thought you might be comfortable in here."

"Ho-o-ly." Bridget walked to the center of the room and turned in a circle. "You could fit my entire family in that bed."

She wasn't wrong either. The room was beautiful and mad as she was, Ellie had to admit it. Cream walls and honeyed wooden floors made the room warm and inviting. Eau de Nile draperies around the windows and bed picked up the shades of another beautiful carpet taking up most of the floor space.

Light flooded through the entire wall of windows. A chaise was positioned before the windows, perfect for whiling away the day and soaking up the warmth.

"Mrs. Pierce?" The butler intruded on her examination of the room. "Is this tolerable? We can move you if it is not to your satisfaction."

Ellie stopped in front of an oil painting of lilies that hung above the large hearth. "It's beautiful."

The butler bowed. "Mr. Mansfield will be pleased to hear so. He was most particular that we see you settled well."

Oh, she'd bet Cole would be pleased. To be fair, he'd never outright told her he wasn't rich, but he had let her go on thinking he was a man who lived on the next turn of the cards.

"I am sure you would like to rest." The butler motioned a still chattering Bridget out. "Dinner is served at eight."

"Actually." Ellie wanted to be alone with her thoughts. "I'm not that hungry. I won't be down for dinner."

"Very good, Mrs. Pierce" He bowed. "In case you find yourself peckish, I will have a tray brought up to you."

"No, you—thank you." She may as well enjoy this lovely room. It wouldn't be nearly as nice with Cole's blood speckled over that silk counterpane. She kind of knew she was being an ass, but she felt misled, deceived, and completely out of her depth. Seeing his house, she couldn't pretend she and Cole were like each other.

"Bye, Ellie." Bridget waved to her. "If you get lonely, I can always come and visit."

"No." It came out louder than she intended, and she moderated her tone. "Thanks, Bridget, but I'm tired and have a bit of a headache.

Bridget frowned and looked like a perturbed angel. "Oh, Ellie, you should have said something. And here is me chattering and chattering and chattering. Why, I must be making your head hurt."

"Miss Bridget." The butler held the door open for her. "Follow me to your room. It's pink."

"Pink." Bridget squealed and clapped her hands. "Do you hear that, Ellie? My room is pink."

The butler glanced at her, and Ellie was almost certain she

caught the ghost of a smile on his thin, grave face. "My name is Roberts, Mrs. Pierce, and we are pleased to serve you at Mansfield House."

After they'd gone, Ellie wandered through a door at the far end of the room, and into her own bathroom.

Someone tapped on the outer door.

Ellie crossed to it and let them in.

A young maid with a big smile stood on the other side. She bobbed a curtsy. "Good afternoon, Mrs. Pierce. I'm Molly, and I'm here to help you."

Behind Molly stood two of the male servants from earlier.

Molly motioned them. "I took the liberty of having bath water drawn for you."

A bath in that lovely bathroom sounded like heaven, and opening the door wider, Ellie let Molly and her entourage in.

Molly went through another door, and Ellie followed her into a closet. Her bags were already there, and Molly set about unpacking them. Her few belongings would be entirely lost in a closet that size.

Ellie felt awkward standing there and watching Molly work. "I can do that."

"Oh no, Mrs. Pierce, it's my job." Molly gently pried a shoe out of Ellie's grasp. "And I'm happy to do it."

"I can help."

Molly turned and smiled. "Or you could have a nice hot bath while I finish."

Feeling managed, Ellie backed out the room.

Molly lost no time in hurrying her into a bath. She picked up Ellie's travel-worn clothing from the floor. "We'll get these washed and pressed and looking better than ever."

She stayed in the bath until her skin pruned and the water had cooled. Molly brought her a red robe in a wool so soft Ellie suspected cashmere. It wasn't hers, but she wasn't about to say no to something so lovely.

Molly left, and Ellie sat on the lovely chaise and looked into the evening. A glorious sunset painted the sky in vivid pinks and reds. It was like a daydream into another world. Chances were this was her first and last time to experience that sort of luxury. It could have been the lovely room, or the delicious dinner, or perhaps even the two glasses of wine, but Ellie was feeling much more relaxed.

A firm knock sounded on her door. "Ellie?" Cole said.

"Come in." They might as well get it over with. Cole owed her some explanations.

Even without his jacket and in his shirtsleeves, his waist-coat open, this Cole didn't look like her Cole. His black evening trousers fit him like they were made for him, which they probably were.

He stood in her doorway with a decanter and two glasses in his hand. "I came offering an olive branch."

"You lied to me." Ellie motioned him in.

"Technically, I didn't lie." Cole pushed the door shut with his foot and strolled deeper into the room. "Is the room all right?"

"It's beautiful, Cole." This Cole was a stranger to her. She felt cast adrift like he had dealt the deck differently, and she was still clutching a fist full of old cards. "Everything is beautiful. You know that."

"You're mad." He perched on the window ledge near her feet and put the glasses and decanter down beside him.

"I was when I first arrived." She took one of the filled glasses from him. "You made me think you were a gambler."

"I was." He poured another glass for himself. "I am still, except now I gamble on things other than cards."

"Apparently." She sniffed her glass. "Whisky?"

"What else?" He flashed his gorgeous, wicked grin at her.

There he was, the man she knew, and a weight shifted from her shoulders. The house had made her think she didn't know Cole at all, but she did know him. At least one side of him. "So." She motioned with her glass. "How did you go from five card stud to all this?"

"Practice." He chuckled at her look of disgust. "I got my stake gambling. You know, I was good at it. But I always knew when to stop. I took my winnings and invested them." He shrugged and sipped his whisky. "Denver is a town growing like a weed. Treat her right, and the lady will repay the favor."

"You were always a charmer." She really had no reason to be angry at him. "Why the secrecy?"

"A precaution." He lifted her legs and sat on the end of the chaise. Placing her legs on his lap he stared into the darkening evening. "I was going to sell this house, but I think I'll keep it for a bit."

"Why?"

"Reasons." He winked at her. "Are you still mad at me?"

"Not really." Them sitting there like that was disconcertingly intimate, like a married couple enjoying the end of the day together.

Her senses woke to the possibilities of them being there like that. The bed was only a few paces away, and there would be no interrupting them tonight. If Cole kissed her, what would she do?

She almost snorted out loud. Like she would do anything other than melt like butter on hot toast. Lying to herself had never gotten her very far, and she finally admitted a truth she'd been dancing around for years. From the moment Cole had walked into the Four Kings and given her a look loaded with desire and determination, she had been his. Only the timing had never been right.

"You're frowning." Cole wrapped a big hand around her ankle. "What's making you frown?"

"Nothing."

"Uh-huh." Those lion eyes of his called her a liar. He refilled the drink she hadn't been aware of finishing. "Tell me."

She toed the line of the truth. "I was thinking about when I first met you."

"Yeah?" He raised his eyebrows. "That was some time ago."

"Right." And yet she could recall the exact shade of gray of his jacket and the blue watered silk of his waistcoat. He'd worn a white rosebud in his lapel and given it to her along with that rakish grin that had been playing merry hell with her since the first time she'd seen it.

"Shall I tell you what I remember of that day?" His gaze warmed like poured gold.

She doubted he remembered it as clearly as she did. "Tell me."

"You were sitting on the bar, holding court to an audience eight horny cowboys deep." Soft smile on his perfect lips he stared out the window. "Shit, Ellie, I'd never expected to see anything like you in the Four Kings. I came to play cards and ended up offering all the money I had in the world for one night with you."

As much as his words thrilled her, she couldn't afford to believe them. Cole could drag her deeper under his spell with his sweet talk, and she couldn't afford that. "You knew I would turn you down. That's why you made that crazy offer."

"No, Ellie, actually I was praying you would say yes." He turned to her with a face bare to the truth. He let her see behind his carefully constructed mask to where his desire was painted in bold, clear colors. "I still am."

Her mouth dried and she took a hasty swallow of whisky. It scraped down her throat, hit her belly and spread its warmth.

"What's it to be, Ellie?" Cole put his glass on the floor. "Time to let me know. Personally, I think we've both waited long enough."

CHAPTER

TWENTY-THREE

U nable to hold the connection, Ellie dropped Cole's gaze. This was it. Her opportunity to experience the missing part of her story, and she wavered.

She'd made her escape from the cathouse, and she wouldn't go back. As for marriage, it wasn't for her. It seemed even whores had more say over their lives and bodies than most married women.

"Ellie?" Cole leaned his elbows on his knees and studied her. "Is your silence a no?"

"Um, it's not a no." She didn't know what was wrong with her. She'd seen more naked men than most women, certainly heard enough stories about copulation not to be ignorant. Yet, she sat there with her heart thundering and her palms sweating.

"I see." Cole laughed. It did great things to his beautiful face. The sort of things that made her want to get close to his warmth and generosity. Taking her hand, he tucked it between his. "Are you nervous, Sugar Ellie?"

"Yup." And she couldn't even look at him as she said it. It

was downright humiliating. In her head, things had gone a whole lot different. For one, she was wearing something more alluring than a robe, albeit cashmere. Also, somehow, she'd had it fixed that she would be doing the luring and seducing. Fat chance of that when she couldn't even answer the man's polite request. She took shelter behind the facts. "I think we should establish the rules first."

Up went his eyebrow. "Rules? Why, Sugar, I didn't know you were that kind of girl."

"Wha—" Then she got it. "You're teasing me."

He threaded her fingers through his. "Set your rules, Sugar."

"This is a once off thing." She motioned between them. Her gut screamed that she had to keep it that way. Already, she liked Cole way more than she wanted to. Being intimate with him would only increase their growing connection, and she wouldn't risk herself like that. "A friend helping a friend out."

"Um." Cole held his forefinger up. "In the interest of honesty, I feel the need to point out this is something I've been trying to make happen for a long time."

"Yes, but not seriously. You were never going to pay all those thousands of dollars to lift my skirts."

Cole shrugged "I guess we'll never know for sure."

"But—"

"Is that the end of the rules?"

Ellie got the feeling she was missing something, but Cole's closed expression didn't look like she would be getting any answers. "No. You're leaving, Cole. Whatever we have ends here, and I think that would be best for both of us."

"Agreed." His expression darkened. "Ellie, you know I'm not free?"

Schooling her expression, Ellie nodded. "I know that. You and Victoria. Your heart belongs there."

"Yeah." He frowned. "To be honest, I don't know if it does, but I need to find out."

"I understand."

He stood and strode to the empty hearth. "Ellie, this is dumb idea, and I shouldn't even be entertaining it, but you opened a door that night in the hotel and I can't get the thing closed again."

"I know what I'm doing, Cole." She recognized a man ready to retreat. Time to take a firmer hand in matters. "I know what this is, Cole. We both do." She stopped in front of him and looked up. "If it hadn't been for my inconvenient virginity, we would have gotten to this point before. Or maybe I misread you?"

"You didn't misread me." He touched the neck opening of her robe. "But this is your first time, and you've waited this long. It should be special, Ellie."

"It will be." She rose on her toes and pressed her mouth to the hard line of his jaw. His skin felt warm and slightly prickly from light evening stubble. "Along with everything else, you're my friend, Cole Mansfield." He smelled like leather and soap and she pressed her nose into his neck. "You're the man I choose. The man I choose, and not one chosen for me."

"What if you find someone more worthy?" He cupped her face and tilted her head up to him.

Ellie gripped the sides of his slim waist. "Then the widow Pierce will take herself a lover."

"Ellie." His eyes blazed. "Why me?"

"Because you're you." She could write him a list of all the reasons she chose him. One day she might write that list, when she was old and gray and remembering him with fondness. "And you'll make it good for me." She wrapped her arms around his neck. "Won't you, Cole?"

"Yes, Sugar Ellie." He slid his arm beneath her knees and

picked her up. "But we're going to make this good for each other."

The bed was soft at her back as he lowered her to it. "Cole?"

"Hmm?" He stretched out by her side and propped his head on his elbow. "More rules, Sugar?"

Ellie pointed to her bedside table. "I don't want to get pregnant. I have something to stop that."

"That's good." He smiled at her. "Any more rules?"

"Not that I can think of." She wanted him to take control. Knowing how a thing was done, was apparently not the same as doing that thing. She shook her head. "No."

"Okay." He untied her belt robe. "Then I have some rules I'd like to lay down."

He looked like he was being serious, and fair was fair. "Okay?"

"First." He smoothed the skin between her eyes. "There will be no frowning."

That she could agree to, and she smiled. "No frowning. Got it."

"You're a very good listener, Sugar Ellie." He eased his finger under her robe opening, touched the indent at the base of her throat. "Second rule. No fretting."

"I'm not fretting."

Cole gave her claim the look of doubt it deserved. "I've got you, Ellie." He trailed his finger down her chest, nudging the robe open as he went. "Think of me as your guide through this journey into uncharted lands."

"My guide?" His silliness made her laugh.

He reared up, looking affronted. "You doubt my credentials?"

"I don't know about your credentials." She met his stare and held it. "All I'm getting so far is a lot of jawing."

"Oh, Ellie." He shook his head and looked regretful. "You're going to be real sorry you said that." He spread the plackets of her robe open. "Now, for your instructions."

Her smart response died on her lips as he ducked his head and kissed her neck. His mouth seared the delicate skin as he dragged the caress to her shoulder and back again.

"You may say the following things."

She'd forgotten what he was talking about.

His lips found her earlobe and he breathed into her ear. "You get to say, 'Yes, Cole.'"

"Yes, Cole."

"Good girl." He pushed her robe off her shoulder. "You also get to say, 'More, Cole.'"

"More, Cole."

"More what?" He touched his mouth to hers and withdrew. "More of this?" He pressed his mouth to hers for longer. "Or more of this." His hand slid down her chest toward her breast and stopped frustratingly close to where she wanted him.

"More of both."

"Such a greedy girl." He cupped her breast and sent sensation arcing through her. Her moan was swallowed in his kiss. Unlike his other kisses, this one was a possession, a clear statement of ownership, and he took his time exploring her mouth.

His thumb caressed her nipple as he kissed her, making it so sensitive she wanted to cry out, but then he might stop, and she definitely didn't want that.

"Ah, Sugar." His hand moved from her breast and she made a noise of protest.

"Please."

"I aim to, Sugar." He studied the progress of his hand down her ribs and over her hip bone. Then his hand made a slow journey back to her breast. "I've waited a long time to have you like this."

Tired of his slow pace, she cupped his nape and dragged his mouth to hers. "You talk too much."

He let her take command of the kiss, hanging back and letting her explore him.

The sense of power surged through her blood, and Ellie sat up and unbuttoned his shirt. She spread the sides away from his lovely flesh like it was her own special present.

Cole was a sensory delight and she ran her hand from the dark, flat discs of his nipples, over the ridges of his belly to his waistband. She retraced her caress and tugged at his shirt. "Off."

He sat up and shrugged out of his shirt. "Now what?"

He was hers to do with as she chose, and Ellie straddled his thighs.

Cole sucked in a breath and gripped her hips. "I thought I was the guide."

"I learn fast." Ellie pressed her mouth to the hot skin of his neck. Through her robe, his chest pressed hot and hard, and she gloried in the differences between them, tormenting herself by brushing her nipples over his chest.

"Ellie." He groaned her name. "You feel better than I imagined."

Tugging at her robe, he slid both palms over her bare thighs.

His hands on her skin only made her crave more. "Yes, Cole." She nipped at his bottom lip. "More, Cole."

"More like this?" His hands slid up her thighs and gripped her bare bottom.

"Yes, Cole."

At the apex of her thighs his erection pressed, a bold reminder of his desire.

Ellie rotated her hips against him.

He groaned and threw his head back. "Jesus, Ellie. You need to slow down."

"You need to hurry up." She went right on tormenting them both. "You're not the only one who's been waiting."

He gripped her bottom tighter and moved.

Suddenly, Ellie was on her back, staring up at him before she knew what he was about.

He tugged open the edges of her robe. "Ah, Ellie." He gazed down at her, taking in every inch of exposed skin. "You sure are something sweet."

Under the heat of his stare, she felt more beautiful than she had in her entire life. He looked at her as if he wanted to consume her.

He stroked the flat plane of her belly and cupped her hip. His touch branded her skin, marked her as his in the same way his gaze did.

Pressing her back into the bed, he kissed her. This kiss was gentler, like he was savoring her. His hand stroked her thigh to her knee and pressed at the crook of her knee.

Ellie bent her leg for him, and his hand swept up to her hip again.

He pulled her leg over his hip, the soft wool of his trousers stroking her overheated skin.

He'd taken control of them again, and Ellie was happy to let him. He released her mouth and pressed hot, sucking kisses down her neck and on her chest.

His mouth closed over her nipple and Ellie arched off the bed. The heat of his mouth was like nothing she'd ever felt. She wanted more of it. The suction speared through her tummy and made her privates throb.

Between her thighs, she was wetter than she could have believed. The girls had told her about this, but the reality was so much better.

And then he slid those long fingers between her thighs, and she lost the power of thought. Her whole being seemed poised on his caress. He slid his fingers through her and found her pleasure spot. Her hips jerked in response to the stroke of his fingers.

"That's it, my Sugar," he whispered. "Let your body tell me what it likes."

He moved to her other breast and gave it his attention.

Ellie gripped the back of his head and held him there. Her body was alive with sensation, from the hot suction of his mouth to the slow, strong stroke of his fingers between her thighs.

His mouth left her nipple and traveled down her ribs to her belly. He pressed his face into her belly, his teeth scraping her soft skin. He bit the jut of her hipbone and drifted lower.

Ellie tensed. She'd heard about this too, and doubt flickered. This was impossibly intimate, and she felt suddenly self-conscious. "Cole?"

"Mmm." He pressed her thighs apart. Raising his head, he peered at her over the length of her body. "Is that a yes, Cole or a more, Cole?"

"It's a—" His mouth opened on the inside of her thigh, so hot and so silky and she couldn't think.

Then he put his mouth there and she lost all coherent thought. Dear God, it was like a sensation overload. The heated slide of his mouth over her intimate flesh released a need in her that demanded satiation.

With his lips, his tongue and every so often the brush of his teeth, Cole introduced her to a whole world of new sensation that made a slave of her. Time and place dropped away as her being narrowed to the point of where he was driving her out of her mind.

Her climax unfurled through her belly and her thighs. She

exploded beneath him, arching into his touch, and staying suspended in the moment of her completion.

Cole rose and gathered her close to him. He held her while her heartbeat slowed.

Ellie knew enough to know only one of them had gotten satisfaction. "Cole?"

"Yes, Cole or more, Cole?" He stroked her back and gripped her bottom.

And there really only was one answer. "More, Cole. I want all of you."

"Really?" He shifted her until she was straddling him. His cock was even harder, and it lay hot between them. Reaching over, he grabbed the protection and slid it on.

Ellie parted her thighs over his thighs. "Show me how."

Sliding his hand between her thighs, Cole touched flesh that was almost too unbearably sensitive.

"It would be my pleasure, Sugar." He gripped her hips and positioned her over him. "Put me inside you, Ellie."

She closed her fist over his velvety length and stroked. It felt silkier than she'd imagined. Positioning him where she most wanted him, Ellie eased onto him

There was an uncomfortable moment of stretching and then her wetness eased the passage and he slid inside her.

Cole clenched his jaw, sweat beading on his face as she took him in careful bit by careful bit.

The sense of completion surprised her, and Ellie took a moment to appreciate the sensation of being joined to him in the most elemental way possible.

"Ellie." Cole gripped her hips and moved her on him. "I'm not gonna last much longer, baby."

Carefully, firmly he showed her how to move on him.

Watching the play of emotion and pleasure on his face was fascinating. It increased her own pleasure as her body opened and responded anew to him. Another climax built, and Ellie abandoned herself to the gathering sensation.

She fell over the edge into the sweet dark beyond.

Cole followed her with a shout and a tightening grip on her hips.

With her wrapped around him, Ellie's drumming heart matched his. This moment belonged to them, and nobody else in the world existed. She had expected some physical pleasure, not as much as she had gotten, but some. What she hadn't expected was the intimacy. Whores talked about the mechanics of sex but never the intimacy.

In this moment, she and Cole were connected on a level that transcended their reality.

TWENTY-FOUR

Ellie woke to the clatter of her drapes being drawn.

Molly stood at the window, grinning. "Sorry." She shrugged. "Did I wake you?"

"It's fine." Her eyes watered in the bright morning sunlight. "What time is it?"

"It's after ten, ma'am." Molly had a soft Irish lilt to her speech. Large green eyes dominated a rounded face that would have been plain without the scattering of freckles. "I brought up some coffee and sweet rolls for your breakfast." She grabbed a tray and rattled it over to Ellie. "Unless you'd prefer something else?"

"No, that's fine." The smell of coffee and pastries perked her up. "It's perfect, thank you."

"You're welcome." Molly picked up her dress from where Ellie had hung it over a chair and bustled into the closet. She came back with one of Ellie's new dresses. Holding it up to the light, she examined it. "As widow's dresses go, this is lovely."

"Thank you." Ellie added sugar and cream to her coffee and

took a sip. The rich coffee sweetness crept through her and warmed her outlook.

Cole must have left in the night, because there was no sign of him in her room. Not even the discarded robe. She had a vague memory of stumbling around sometime in the wee hours and finding a nightgown.

Molly examined the stitching on her gown. "Whoever did this has a good hand."

"Thank you." The praise puffed her up. "I bought it ready-made and then did some alterations." Ellie losing herself in sewing may very well have saved Bridget's life as they traveled.

"You did this?" Molly's eyes grew even larger. "Well, I never would have thought that. I would have thought one of those fancy dressmakers."

"No." Ellie bit into one of the sweet rolls and moaned. "These are delicious."

"I know." Molly giggled. "Don't tell Mr. Roberts, but I like to sneak one or two."

Ellie stuffed the rest of the roll into her mouth. "I don't blame you."

"Oh, Lord!" Molly clapped her hand over her mouth. "I got so busy chatting, I forgot." She flapped her hands at Ellie. "You must get up. Mister Cole said to tell you he'd like to take you somewhere today."

"Where?"

Molly rolled her eyes. "Well, I don't know that now, do I? He said to get you ready to go out."

Grabbing another roll, Ellie scooted out of bed. Her body told the story of how she'd spent the night with a collection of aches and twinges. "Is Bridget about?"

"That one?" Molly rolled her eyes. "I never saw a lovelier girl, but I also never heard one talk quite so much either."

At least Bridget had started speaking again, even though it

was interposed with long periods of sighing. "Is she coming with us?"

"Mister Cole said no." Molly giggled and poured warm wash water for Ellie. "She didn't mind though. She took herself off to the kitchen, and she and Cook are getting on like old friends. Cook is not much of talker, and for all her chatter, Bridget is useful in the kitchen."

As quickly as Molly could chivvy her, Ellie was washed, dressed, with her hair stylishly arranged, and eased out of her bedroom.

Molly picked up the basin of wash water to return to the kitchen. "You call for me when you get back and I'll take care of you."

Ellie didn't think Molly would give her any other choice. "I'll do that."

Downstairs, Robert's pointed her to Cole's study, where Cole was waiting for her.

Cole's secretary looked up from his desk close to the door as she entered. He stood. "Good morning, Mrs. Pierce."

"Good morning. I'm sorry I don't know your name."

"Sebastian," Cole said from deeper inside the room. Sitting behind his desk like a relaxed monarch, he smiled at her. "Good morning, Mrs. Pierce. I trust you slept well."

"Passing well, thank you." Did he think he could make her giggle and blush? That roguish light in his eyes said he did. "Tell me, Sebastian, do you have vermin in the house?"

"Vermin?" Sebastian paled. "I sincerely believe not."

"It must have been a dream then." Ellie smiled at him. "But I was sure something crawled into my room in the middle of the night."

Cole's grin broadened. "How very uncomfortable for you." He glanced at Sebastian. "Will you see that Roberts looks into it?"

"Of course, Mr. Mansfield." Sebastian scurried for the door. He stopped and went pink to his hairline as he looked at her. "And rest easy, Mrs. Pierce, if there is a filthy creature in this house, we will rid ourselves of it immediately."

"You've set them an impossible task," Ellie said as the door closed behind Sebastian.

"They'll be fine." Cole rose with feline grace and sauntered toward her. "That will teach Sebastian to ogle my girl."

Ellie steeled herself against the easy charm of his smile and the heart racing possibilities gleaming in his eyes. "First off, Sebastian didn't ogle me." He stopped right in front of her, and she had to tip her head back to maintain eye contact. "And I'm not your girl."

"I was thinking about that." His gaze touched as firmly as a caress on her curves. "I know we said last night would be a once only thing, but I've been reconsidering that."

Ellie's heart beat like a bird against her ribcage. "Cole, we both know this can't last. We went into it knowing that."

"I understand that, Sugar." She wished she knew how he could make her name sound like a heated touch. "But maybe there's something between forever and never again."

He smelled good enough to scramble her thoughts. Here she'd thought scratching the itch would help alleviate it. Turns out, it didn't work like that. She wanted more, and knowing exactly what more felt like, sharpened her hunger for him. "What did you have in mind?"

"A widow is a woman of some experience." He slid an arm about her waist and brought her to rest against him. "It would be remiss of me to send you into the world having only a taste of what is available to you."

"Hmm..." She pretended to mull his words. It was hard to concentrate with the warm strength of him pressed against her. Taking a deep breath, she gathered her scattered thoughts. "You want to visit me again?"

"Sugar Ellie." He growled her name, and the sound skittered over her skin like a cat paw. "Turns out you're even sweeter than your name implies. Sweet enough to make me want more."

"More?" It was wrong and dangerous how her heart skipped at those words. Whores were always warning against getting their feelings engaged. After last night, however, Ellie was afraid that was already a lost cause. She didn't care to examine how deep her feelings were, but caution whispered to her. "You're going to have to spell that out, Whisky."

"I'm not in New York yet." He shrugged, but she sensed the tension he wasn't showing. "And we still have to see you set up in Denver before I go."

That had never been the deal. "Cole, I—"

"I'm not leaving until I know you're safe and set up." His face hardened. "So don't even suggest it."

"Okay." She was so stupid that for a moment she had entertained the vague possibility he wouldn't go to New York. Of course he was going to New York. He'd lived most of his adult life getting to this point. "And you want us to be together until you go?"

Cole winced. "That sounded bad. I didn't mean it like that." He looped his other arm around her waist. "I know I sound like the biggest cad out there, Ellie, but if you were willing, I wanted to see if we could enjoy the time we had."

No. The sensible answer was hell no. Risking getting any closer to this man was a carriage wreck into hell. Dear God, but she craved it anyway, and a lifetime spent not having what she wanted had taught her to take what he offered with both hands. "Like a love affair?"

"Exactly like a love affair, Sugar." His beautiful face would probably haunt the rest of her days. "For as long as it lasts."

There really was only one answer. "For as long as it lasts."

"Is that a yes, Cole?"

For as long as she could, she would take what she wanted. "That's a yes, Cole, and definitely a more, Cole."

"I like that." He dipped his head to her ear. "Now this is how I greet my lover." The kiss he gave her left her breathless. "Good morning, Ellie."

The world seemed a brighter place this morning. "Good morning, Cole."

"Right." He pulled his arms away from her. "As much as I'd like to take this celebration upstairs, we have an appointment."

"We?" As far as she knew, the only people she and Cole had in common were her brothers and the people in this house. "Who with?"

"You'll see." He rested his hand in the small of her back and guided her to the door. "Trust me."

Probably the only person in the world whom she did trust.

The carriage waited outside for them, and Cole climbed in beside her. His face grew serious as they set off. "I want to make sure nobody can ever force you into doing something you don't want to do again."

"Cole, that's not your responsibility." Her carefree gambler had a serious side she was only learning about now.

Cole got that hard look on his face again. "I don't see it that way, Ellie. And I'm going to make sure you're okay whether you like it or not." He got his dander up every now and again and assumed she'd let him boss her around.

"Indeed. We need to talk on that some more."

"Ellie." He raised an eyebrow at her. "At least hear my plan before you get all independent and bloody minded."

"I'm not bloody minded."

"You can be," he said. "And sometimes too stubborn for your own good."

Now that was fighting talk and Ellie gathered her ire to let fly with it.

"We're here," Cole said before she could get started.

Despite her annoyance, Ellie was curious, and she peered out the window. They were stopped on a busy, broad street with buildings on either side of it.

Ellie stepped out the carriage and gawped. She couldn't help it, but she'd never seen so many people or buildings this size. The clatter of carriages, the voices of all those folks, hammers going, and horse's hooves crowded around her.

"What do you think?" Cole stood by a boarded-up building with an expectant look on his face. "I mean, it needs some work, but it wouldn't take much."

Ellie had missed something vital as she looked from Cole to the building and back again. "What's it for?"

"You." He threw his arms wide. "You want to be dress-maker, and a dressmaker needs a store."

Words failed her, and she stood there gaping like a landed fish. "I don't understand."

"I own this building." Cole took a key out his pocket and fitted it into the door. "And the tenant recently vacated."

A man crowded behind her and then stepped around her with a noise of impatience. She was blocking the flow of people on the sidewalk, so she ducked into the building after Cole.

Inside was quieter, and she had to blink against the sudden dark.

"The street gets plenty of traffic." Cole opened some shut-ters and light spilled across the dusty floor. A couple of empty glass counter cases stood at one end of the space. Empty shelves rose behind it. The sort of shelves for goods, or bolts and bolts of lovely fabric for women to choose from.

She could see what Cole did.

The glass cases could be used for accessories and ribbons. In the center, she could position a couple of chaises for women waiting for a fitting. She followed Cole through a door into the back.

It was even larger with plenty of room for seamstresses and even an office. She could partition off one section for women to be fitted. Hell, she had enough space for more than one fitting room.

Reality crashed into her dreams. "Cole, I don't know how much the rental is, but I'm pretty sure it adds up to more than I can afford."

"Here's my proposal." Cole grabbed her hand and tugged her closer to him. "I believe in you, Ellie, and I'd like to stake you to start your business. I provide you enough funds to get started and this space. I'll be in New York, so a silent partner. What do you say, Ellie?"

"I say this feels like charity." Her dreams drifted so close, and she wanted them so bad.

"It's not charity if I have a stake in the business." He wrapped his arms around her. "And I'm a demanding business partner."

The look in his eyes lit her like a candle, and she softened against him. They were lovers now. That meant she could lean into him, rise on her toes and kiss him as if he belonged to her.

Cole groaned into her mouth. "Ellie. Is this a yes, Cole?"

"This is a yes, Cole." She pressed her breasts into his chest. "This is also a more please, Cole. Now."

CHAPTER

TWENTY-FIVE

Cole insisted on taking her to lunch afterward. It was the first time Ellie had been in a restaurant so grand and she prayed she wouldn't do anything stupid like pick her teeth with her knife. Not that she'd ever picked her teeth with her knife, but still it could—

"Ellie." Cole laid a hand over hers. "Breathe."

She stifled a nervous giggle. A woman seated by the picture window turned and stared from beneath her enormous, plumed hat.

Ellie took in the gleaming wooden floor, the crisp white tablecloths, the crystal and the polished silver and said, "It's very grand here, isn't it?"

Cole glanced around them. "I suppose. Would you like to go somewhere else?"

"No, this is..." Not her, and everybody in there could see how out of place she was. "Cole, I don't belong here."

He stared at her across the tablecloth that Ellie knew they starched. "Sugar, you can be whoever the hell you want to be, and you can go wherever you want." He picked up her hand

and kissed her knuckles. "You, Sugar Ellie, are a powerful force of nature."

Well, when he put it that way. Her cheeks flushed and she sipped from her crystal water goblet. She'd never seen crystal in her life, but she'd bet her best bustle this was it.

A waiter dressed in black tails appeared at their table. "Good afternoon, Mr. Mansfield. We are pleased to have you back."

"Thanks, Gerald. We'd like a bottle—"

"Sugar?" a man called. "Sugar Ellie, is that you, honey?"

The beautiful room with the elegantly dressed men and women faded away, replaced by the sawdust floor of the Four Kings and the smell of stale beer, dusty range, tobacco and sweat.

"Well, I never." A tall man with a thin mustache and dark, slicked back hair appeared at their table. "I thought it was you, but I couldn't be certain." He looked at Cole with a gleam in his eye. "I didn't know you—"

"You still don't know." Cole stood as tall but broader and oozing quiet menace. "Now, say your hello and move on."

"I—" The man swallowed and nodded. "Sorry, Whisky. I didn't realize...mean to say." He cleared his throat and smoothed a hand over his jacket. "Nice to see you, Sugar. You look great."

He hurried away and out of the restaurant.

Ellie didn't even know his name. He could be one of thousands of men who had passed through the Four Kings in her time there, another gambler with a taste for adventure and a hankering after some easy money.

"You okay?" Cole took his seat, anger still stamped on the lines of his face.

Was she? Not a chance.

The woman with the huge hat was looking at her again,

and Ellie felt she could see past her widow's dress and straight into the madam she had been. She felt exposed, naked, like she was sitting there in her ankle boots, stockings and satin corset. Suddenly, she was Sugar Ellie. The woman she'd been running from had caught up with her.

Cole stood and held out his hand. "Let's go."

Forcing herself to keep walking, Ellie restrained the need to run as far and fast as she could. Would that be far enough to escape who she had been all these years?

She didn't believe so.

Outside the restaurant, Cole helped her into his carriage and got in beside her. He took her hand, and she could feel his gaze on her. "Ellie?"

"She's always going to be there." She had never spoken her fear to anyone. To be fair, she'd had nobody who would listen before today. "Sugar Ellie is going to outlive me."

"Sugar Ellie isn't so bad." Cole wrapped an arm around her shoulders. "I used to make a trip out to Rattler's Gulch, through the dust, dirt and whatever the hell else it kicked up, to see Sugar Ellie."

He didn't really get it. "Sugar Ellie is a whore."

"Sugar Ellie is a woman who did what she needed to survive, and she never hurt anyone doing it." He kissed her temple. "Sugar Ellie is sweet and sassy and beautiful. She's got a heart even bigger than her gumption, and she's got plenty of that."

He was comforting her, trying to make her feel better, and it was working a little too. It was also making her aware of something that had never crystalized in her thinking before. Even before he'd known she wasn't who she portrayed herself to be, Cole hadn't judged. He had accepted Sugar Ellie for who she was and the choices she'd made.

"You don't really get it." She stared out the carriage

window at the bustling city she had hoped to make a new start in. "Because you don't see me and see a whore, you see the woman."

"When you look at me, do you see a man who's killed, cheated and lied to survive?"

"No." She saw Cole, a man who was coming to mean too much to her.

"Right." He shrugged. "But I've done all of those things and more besides." He rested his cheek against her head. "This is a tough world we're part of, Sugar, and sometimes we all have to do what it takes to stay breathing."

He was right, but it still didn't alleviate the pressure on her chest. Theo used to call her Sugar when she was younger, and when she stepped into her role at the Four Kings, Sugar had stuck with Ellie added to it. Sugar Ellie had chosen her, and she wasn't going to disappear without a fight.

The carriage stopped, and Cole helped her out.

Looking so out of place it would have been laughable if she hadn't been so shocked, Pete and Isaac sat on the top steps of Cole's house.

Roberts stood in the doorway, a look of relief as he spotted Cole. "I am sorry, Mr. Mansfield. These persons insist on speaking with you and will not be deterred."

"That's all right, Roberts. Take them to my study and bring some refreshments."

Roberts took it in his stride and nodded. "Very good. Gentlemen? If you would be so good as to follow me."

"Huh?" Isaac blinked at Pete.

Pete boxed his ears. "Git after him." He looked over at Cole and grimaced. "We need to talk. I can't get a lick of work outta him since you left with that girl."

Dumbstruck, Ellie followed Cole into the house. At the door, she handed her hat and coat to a hovering Molly.

Jerking her head at Pete's disappearing back, Molly whispered, "Who's that?"

"I suspect he will be Bridget's father-in-law."

Molly gaped and then sniffed. "Well, I don't like the look of him. Looks mean."

Pete had his moments, and as the woman he'd abducted, she certainly didn't have too much good to say for him, but she'd come to no harm at his cabin and he genuinely cared for his son. "He's a bit odd."

"I'll say." Molly snickered.

"Miss O'Rourke?" Roberts glided down the corridor. "If you have successfully retrieved Mrs. Pierce's outerwear, I suggest you take it to her chamber." He glared down at Molly, hands behind his back. "And then Bertha requires some help in the laundry."

Molly looked at her and winked. "We're not supposed to gossip about the guests."

"Miss O'Rourke!"

"All right, Uncle Dan, but I still think it's strange someone like that showing up to a house like this."

Roberts kept his face impassive and motioned Ellie forward. "Mr. Mansfield requests you join them in the study."

Like she would miss what Pete had to say. Ellie hurried to join them.

Cole looked relieved to see her.

Beside the window, Isaac stood mangling his hat between his hands.

Pete accepted a glass from Cole and sniffed it. Deciding it met his standards, he downed the glass.

Raising an eyebrow, Cole refilled Pete's glass and sipped his own drink. "You're here about Bridget."

"Is she here?" Up came Isaac's head, hope beaming from his eyes.

Ellie took pity on him. "I think she's in the kitchen helping Cook."

"May I see her?" Isaac edged for the door. "Just for a moment."

Roberts appeared in the doorway and on a nod from Cole took Isaac with him.

"Now, I know you aren't partial to my method of getting my boy a wife." Pete held out his empty glass for a refill.

A refill of a whisky, Ellie suspected, cost more money than Pete saw in a year.

"You kidnapped me," Ellie said. However Pete tried to dress it up, he'd knocked her out and toted her on the back of a mule.

Pete gaped at her. "Well, if I'd asked you, you would'a said no."

"That's true." Laughter glittered in Cole's eyes as he turned to look at her. "You would have said no."

Ellie gave up on the two of them. "Why are you here?"

"I reckon we should have us a wedding." Pete went in for glass four.

Ignoring Pete's outstretched glass, Cole looked at her. "I hadn't sent anyone to Pete yet, and you know how Bridget's been."

"How's she been?" Pete stomped over to the decanter and helped himself. "Sighing and pining like that idiot of mine?"

"Something like that." Ellie was gladder than she could say that Pete and Isaac had made the trip before receiving any message. They really did care about Bridget, cared enough to make the long trip and put themselves at her and Cole's mercy.

Pete sniffed and hitched his pants. "I reckon Isaac and I could add an extra room on the cabin. Young people need their privacy and all. Then maybe when the little 'uns come, we can expand a bit more. We got plenty of land out there."

"How do I know she'll be safe, and you won't hurt her?"

Ellie wasn't about to miss her chance to make Pete squirm a bit.

Pete took a grubby cloth from his back pocket and wiped his mouth and beard. "Because I didn't hurt you none, and I had plenty of chance before your fella showed up."

"You kidnapped me." Ellie felt the point needed belaboring.

Pete shook his head. "You keep harping on that."

"Because you can't go around kidnapping women."

Looking unconvinced, Pete stared into his empty glass. "Then, I guess I'll apologize. Will that make you happy?"

"Fine." At some point, she had to give up and let the greased pig run free. She stared at Pete.

Pete stared back. "What?"

"Go ahead and apologize." He was lucky she wasn't insisting on some groveling with it.

"I just did."

"No, you offered to apologize, and I said fine. You still have to do the apologizing."

Heaving his pants up, Pete rolled his eyes. "I am sorry for kidnapping you. I recognize that I was wrong, and I pledge never to do such a thing again. I also give you my word, on my late wife's soul, that no harm will come to Bridget." He nodded. "Kin's kin, and I look after mine."

"Ellie?" Cole looked to her.

She already knew what her answer was, but it wasn't her proposal to accept or reject. "The only person who gets to decide if there's going to be a wedding here today is Bridget."

TWENTY-SIX

B ridget and Isaac—Isaac Fisher, it turned out—were married the next day in Cole's palatial living room. Cole had unearthed a willing preacher, and Roberts and Molly stood witness with Cole and Ellie.

The night before, Ellie and Molly had worked all night on a dress, and Bridget got married looking heartbreakingly beautiful in a green and silver gown and wearing fresh flowers in her hair.

Cole offered them and Pete a room for the night, but they all declined. They wanted to get back to the cabin as soon as they could.

Pete did accept a wagon and four new mules to pull it, however, along with a crate of whisky and some bits and pieces to make Bridget's life more comfortable.

Standing on the porch beside Cole later that morning, Ellie waved Bridget goodbye.

Turned around in her seat, Bridget kept waving until the wagon lumbered around the corner and they were out of sight.

Ellie really hoped Bridget would be all right.

"That's a big sigh." Cole wrapped his arm around her shoulders. "Worried about her?"

"A bit." Ellie allowed herself to be led back into the house. "There won't be anyone to help her if she needs it."

Cole opened the library door and shut it behind them. "If it worries you, I can always send someone out to check on them."

"Pete would shoot them."

"Not if they bring free stuff with them." Cole picked up a bottle of champagne leftover from the wedding toast and handed her a glass.

Ellie took a sip. She was developing a fondness for champagne. Once Cole was gone though, she'd be back to beer. "I think she'll be fine. Happy even. Pete never hurt me, and after you were stabbed, he could have finished the job, but he didn't."

Cole stopped with his glass halfway to his mouth and looked at her. "I, for one, am very glad he didn't finish the job."

Giggling, Ellie set down her glass, closed the distance between them and wrapped her arms around his waist. "Me too."

"I've been thinking." Cole looped his arms around her. "About you."

"Hmm?" She liked the sound of that. She also liked the sharp line of his jaw and she craned her neck and kissed it. His skin was warm against her lips, and he smelled like sandalwood and whisky. "What sort of thoughts?"

"Not those." His voice went deeper, and he drew her closer to him. "Or should I say, not only those thoughts."

Ellie tasted the strong column of his neck, still smooth from his morning shave. "I missed you last night."

"You were busy." He dropped a kiss on her mouth. "Now stop that so I can speak to you."

"Speak?" Ellie slid her hands inside his jacket. "I may be

new to this love affair thing, but even I know it doesn't involve a lot of speaking."

"Complaining already?" He pressed her hips to his. "We'll get to the loving later, but listen up, this is important."

"All right." She stepped away from him and picked up her champagne glass. Robbed of her first choice of pleasure, she took an enormous swig of her second.

Cole refilled her glass and poured himself a whisky. "You can't stay in Denver."

"Not without people knowing who I am." Her mood crashed into despondent. "And if that man spotted us yesterday, it won't be long before my brothers find us."

Nodding, Cole sipped his whisky. "That's what occurred to me last night. You can't stay here, and you can't go back." His gaze grew more intense. "But you can come with me to New York."

Ellie laughed. She couldn't help it. It was an absurd idea, and Cole was clearly joking. Only he kept looking at her as if he were dead serious. Her mirth disappeared. "Cole. I can't come to New York with you."

"Why not?" He had a set line to his jaw that meant he was going to be difficult.

Ellie couldn't believe she had to spell it out for him. "After all this time, how do you think Victoria is going to feel about you showing up with another woman?"

"I'll explain that you're the widow of a good friend and I am setting you up in business as per his instructions." Cole took a seat in a large leather chair. "If it even comes to that. New York is a huge place, and once I set you up, you and Victoria may never cross paths."

He made sense, but it was still a crazy idea. Denver was the biggest city she'd ever been in, and it intimidated her enough. However, Cole was right about New York being big enough for her to get lost. Her brothers would never find her in a city that size. Jake and the twins she was glad of, but not Theo. "What about Theo? If I go to New York, he'll never find me."

"I've thought of that too." He stretched out his long legs and crossed them at the ankle. "Whether you come to New York or not, I'm sending someone to find Theo."

"I'm not sure where to even look." Ellie could go to San Francisco. That or stay there waiting for Jake to catch up with her, and that really was no choice. "I think I should go to San Francisco."

Cole's stare hardened. "If you think I'm going to let you go to San Francisco on your own, you've lost your mind."

"I beg your pardon." Where did he get off with being so bossy?

"I said." Cole spread his arm over the back of the chair. "That you're not going to California on your own."

"Who are you to stay I'm not?"

"I'm saying it." He sipped his drink. "And if you try it, I'll follow you and drag you back."

He was being impossible, and she needed to set him straight. "You wouldn't dare. And anyway, you're off to New York in a day or two."

"I'm off to New York in the morning," Cole said. "And you're coming with me."

Ellie didn't bother with keeping her voice down. She was frustrated, and he wasn't listening. "I can't go to New York."

"Why not?"

"Because...what would I do there? Where would I live?" Cole looked so calm and collected, she wanted to smack him.

He sipped his whisky. "You will do exactly what you planned to do in Denver. You'll open a dress shop for women who can't afford the expensive modistes. I'll stake you a start in your business, same as I was going to do here."

"Yes, but…" She couldn't finish her sentence because her reasons against were running out.

"You can stay with me at a hotel for a bit. We'll find you somewhere to live close to your business."

Cole made it sound so reasonable, so plausible. All she had to do was get on that train with him tomorrow.

"You know it makes sense, Ellie." Cole stood and put his glass on the side table. He took both her hands in his and pulled her arms about his waist. "I know it wasn't the plan at first, but plans change. We can do this. I think your idea will go down even better in New York, where there are plenty of girls who need what you offer."

Still not willing to believe the solution was so easy, Ellie pressed her cheek to his chest. "If I agree to this, it's as your business partner and not your lover."

"Why can't we be both?" He rubbed her back with his big hands.

Already she was in too deep with Cole. Once he got back with his Victoria, she'd never be able to share him. She wasn't made that way. On this point, she needed to stand firm, for the sake of her poor heart. "If we go to New York, we will be business partners only. Whatever this is between us ends the moment we step off the train to New York."

"Done." Cole's eyes gleamed. He bent and lifted her off her feet. "Ever imagine you'd conduct a love affair on a train?"

"No." Ellie wrapped her legs around his waist.

Cole gave her a wicked grin. "Well, get ready, Sugar, you're about to."

TWENTY-SEVEN

I n all her speculating about a love affair, Ellie had never thought of having one as fun. Turns out Cole was all about fun.

They'd taken his private rail car from Denver to Cheyenne, and then hitched to the New York train. Just last year, the Transcontinental Express had left New York and arrived in San Francisco eighty-three hours later. Ellie kind of wished they still went slower.

After she'd gotten over the surprise of going to New York, she'd made the decision to enjoy the life out of whatever hours she had with Cole.

Like now, sitting in her chemise on the huge rumpled bed where Cole made love to her any time the fancy took—and the fancy took often—as he taught her to play poker.

She had a working knowledge of the game, but Cole was trying to instruct her on the finer points. If he hadn't been sitting there shirtless, his beautiful chest the subject of her slavish admiration, she might have absorbed more of the lesson.

"Sugar." He gave her a reproving look over his cards. "You cannot see me without meeting the bet."

Not with this fistful of nothing she had. "But I don't want to."

He looked torn between the desire to laugh or shake her. "Then you shouldn't have played."

"Pfft!" She waved her hand at him. "Maybe it's all a ploy to get you to think I don't know what to do. Then you'll bet big, and *bam*, I got you." She raised an eyebrow at him. "Did that ever occur to you?"

"No, Sugar." He drawled her name like honey poured into whisky. "That did not occur to me for one minute, and neither does it occur to me now. You're not concentrating."

"Oh, I'm concentrating all right." She leered at him.

Cole's expression warmed immediately. "Is that so?"

"Uh-huh." She shrugged and the sleeve of her chemise slid down her shoulder.

His eyes tracked the fabric's movement. "So what's your next move?"

"I pay to see you." She shoved her rapidly dwindling pile of pennies into the middle of their game.

"Right!" Cole tossed his cards over his shoulder and lunged. He caught her around the waist and bore her down to the bed beneath him. "Consider this me showing my cards."

Giggling, Ellie wrapped her arms around his neck. Most of the time, he didn't need to lay a finger on her for her to want him. A look from those molten gold eyes, or just looking at all the gorgeous male sharing a train car with her, and she craved him. "We should get up and get dressed."

"That's where you're wrong, Sugar." He left a trail of hot kisses up her neck to her mouth. "You get dressed, and I'm only going to take all your clothes off again."

"You're so demanding." And it might be her favorite thing

about him. Along with the way he made her feel like the world centered around her. Or how he could always make her laugh, and he never spoke down to her when he discovered gaps in her education.

Ellie bet Victoria didn't have those gaps in her education. When Cole spoke about stuff with Victoria, she would have an intelligent opinion.

"Hey!" Cole framed her face with his hands. A small frown creased his brow. "Where did you go?"

"I'm here." She wriggled beneath him to prove her point.

Cole didn't play. He continued to look into her eyes as if he could see her thoughts. "You went somewhere else." He kissed her temple. "Your head left us."

He also read her like one of the many books he kept in the car. "It's nothing." She slid her hands over his shoulders and down the fascinating swells of his arms. "I was thinking you spoil me."

"I like spoiling you." He took her lead, but his eyes said he didn't entirely believe her. By unspoken agreement, they kept their discussions light. They steered clear of anything concerning the future. "And I have an obscene amount of money with which to do so."

"I don't think it's polite to talk about how rich you are."

He pulled a face. "You may be right. But you know what else isn't polite?"

She shook her head. From the heat in his eyes, she knew she was going to really like the answer.

His lips trailed her chest and fastened over her nipple. Through the fabric of her chemise, he sucked it into the heat of his mouth and released it. "It's not polite to tell a woman how much you want to bury your face in her breasts." Sitting up, he tugged her chemise over her head and threw it away. He slid down her body to her belly. "Or here." He parted her thighs and settled between them. "And it's definitely the height of bad manners to bury your face between her thighs."

With a small scream, Ellie arched into the caress of his mouth. Cole brought her to completion before crawling up her body. He shrugged out of his trousers.

Ellie wrapped her legs around his hips and let him take her there. Every time he loved her, it felt as good as the first time, better even. He taught her about her pleasure, and about his.

With every lesson he gave, Ellie fell deeper and deeper under his spell. Every touch bound him closer to her. Every time he loved her, he took another piece of her heart with him.

Hours later, Ellie lay beside a sleeping Cole, laying partially on his stomach, his right arm stretched out and resting across her belly.

The train rushed into the night, taking them with it. With every mile of grassland passing the window, her time with Cole drew to a close. Soon they would arrive in New York, and their love affair would be over. Only then, would she allow herself to tally how badly she'd miscalculated. Leaving Cole would plow a furrow straight through the middle of her.

THEIR TIME RAN out a day and a half later. Ellie pressed her face to the window, staring into the bustling mammoth that was New York City, and hiding her steadily tearing heart.

"Almost there." Cole sat beside her, his face shuttered as he stared into the city where he had grown up.

Ellie tried to read his thoughts. "Does it look different?"

"It does, and it doesn't." He tried for a light shrug, but she was coming to know this man. "It's bigger, for sure."

The train had slowed as they passed tall buildings all packed side by side.

From the safety of her carriage window, she eyed the heaving streets with trepidation. So many people and so many horses and carriages, they blurred into a mass of busy and impatient.

She wanted to ask him about the stuff she saw, but returning home must have been difficult for him. "How long since you've been in New York?"

"Twelve years."

A lot changed in twelve years. For his sake, she hoped Victoria wasn't one of those things. For hers, and this was the really pathetic part, she didn't hope any different. She wanted him to be happy. Besides, the pragmatist in her insisted that even if Victoria never took Cole back, he'd already made his choice.

CHAPTER
TWENTY-EIGHT

C ole stood on the sidewalk in front to the towering mansion, morning sun beating on his head, the humidity already making him want to fidget, and waited. What for, he couldn't say, but he waited anyway. Twelve long and grueling years had brought him to this point, and now he was struggling to take the next steps. Literally take the steps up to the mansion's front door so he could ring the bell.

When he had been engaged to Victoria, she'd lived with her parents. He'd never been inside this house. It belonged to her late husband. Giles Bonnington had been one of the set he and Victoria ran with back then.

If pressed, Cole could form a vague image of light brown hair and average height. Victoria, however, was painted as vividly in his mind as she had been the day he'd left.

Tall and slender, Victoria moved with an innate grace that made her seem to float on her own air bubble. The quintessential upper crust debutante, her manners were impeccable, she spoke conversational French, could play the piano and sing, and dabbled in watercolor painting.

He had heard other girls complain at the time that everything Victoria did, she did better than anyone else. He'd felt like king of the world the day she'd said yes to his proposal.

The door opened and a stiff looking butler stared down his nose at Cole. "Mrs. Bonnington bids you enter, sir."

That would be Victoria now, Mrs. Bonnington. Had she seen him standing outside? Did she recognize him?

Instead of standing there like a limp noodle, he needed to get in there and find out for himself. He pressed his sweating palms to his trouser legs. Every dime he'd scrabbled for, every hardship he'd overcome had been so he could come back and prove to Victoria he'd changed, and she could put her faith in him, this time forever.

Inside, the mansion smelled like wax and furniture oil. They were the scents of his privileged childhood, and they surrounded him in a rush of sentiment. He almost expected to turn and see his mother standing at the top of the large, curving staircase.

Heart still pounding in his throat, he followed the butler across the black and white tiled foyer. Bonnington had been a man of means or had come from a family that was. The house was large but beautifully furnished. He'd bet his left jewel Victoria had something to do with that.

The butler opened the door into a salon and stepped back.

And there she was.

Victoria.

He stood one pace inside the salon and stared at her. She'd matured, her figure fuller and her face missing the soft edges of a young girl.

Standing with her hands clasped in front of her, she was

staring at him too. "Cole?" she whispered, alarmingly pale in her stiff black widow's gown.

The gown made him think of Ellie, now Widow Pierce. Her austere black gowns provided a fetching foil for her vibrant beauty. Thinking about Ellie grounded him somehow, and he found his voice. "Good morning, Victoria, or would you prefer I call you Mrs. Bonnington?"

"Cole." She blinked and sat abruptly on the chair behind her. "I couldn't believe my eyes when I looked out the window and saw you there."

He moved deeper into the room. Her voice was the same, light and sweet. Even in his last dreadful days in New York, she had never raised it in his presence. "I was working on the courage to knock on your door."

"You look..." Her large brown eyes catalogued every inch of him in a manner she would have found ill-bred in someone else. But twelve years was a long time not to see the man you'd pledged your life to. "You look well."

And just like that, her breeding came to the rescue and her spine snapped erect and she schooled her expression.

"I know I have no right to be here, but I couldn't not come." He moved deeper into the room. She motioned him to sit and he did. "I needed to see you."

"Have you been in New York long?" She folded her slim white hands on her lap.

Cole wanted her to react somehow. Instead, she sat as she'd been taught to do and showed precious little of her thoughts or her feelings. Jesus, Ellie would either be whaling on him for leaving her for so long, or demanding to know where the hell he'd been, and what the hell he thought he was doing showing up on her doorstep. "I arrived yesterday evening," he said. "You are the first visit I made. I will try to see my mother next."

"My condolences on your father's passing." Victoria inclined her head like she was bestowing a queenly blessing on him. "If it's any comfort, he did not suffer."

It was no fucking comfort. The old bastard should have gone slow and painfully. He'd certainly made his family's lives a living torment when he'd been alive. "Thank you, and I was sorry to hear about Bonnington."

"It was a shock." She cleared her throat. "A sailing accident."

Of course it was. Nobody in New York got dead in a high noon shootout or beaten to death for cheating the wrong man at cards. At least, not in the part of New York he'd been part of.

The clock over the mantel ticked away in the silence. From the street, faint noises drifted inside the mansion. But they were genteel noises, the scrunch of carriage wheels, the clop of horse hooves, the gentle chiding of a nursemaid to her pampered charge.

Twelve years of living a different kind of life robbed him of the ability to sit there and let the minute hand count off the acceptable time for a social call. Life was too short and too precious. It could be snatched away at any second.

"Victoria." Cole sat forward, sweating and his gut tight. "I've never forgotten you."

She jerked and stared at him. "I don't...Cole. You can't..." Then she softened. She was so beautiful, he forgot to breathe as she whispered, "Really?"

"I thought about you almost every day." He took her softening as an encouraging sign. "There were days when the memory of your face was all that kept me going."

"Oh." She flushed and her eyes sparkled. "I was a married woman."

"I know that." And it had been his fault she'd married elsewhere. "And I respected your decision. God knows, I deserved no less."

Dropping his gaze, she stared at her hands as she twisted her skirts between her fingers. Ladies like his mother and Victoria didn't fidget, unless they were deeply perturbed. "Why, Cole?" She looked haunted by the question. "Why did you do it?"

"Accept that challenge? Or break off our engagement?" There was a strange disassociation within him to those events. Pivotal as they had been, they now belonged to another version of himself. A young man, a stranger now, had accepted a duel on some imagined slight. His father had forbidden him from dueling, but he'd done it anyway. Both duelists had been arrested, and only his father's influence had kept Cole out of more trouble. But society had heard the news, and added to the tally of wild misdeeds he'd already accrued, Cole had been out.

"The challenge." She kept her head lowered. "And my father broke off our engagement before you tried to see me that day."

He had stood outside her father's house for nearly two days straight waiting for the girl he had loved to come out and speak to him. In the end, her brothers had forced him away at gunpoint. About ten minutes later, he'd boarded a train going west.

"Whatever you believe about that day, know this." Needing to bridge the gap between them, he took her hands. Cold, white and delicate, they looked fragile against his sun darkened, calloused palm. "I loved you. Nothing that happened all those years ago was because of lack of love for you." She left her hand in his. "In my arrogance and stupidity, I was careless with your love and lost it."

"Oh, Cole." She took her hand away and pressed it to her

mouth. "There were so many months I wished you would come to me and say the things you're saying now." Tears shone against the stark black of her lashes. "But it's too late now. Too many years have passed."

"I don't believe that." He hadn't been naive enough to think she would throw open her doors to him. He had hurt her, changed the course of her life, as well as his, through his thoughtless actions. "All I ask is that you give me the chance to mend my fences."

She stood and walked to the window. She held her head like a queen, her back slim and straight in her heavy black gown. "What do you want from me?"

"A chance." He went with the truth. "A chance to mend the rift as much as you will allow."

With her back still to him, she sighed. "Again, I must ask why?"

"Because I have never forgotten you. You were my everything, and the end to our story has never been written."

She turned, her expression strained. "I cannot think. I don't believe I am yet over the shock of seeing you standing on the sidewalk outside my house." She gave a tight little laugh. "You have barely changed, you know?"

"I think you'll find I am much changed," he said.

"But you look nearly the same." She studied his face. "Actually, that's a lie. You have only gotten handsomer with age."

That was definitely a good sign, and Cole closed the distance between them. "Look, I know this is a shock. I don't expect you to say or do anything now. Take some time and think, but while you're doing that, know that I am more sorry than I can say for hurting you. If you decide you want nothing more to do with me, I'll accept that, but if you give me a chance, I'll do everything I can to make it up to you."

Cole left shortly after. The meeting had gone as well as he

could expect. The weight of his next visit still pressed on him and made it impossible to relax.

Elegant brick exterior peering down at him, his childhood home looked nearly identical. Except the oak in the front of the house was much taller and stouter now, and the door had been painted a cheery blue.

Taking the stairs two at a time, like he had as a boy, he took a moment to breathe before he knocked.

Time stretched slowly as he waited for someone to answer. Finally, the handle turned, and the door opened.

Expecting to see the old family butler, he was nonplussed by the shorter, younger man standing and looking at him politely. "May I help you?"

"Yes." He cleared his throat. "Is my moth—is Mrs. Mansfield in?"

"I shall enquire." He inclined his head. "Who may I say is calling?"

"Tell her..." He hesitated and then spurred forward. "Tell her Cole Mansfield would very much like to see her."

The man showed no reaction to his name, but after asking Cole to wait, closed the door.

Cole cursed himself for being all kinds of a fool. He should have written, sent a fucking telegram, for God's sake. His mother might not believe the butler or get the shock of her life.

The door wrenched open and Brett stood in the doorway.

"Jesus!" Brett looked at him from top to toe. "I couldn't believe it when Mellor told us you were at the door."

"It's me." Cole took in the changes the years had wrought to his older brother. He'd grown muscular and heavyset in his thirties, looking more like their paternal grandfather. "How are you, Brett?"

"Are you serious?" Brett scowled at him. "After all this time, you show up on my doorstep and expect what?"

"You're right." Cole didn't want to fight with Brett. They'd never gotten on as younger men, but this could be a new beginning. "I should have written, or at least sent a telegram. I didn't really think this through past seeing everyone again."

"What a surprise." Brett folded his arms. "Cole didn't think things through before he acted. Nice to know you haven't changed."

But he had changed. More than he could say. "I'd like to see Mother. And you. May I come in?"

"You think because he's dead you can have free run of this house?" Brett shook his head, the cold censure of his face so reminiscent of their father.

"We both know he wouldn't have let me in the house," Cole said. His father had told him to go away and stay away, and Cole had believed him. Quentin Mansfield had not made idle threats or said things he didn't mean. It was a pity that most of what he meant and said was cruel and ugly. "The question is, will you, Brett? Will you let me in the house?"

"No." Brett relished the word. "You're not welcome here or anywhere the family is. You're not part of us anymore, and we've gotten on fine without you." He started closing the door. "Go away, Cole. Crawl back into whatever hovel you've been living in and stay there."

CHAPTER
TWENTY-NINE

Ellie spent her morning lounging in her hotel room, trying not to fret about Cole. Other than Cole's house in Denver, she'd never seen such luxury. Gas lights and a water closet, plus a bath she could fill from her bathroom.

She spent a good fifteen minutes turning the water on and off again, just because she could. A shared sitting room sat between her bedroom and Cole's, and she unearthed some books and a pack of cards. They kept her entertained for a while. Cole hadn't said when he would be back.

At noon, she ordered lunch to be brought up and ate it looking at the bustling street outside her window. There were an awful lot of people in an all-fired hurry out there. She didn't know how she was ever going to find her place among them.

After lunch, she read a book until Cole walked into their sitting room. The pensive look on his face made her heart sink. She'd been bouncing between what she wished for Cole all morning. Her selfish heart wanted things to go badly with Victoria, because her heart tried to convince her brain that if

Victoria rejected him, he would come back to her. Most of her wanted him to have what he desired.

She stood and went to him. "It didn't go well?"

"Ellie." His expression gentled and he brushed her cheek with his fingers. "I'm glad you're here."

And didn't that set her stupid heart off again. Hiding her reaction from him, she poured him a glass off whisky from the decanters and gave it to him.

He smiled his thanks as he took the whisky, shrugged out of his coat and draped it over a chair.

Ellie thought about pouring one for herself but resisted. For both their sakes, she needed to keep her defenses up around him. Already all she wanted to do was wrap her arms around him and love him until he lost that hollowness in his eyes.

"I saw Victoria." He lowered himself into a chair by the fire. Putting his head back, he closed his eyes and stretched his legs out in front of him. "She looked...well. Beautiful."

It was what she had wished for him. There was no reason for the pang his words caused. "And?"

"I'm not sure." He opened his eyes and smiled at her. "I told her I was back, that I was sorry and left it to her if she wanted contact with me again."

"Is that where you were all morning?"

"For some of the time." He held out his hand to her. "I also went to see my mother."

Ellie slid her hand into his and squeezed. "Was she happy to see you?"

"I don't know." He tugged her closer to his chair. "I couldn't get past my brother." His laugh held a wry edge. "My brother, it should be noted, was not in the least happy to see me."

The cause of his upset became clear. Ellie ached to hold

him, touch him, comfort him. She settled for squeezing his hand. "Give him time. It must have been quite a shock to see you after all this time."

"Brett doesn't need time." He kissed her knuckles then turned her hand over and kissed her palm. "He hated me when we were boys, and his feelings haven't changed.

Ellie eased her hand out of his and curled her fingers over the warm tingling where his mouth had been. "So your mother might not even know you're back?"

"I don't know." He downed his whisky and stood and poured himself another. "Maybe she does and feels the same about seeing me as Brett does."

"And maybe she doesn't." Ellie hated to see him defeated. "You did all of this, came all this way, don't give up on her before you know for sure."

"You're right." He put his glass down. The sultry heat in his eyes called to her, a song of want her body answered instantly. "What are you doing standing all the way over there?"

"Maintaining a safe distance." She locked her knees to stop herself from closing the gap between them and giving him the most elemental comfort of all. How she felt about him was irrelevant, and she would not allow her brain to unfurl that thought yet. When he was with his Victoria and she was on her own again, then she would think back to this man and how much he'd meant to her, would always mean to her. "I'm sorry about your brother, Cole. I don't have much luck with brothers either."

He stopped in front of her. "No, you don't." His eyes went molten as they caressed her face and then slid down her body. "I know we said we would go our separate ways in New York, but I think we should reconsider."

His kiss landed as a gentle touch of his mouth to hers.

For a moment, Ellie allowed herself that much. She closed

her eyes and sank into his kiss. His sandalwood and leather scent, she drew deep into her lungs, letting it settle there. This small taste of him would have to last her a long time. Fighting every instinct and desire she had, she ended the kiss and stepped back. "Our time together was incredible." From somewhere she dredged up a smile. "I could never have dreamed of such a wonderful love affair, but for both our sakes, it needs to end now."

He studied her face for a long silent moment, and then said, "If that's what you want, Ellie, that's how it will be."

What she wanted didn't come into it. Ellie could write him a book on how much she didn't want it that way, but the truth she couldn't deny was that when all was said and done, she was the only one who really wanted things to be different.

Cole stayed long enough to share a whisky with her, and then went off to see his business manager. He didn't say why, and Ellie didn't ask. She wasn't entitled to ask him questions like that. Those were questions for a wife.

She busied herself improving her widow gowns until a knock on the door interrupted her.

Opening the door, she found an older woman standing outside dressed in the most beautiful plum colored dress Ellie had ever seen. "Good afternoon."

"Oh." The woman blinked at her and frowned at the door. "I thought this was Mr. Mansfield's room."

It was the eyes that gave her away. The same burnished gold as Cole's. He also got his fine bone structure from his mother. "Are you Mrs. Mansfield?"

"Why, yes, I am." She looked relieved. Beneath a black hat

with a wonderful plume, she looked pale and anxious. "Is Cole...Mr. Mans—is my son here?"

"Not at the moment." Ellie opened the door wider. "But he will be soon if you'd like to come in and wait for him." She was so relieved to be right that his mother wouldn't have refused to see him. "Please stay and wait for him. He so wants to see you."

Mrs. Mansfield studied her and then entered the sitting room. "I take it you know my son well."

"As well as any." Ellie was relieved she was dressed in her respectable widow's garb. The way Cole's mother was looking at her promised probing questions on the way. "Cole keeps to himself a lot, but I journeyed here from Denver with him."

"Denver?" She made a stifled sound, half sob and half laugh. "Is that where he's been all this time?"

"I don't know about all the time." Ellie ached for the way Mrs. Mansfield held her pain close and tried not to show it. "I know he did well for himself in Denver. As a respectable businessman."

Mrs. Mansfield smiled, but it held the weight of her sadness. "If you know my son well, then you know he is not always respectable."

"Maybe not." Ellie didn't want his mama thinking bad of him. "But he's a good man, and a generous and kind one. I got into some bother, and Cole rescued me. That's the reason he brought me to New York."

"Hmm." Mrs. Mansfield motioned a chair. "May I?"

Where the hell were her manners? "Of course." Ellie rushed to pull the dress she was working on off the chair so Mrs. Mansfield could sit. Then she tried to tidy up her sewing paraphernalia.

"You sew?" Mrs. Mansfield tilted her head in a gesture so reminiscent of Cole, Ellie stared at her for a moment.

"Er...yes." Ellie folded her dress over her arm. "That is, not

this one. Well, I am making it better, but it was readymade."
And would her mouth stop flapping?

Folding her hands on her lap, Mrs. Mansfield looked about
the sitting room. "Might I ask a favor, Mrs..."

"Pierce." Of course a widow was a missus first. "Ellie Pierce,
but I prefer to be called Ellie." Actually she liked Cole calling
her Sugar in his deep, smooth drawl best of all, but she wasn't
going to share that with his mother.

"Ellie, then." She inclined her head. "I'm not sure how
much you know of Cole's history."

"I know he left here under a cloud," she said. "I also know
he's spent the last twelve years desperate to get back and prove
he's changed."

Mrs. Mansfield pressed her lips together and stared down
at her hands. She swallowed and cleared her throat. "Could
you tell me about him?"

"Eh?" Ellie wasn't sure what the woman was really asking.
"You're his mother. You know him better than I."

"I know the boy." She pressed her gloved fingers to her lips
and blinked rapidly. "And I knew him as a wild young man, but
the Cole you know is a stranger to me."

They seemed to be straying into some dark waters, and so
Ellie said, "Shouldn't you wait for Cole to tell you."

"I should, yes." Her voice shook. "But I haven't seen my son
in twelve years, Ellie, and I would like to know more about the
man I will meet."

"All right." Ellie kind of understood what she wanted. She
hesitated, wondering where to start.

"How did he live?" Mrs. Mansfield provided the starting
point. "His father threw him out with nothing more than the
money in his pockets. Why not start there?" The anger in Mrs.
Mansfield voice spoke of a wound still festering. Ellie took

hope from Mrs. Mansfield sounding like she violently disagreed with her husband's decision.

"Well, and I can only tell you what he told me because I wasn't there."

Mrs. Mansfield nodded.

"He said he went to the station and bought a ticket for as far as his money would take him."

Mrs. Mansfield made a soft noise of distress. "For the first time I am glad he didn't have more money on him."

"Mostly he played cards at first."

"Gambling?"

Ellie really didn't want to create a bad impression. "Well, yes, but the west is a different place from New York. You have to do—"

"Ellie." Mrs. Mansfield leaned forward and patted her hand. "I'm not here to judge his decisions. I want to know him. I want to somehow bridge the gap of all these years."

"All right then." Ellie took the seat opposite her. "They call him Cole Whisky Mansfield," she said. "On account of his eyes. Eyes like yours, I see, and also on account of his habit of insisting on the finest whisky wherever he drinks regularly."

"That sounds like my Cole." Mrs. Mansfield chuckled. "Cole Whisky Mansfield? I like it."

"He's known as having the devil's own luck with the cards and the..." Ellie didn't want to finish that.

"Ladies?" Mrs. Mansfield raised a finely sculpted dark brow.

"Er...yes." Ellie felt all kinds of stupid now. "But there aren't that many I would call ladies out west."

"Except for you?"

"Er...no." But she wasn't going to get into that. "Out west, you need to be able to look after yourself, and Cole also has a reputation for being a fast gun."

"Fast gun?" Mrs. Mansfield blinked at her. "Are you saying my son is a gunfighter. Like one of those men in those dreadful dime novels?"

Ellie hadn't read one of those. "Not really." She searched for a way to put it that wouldn't have his mother running away in horror. "The west is tough, and you need to be tough to survive. Anybody who made their living on cards needed to be able to defend themselves from sore losers."

"I see." Mrs. Mansfield sharp gaze did indeed see, and possibly more than Ellie intended her to. "Tell me more."

"I only found out a few days ago that he'd been taking the money from his gambling and investing it. He's a legitimate businessman now."

"Are you and he...close?"

Well shoot, she should have expected that. "We're friends." Ellie stressed the word friends. "I met Cole some years back when he was passing through our town. We got to chatting every time he came through." Then she thought of something his mother ought to be proud of. "Every time he came through, he would bring me a book."

She smiled. "Do you like to read?"

"Ellie loves to read." Cole spoke from the doorway. "Good evening, Mother."

THIRTY

C ole was in serious danger of bawling like a baby. There was something about seeing one's mother that cut the toughest bastard down to his short pants.

Downstairs, the clerk had informed him of his visitor. Heart pounding, he had climbed there, knowing it could only be one of two women: his mother or Victoria.

He'd stood at the door for a few minutes as she spoke to Ellie, just looking at her. The years had touched her kindly and she was the same beautiful mother he remembered.

"Cole." She shot to her feet and looked at him. For a moment she went pale and then burst into tears. "My darling, Cole."

And now Cole did choke up as she wrapped him in a hug redolent of all the scents and experiences of his childhood, her floral perfume that she still wore, the rustle of silk as she put her arms around him.

Her head barely reached his shoulder, and somehow, he'd remembered her as taller.

It was a long time before either of them could speak, and then his mother pushed away far enough to see him and cupped his face in her palms. "My beautiful boy." Her eyes filled anew with tears. "I thought I'd never see you again. I'm so sorry." She crumpled, and he had to help her into a chair. "I should never have let him send you away. I should have found you. I tried, darling, I tried but—"

"Mother." He crouched at her feet and took her hands. "I'm the one who's to blame for being sent away."

She shook her head. "No, Cole. You were young and impetuous. We were your parents. It was our duty to teach you better, not send you into the wilds alone."

"It made a man of me." He squeezed her hands. "Look at me, Mother. I'm alive and well and, I like to think, a better man than the one who left here."

"When Brett told me he'd sent you away, I nearly hit him." Her eyes grew flint cold. "He had no right to do that."

He didn't want to talk about Brett. He chose not to get lost in the anger and bitterness of the past. Everything he'd done was to create a new way forward. "It doesn't matter anymore. You're here, and I'm here."

"Oh, Cole." Fresh tears tracked down her cheeks. "I've prayed for this every day since you left."

Cole laid his head on her knee. "I missed you, Mother."

"And I missed you." She put a hand on his head.

At some point, Ellie must have left them alone. Cole stood and found a handkerchief for his mother and poured them both a stiff drink.

"Whisky?" Mother looked up at him with laughing eyes.

Ellie must have been telling stories. "But only the best whisky."

"How on earth did that come about?" Mother sipped her whisky and sighed. "I think we could both do with this."

249

"Like a lot of things out west, a little bit of an accident and a whole lot of exaggeration." He needed to say it before they went further. "I've done things you wouldn't be proud of. I've done things I'm not proud of, but I came here hoping for a new beginning."

"You have it." She quaffed her whisky and held the glass for a refill. "You can tell me as much as you like or as little. Although I do hope you'll tell me where you met the delightful Ellie. I like her." She swirled her drink in her glass. "I have no right to judge what you did to survive. Or even how you fit into your new world. I'm the woman who let her son be cast out and did nothing about it."

"What could you have done?" Cole's memory of his father hadn't dimmed over the years. One look at Brett's mulish, angry expression had brought his father back again. "His word was law in our house. He never brooked any argument or opposition."

"You were my son." She sighed. "And I should have fought for you."

"It wouldn't have helped." He could acquit her of any guilt she felt. He'd never once blamed her for what had happened. His memories of his mother were of the one soft and beautiful thing in his childhood. However tough the old bastard had been, she'd been there with a gentle word and a loving touch. "He made up his mind about me, and nothing would have changed that."

"Maybe not." She shrugged. "But we will never know now, will we?"

"No."

The silence of so many memories and regrets settled around them.

Mother cleared her throat. "Tell me about Ellie."

"I think that's her story to tell."

Mother laughed and the sound took him back to happier times. "That's what she said about you. She must be special to you."

"Ellie is..." How to sum up the vibrancy and force packed into that small woman? "She's the bravest, strongest woman I've met, and for a time, she was my only friend."

He told her all about Ellie and her dreams of a dress shop. He even hinted at how she was running away from her brothers.

Nodding, Mother studied him. "What of Victoria?"

"I'm here to see if she will give me another chance." The words didn't fit comfortably, and he avoided making eye contact with his mother. "She's all I ever wanted, and I owe it to myself to see if there's hope for us."

COLE ARRIVED at her house the next morning to collect Victoria. She'd agreed to a stroll with him, and the late morning was warm and fine. He'd forgotten how close and damp the air was in New York. Beneath his stiff, formal suit, perspiration slid down his sides.

Here he had thought he missed his fine duds, and right now, he'd give his right jewel for some denim and a bandanna to keep the stench of the city out.

Victoria appeared in her doorway, elegant and subdued in her light purple dress. A bonnet heavily weighted by silk flowers covered her hair and drooped artfully over one eye.

"Cole." She held her hand out to him, and he dutifully brushed the air over her knuckles. "It's a fine morning."

"Even finer for the company." He offered her his arm.

She snapped open her parasol and tucked her free hand into his arm. "I have been reading one of those dime novels since I saw you yesterday. I must say, it all sounds terrifying."

And parts of it had been. "Not really. Those silly lurid tales exaggerate."

Their strides matched. She was the perfect height for him. During their betrothal, friends had often remarked how well they looked together as a couple. Here they were on a fine New York morning, being a couple again.

"Tell me what you've been up to." He wanted to hear about her marriage to Bonnington, but only if it had been a disappointment.

"I was married," she said and waved to an acquaintance across the street. "But you already knew that."

"Were you happy?" Her infernal bonnet got in the way of him seeing her face and reading the truth of her answer. One of the benefits of making your money at a card table was being able to read the faces of the men around the table.

Victoria glanced at him. "I must say you have grown more direct."

"Have I?" She was probably right. Out west, people didn't have time for dancing around. When they wanted to know something, they asked.

She nodded. "Indeed you have." Raising her head, she smiled at him. "I like it, and I shall answer in kind. Bonnington...loved me and was good to me."

"And you?"

"I was very fond of him." Victoria nodded a greeting to two smartly dressed women walking past them. "He was a good husband."

Which was probably the most honest she would get. Thinking of how Ellie would have answered made him nearly laugh. However Ellie had felt, she would have told you. In fact, he couldn't see her wearing black because it was expected. Then he did chuckle.

"What?" Victoria looked at him with a slight frown. "You are amused by my marriage?"

"Ah, no." He backtracked. "I was thinking of someone...a friend of mine from out west."

She accepted that with a nod. "Will you stay in contact with this friend?"

"Most definitely." He steered the conversation into calmer waters. "Now, tell me all I've missed in twelve years."

Victoria laughed, and it brought so many memories flooding back. He'd been captivated by her from the moment he had first seen her at the theatre with her parents. Immediately he had sought an introduction, which had delighted his mother and even drawn a reluctant nod of approval from his father.

They had made the perfect match. Both families were delighted, and Cole had played by the rules for the first time in his young life.

Victoria was chattering on about a couple they used to know. The wife had apparently been caught cheating on the husband. She'd been sent from the city, and rumor had it she was expecting a child. Rumor was also rampant as to who had fathered the child.

Cole couldn't give a shit, but he smiled and let her carry on to another piece of gossip. Something about two women wearing the same dress.

Eager to win the beautiful Victoria, Cole had courted her without taking one misstep. He had rigidly suppressed his boyish eagerness and ardor, not wanting to take any chance she would turn him away. And she hadn't. He'd asked her father, got the blessing and then asked her.

"Are you listening to me, Cole?" Victoria shot him a coy look from beneath her bonnet.

He smiled and nodded. "Of course I am. Pricilla Honeycutt is said to be finally stepping off the shelf."

"Right." Her eyes sparkled with delight. "You know she is my age and never been married."

Not if she'd gone out west, she wouldn't be. Pricilla would already be sporting the name of one of her choice of desperate men. Wives were the rarest commodity in his world—his old world. "She should have come to Denver."

"I beg your pardon?" Victoria stopped and stared at him. "Who should have come to Denver?"

"Pricilla Honeycutt." He kind of wished he hadn't opened his mouth now, but he would follow through now that he had. If this thing with Victoria was going somewhere, she needed to understand about the life he'd led for so many years. Like grit in a cattleman's skin, it was forever a part of him. "You were saying she couldn't find a husband."

"I'm sure I never said it quite so indelicately." Victoria raised her chin and stared away from him.

"Of course not." He reined in his impatience. What the hell difference did it make how she had said it? The meaning was the same. "But the sort of women you marry are in short supply in Denver. Men would line up four deep for a chance at a wife like Pricilla."

Victoria sniffed. "How vulgar."

Cole didn't think so at all. When good women were in short supply, you didn't hang about and wait for one to drop in your lap, you made your intentions clear. "It's a different world," he said, picking his words carefully. "Men come there alone to make their fortunes. Those who survive get themselves a nice piece of land or start a good business. Then they start looking for someone to share that with, a family."

"Hmm." She gazed at him. "But you did not."

"I beg your pardon?"

"You made your fortune, and yet you did not find a woman to marry."

No, he most definitely hadn't, and Cole raised her hand to his mouth. This time he pressed his mouth to her gloved fingers. "That's because I already had the woman I wanted to marry."

THIRTY-ONE

Ellie faced her morning without enthusiasm.

After a shared breakfast, Cole had left to go strolling with Victoria. *Strolling*? She didn't get it. They could both walk, they'd done it before, what possible joy could two people get from walking around together?

Then she remembered how good it was when she and Cole sat together, neither of them doing much at all. Him having that with Victoria pinched.

She needed to get out of the hotel room. She was in New York. She should be out there looking around.

A knock at the door came as she was putting her bonnet on.

Mrs. Mansfield stood on the other side. "Good morning, I hope you don't mind."

"Not at all." Ellie motioned her in. "But Cole isn't here now." Then she added because this was his mother, and Ellie wanted her to know that she knew all about Victoria. "He went to see Victoria."

"Yes." She smiled and motioned Ellie's bonnet? "Were you on your way out?"

"I was." Ellie felt a bit foolish to confess, "I wasn't really going anywhere, just out of the hotel room."

Mrs. Mansfield's smile broadened, and it was Cole's grin on a woman's face. "Good, I can help on both counts. Get you out of the hotel and find somewhere for you to go."

Ellie had grown up never going anywhere blindly with another person. "Where?"

"It's a surprise." Mrs. Mansfield motioned Ellie to precede her. "But I promise you'll like it." She leaned forward and lowered her voice. "Cole told me of your plans, and this will fit perfectly into those."

"Plans? For the dress shop?" Ellie had to hurry to keep up with Mrs. Mansfield's much longer legs.

They descended into the lobby as Mrs. Mansfield said, "Yes and yes. Come along now. I'm excited for you to see this."

With her shorter legs, Ellie was coming along as fast as they would carry her.

She followed Mrs. Mansfield into a carriage waiting outside the hotel.

Settling herself across from Ellie, Mrs. Mansfield said, "Thank you for telling me about Cole yesterday."

"It was my pleasure." There was something easy about talking to Mrs. Mansfield. "He was very upset when he couldn't see you."

"Yes." Mrs. Mansfield rolled her eyes. "My oldest son assumes too much at times." She waved a dismissive hand. "His heart is in the right place, but he is prone to acting too much like his father."

Ellie would love to ask what sort of man had kicked his child out of his home, but she dare not.

"We were not a love match," Mrs. Mansfield looked at her. "Cole's father was an arranged marriage, but he was handsome and wealthy, had the right connections to please my father, and I was halfway persuaded I might be in love with him."

Women had precious few choices open to them, and most of the women she knew had made the best choices they could. "But you weren't?"

Mrs. Mansfield shook her head. "I was not, but we got on well enough, and I took joy in my children." A deep sadness spread over her lovely face. "There is nothing worse than losing a child, you know. I lost three between Brett and Cole." She sighed, and it came from a bottomless grief that brought tears to Ellie's eyes. "And then, I allowed my youngest to be taken from me."

She took one of Mrs. Mansfield's hands in hers. "Cole doesn't see it like that."

"Cole is too generous." She shook her head and took a deep breath. "Forgive me. This"—she motioned between Ellie and her—"With Cole reappearing so suddenly has made me so happy, but also melancholy. It reminds me of all the years I've wasted."

Cole must have felt the same when he looked at Victoria, all those wasted years and no way to get them back.

"Now." Mrs. Mansfield straightened. "Enough of that. This is supposed to be a good surprise."

"Mrs. Mansfield—"

"Dear Lord, call me Joy." Mrs. Mansfield smiled at her. "And you are Ellie to me."

"Thank you. Joy."

The carriage rattled over some ruts before settling into a smoother rhythm. They didn't seem to be getting very far fast, and Ellie decided she would walk in New York. She needed to find somewhere to live close enough to her business to do so.

Joy peered out the window. "Not long now. Why does Cole call you Sugar Ellie? That sounds like a name with a story behind it."

"When did he call me that?" Ellie played for time. Joy had no idea how much of a story that was.

Joy turned back to her and cocked her head. "Yesterday, when he was telling me about your plans. He also mentioned how you'd been having some trouble with your brothers."

Oh dear. Cole's mother would not be happy to hear the truth. "Sugar Ellie is a part I played."

"You're an actress?" Joy frowned. "Cole never mentioned that. Why we have a number of good theatre—"

"No, ma'am. Joy. I'm not an actress." If Cole had let slip and called her Sugar Ellie, he should have told the whole story and spared her the mortification of telling it now. Joy would look at her with that curl of disgust to her lip and that would be the end of their budding acquaintance. "It's not a pretty story, Joy."

"Hmm." Joy studied her and then nodded. "Ellie, are you or where you a...um...prostitute?"

Ellie froze and blinked at Joy. All thoughts scattered, and she answered before she could stop her mouth. "No, but also yes."

"Now you have to tell me." Joy raised her eyebrow. She didn't look like she might throw Ellie out of the carriage once she knew the truth.

"I'm not a prostitute in truth, but a lot of people think I am. Or at least they think Sugar Ellie is," she said.

Joy frowned. "But you're Sugar Ellie."

"I am." She took a deep breath. Thus far, only Cole knew her real story. "My ma died when I was too little to remember her, and my pa followed the first rumors of gold out to Colorado."

"You must have been very young." Joy looked at her with compassion and not judgment.

"I was, and my four brothers and I followed my pa out to Colorado." She didn't remember any other life but struggling through the thick, red Colorado clay and living in filthy tent camps. "But my pa died when I was young, and my older brother—Theo—he and Jake, that's the second oldest, had this hooch distillery in the mountains near our tent, and after pa died, they started selling the hooch to feed the rest of us."

Joy nodded. "You said four brothers."

"Yes. Theo and Jake and then the twins, Paul and Patrick. I'm the only girl and the youngest."

"They should have taken better care of you then." Joy looked angry on her behalf. "Instead of letting you be...letting that happen to you."

Ellie needed to stop her before she went down the totally wrong path. "They did. At least, Theo always did. The selling hooch grew into a hooch tent, and as the town grew, it became a saloon. Then Jake got the idea to start running girls." Heat climbed her face. She shouldn't talk like that in front of a real lady like Joy. "What I mean is—"

"Whores," Joy said. "Jake wanted to make money from whores."

"Yes."

"Good God!" Joy reared back. "You were not one of their whores. Tell me they didn't sell their own sister into prostitution."

"No." Ellie got in quickly before Joy went off half-cocked again. "Well, not then they didn't because Theo was about."

Joy stared at her. "You better tell me the rest quickly because we are almost there, and I cannot wait until our business is concluded to hear the rest of this."

"Okay then." Ellie locked her fingers together for courage.

"When I was fifteen, and men started looking at me, Theo came up with an idea that would keep me safe, but also close to my brothers all the time. He set me up as the madam of the whores. I dressed the part, painted my face to look older, and nobody thought anything of it. They believed I was Sugar Ellie."

"This is when Cole first met you?"

"Yes, as Sugar Ellie." Ellie decided to skip the twenty-thousand-dollar story. "He came to the Four Kings, that's the saloon, to say goodbye before coming back here. I found out that my brother Jake was planning to blow the whistle on who I was and sell my first night to the highest bidder."

"What!" Joy shrieked and sat up straight. "That's unforgivable."

"Well, I thought so." Ellie shrugged, because she didn't like a nice lady like Joy getting all bent out of shape about her life. "And so did Cole, and he helped me get away from Jake. Actually, my plan was to find Theo, but he's in California, and I'm not sure where." Or if he was still alive, but she didn't want to deal with that possibility yet. "Cole said he could help me find Theo. He was going to set me up in business in Denver, but somebody recognized Sugar Ellie."

"Recognized?" Comprehension lit Joy's face. "Of course! There is no Mr. Pierce and there never was." She chuckled. "Oh, that is very clever, Sugar. Nobody ever questions a widow, particularly not one in heavy mourning."

Ellie nodded. She tried to read how Joy had taken the entire sordid story.

The carriage stopped, and Joy peered out the window. "We're here." She sat back with a smile. "Hopefully the location of your new beginning, and I, for one, am delighted to be even a tiny part of it."

~

TURNS OUT, Joy was even better at picking stores and locations than Cole, and the one he'd picked out in Denver had been perfect.

Joy chose a busy road with businesses all around it that gave work to the sort of women she wanted to cater to. Women working in the businesses would pass by her window every day on their way to work.

The premises had a big work room area in the back, and had been a milliner's before, so long work benches were already set up along with shelving for bolts of fabric. She would only have space for one changing room, but it would do. Best of all, it had a small apartment above it. One room with a tiny kitchen in an annex at the back, but it would be enough for her.

She and Joy returned to the hotel brimming with plans for the premises and dress styles. Joy was invaluable in helping Ellie bridge the gaps in her thinking between Denver and New York.

Dust and dry heat were not quite the same problem in New York as they were in Denver. Also the women who were her customers needed dresses that were practical in the workplace, skirts that didn't drag on the ground, sleeves that couldn't get caught in machinery, and made of hardy fabrics that would justify a higher price.

Ellie had so much to think about. Her mind whirled with ideas as she opened the door to her hotel sitting room, Joy on her heels.

Cole pushed to his feet and strode toward her. "There you are." He wore the most ferocious frown.

"Oh? Were you waiting for me?"

"Ellie." He took a deep and careful breath. "I returned to

find you gone and with nobody any the wiser as to where you had gone. Need I remind you—"

Joy bustled between them and held her cheek up to be kissed. "Good afternoon, darling. If you must be cross with someone, then let that be me. I swooped in and carried Ellie off."

"I didn't mean to worry you." Ellie needed the physical connection, and she took his hand. "I should have left a note."

"Yes, you should have." Cole was still glaring but not quite as ferociously as before. "I would not take kindly to my Sugar Ellie being carried off."

"Neither would I." Ellie smiled up at him. "Pigeon Pete was quite enough of that, thank you."

Joy's face lit up. "Pigeon Pete."

"An old trapper." Cole looked at his mother. "He got it into his head Ellie would make a good bride for his son."

Gaze darting between them, alight with interest, Joy said, "My goodness. What happened?"

"Cole rescued me." It still made Ellie glow inside that he had. "Pete took me to his cabin and Cole rescued me."

Joy studied her son. "I'm sure he had his reasons."

"He's a good person," Ellie said, not understanding the shades of meaning in Joy's statement.

Joy gave her a sweet smile and cupped her cheek. "He is a good person," she said. "And with you, he is especially good."

CHAPTER
THIRTY-TWO

E llie answered Cole's knock on her bedroom door the next morning, heart pounding and already inventing reasons why inviting him in wouldn't be the worst idea ever.

"Good morning." Cole's warm whisky gaze touched her from head to toe and his voice warmed. "Did you sleep well?"

Not at all. She hadn't slept well since she'd slept entangled with Cole in the train car. "I did." She slapped a big smile on her face. "I'm not sure what they do with the beds here, but they're like big clouds."

"Down." Cole propped his shoulder on the doorjamb, slumberous warmth creeping over his expression. His gaze strayed to her breasts, as tangible as a touch. "Goose down. It makes them soft and warm."

"I like it." Ellie wanted his hands, not his eyes, on her.

"I do too."

She could get lost in the husky rasp of his voice. She knew what that voice meant as well. It meant Cole wanted her. "It makes it hard to get out of bed."

"Hard." Cole nodded. "Yup, it sure does make it hard."

"Cole?" The need to giggle overcame her. "Are we still talking about the same thing?"

He chuckled and gave her a sheepish look. "To be honest, I have no damn idea, Sugar. My mind is stuck on how sweet and warm and tempting you are in the morning."

Oh, this man said things that made a sensible girl get stupid. "Did you want anything?"

"So many things." Wicked intent was written all over his beautiful face.

Ellie clenched her hands to stop from reaching for him and dragging him into her bed. "This morning. Did you knock for anything specific?"

"Again, I'm having memory issues." His chuckle grew rueful. "But we're not doing that anymore. Are we?"

Dear God, how much strength did one girl have to have? "No." She found those two letters the hardest she'd ever spoken in her life. "No, we're not doing that anymore. It's better this way."

"I know you're right, Sugar." And the gaze that met hers was stripped of pretense and prevarication. This was a view straight into Cole. "But for the life of me, I can't remember why."

"Victoria," she said, and the name scraped her raw.

Cole nodded and straightened. "Right. Victoria." He held up a piece of paper. "My mother is demanding our presence for luncheon today at the house."

"Demanding?" That didn't sound like Joy.

Cole's smile was equal parts wry and fond. "In the politest possible terms, of course."

COLE'S HOUSE IN DENVER, Ellie discovered, didn't hold a candle to the Maddison avenue mansion the carriage stopped in front of. This was old money, and more of it than she was likely to see in her lifetime.

Feeling like an interloper, she followed Cole into the house.

A butler took their outer garments and led them into a palatial salon.

Ellie stuck close to Cole. She so didn't belong in a place that beautiful.

The room was decorated in shades of blue so pale it was almost white. A grouping of elegant chairs clustered close to the fire. Beneath a bank of windows, a second grouping was positioned to take advantage of the sun streaming through the windows.

Joy rose from a chaise near the window. "Darlings." She held her hands out to both of them. "I'm so glad you could join us."

Ellie stifled her giggle at Cole's quick sardonic glance her way. She obediently kissed Joy's cheek and then tucked her hands behind her back. No way she was sitting on that pale as milk furniture and getting it all dirty.

"Cole." A man entered the room. He looked so much like Cole that Ellie stared at him.

Fortunately, the man was too busy scowling at Cole to notice.

"Brett." Cole's tone was no warmer than his brother's. He turned to Joy. "Is this why we're here?"

"No." Joy smiled at him. "This is why you are here. Ellie and I have a store to get ready." She looked at Ellie as if she had no idea she'd tossed the verbal equivalent of a rattlesnake between her sons. "I thought we'd visit some fabric warehouses. We need to establish what sort of price we can get cloth for."

"Mother." Brett's voice was little more than a growl. "I'm not staying for this."

Cole stiffened. "Neither am I. This is pointless."

"No, it's not." Joy smiled up at him. Moving to Brett, she patted his cheek. "You're both my sons, and I love you both. I've lived the last twelve years without one of you, and I'm not prepared to do it again." She rang the bell for the servant. "I am determined to have both the men I love in my life."

The butler appeared. "Mrs. Mansfield?"

"Ah, yes. Could you have my carriage brought around?"

He bowed his way out.

"This is ridiculous." Brett paced to the window.

Ellie couldn't get over how much he and Cole looked alike.

Cole shoved his hands in his pockets. "Look, Mother, I know why—"

"No." Joy cut the air with her hand. "You really don't know. Unless you're a mother, you couldn't possibly know how it feels to pine and ache for a child every living moment of every living day." Joy sucked in a breath and composed herself. "Now, you can either stay here and talk it out like adults, or I'll lock you in until you do." Her voice hardened. "But I want Christmases with all my children and grandchildren around me. And you two"—she pointed at Brett and then Cole—"are going to see that I get that." Turning to Ellie, she gave her a tight smile. "Shall we?"

THE FABRIC HOUSES Joy took Ellie to were another revelation. Ellie stopped trying to be nonchalant and straight up gawped at everything around her. Never in her life would she have guessed so many different types of fabric existed.

Standing in front of endless shelves of red silk, red in every shade imaginable from scarlet to aubergine and all hues in between. Then there was flocked silk, flubbed silk, raw silk, silk shantung, silk organza, silk charmeuse, dupion silk, crepe de chine, broadcloth and brocade. All of them variations of silk and all of them red.

If she even tried to conceive of all the other colors and types of fabric in one warehouse alone, she would lose her darned mind.

Joy took it all in her stride. Eyes sparkling, and chattering to merchants constantly, Joy looked to be having the time of her life.

"The trick is this, Ellie," she said as she charged after the merchant to where he kept the linens. "Don't get dazzled by the choices. Pick what works for what you need and stick with that."

Easier—a lot easier—said than done.

By the time they'd visited their fourth warehouse, Ellie had a handle on not staring. Her mind, however, was churning, and she desperately needed a break.

"Poor darling." Joy patted her hand. "You look worn out."

"Overwhelmed is more like." Ellie shook her head in disbelief. "My head feels like its crammed full."

"Ah." Joy led the way down the sidewalk. "Just what we need. A cup of tea."

Ellie followed Joy into a light, airy tearoom. A black and white patterned floor spread beneath white iron tables, at which sat elegant women of all ages. Their hats alone made Ellie want to sink into the floor.

"Mrs. Mansfield." A dapper little man in a canary yellow waistcoat closed in on them. "How lovely to see you again."

"Thank you, Andre." Smiling, Joy drew off her gloves. "My friend and I are in desperate need of a cup of your excellent tea."

"Mrs. Mansfield." Andre chuckled and looked coy. "You flatter me. Perhaps I can suggest a little light accompaniment with your tea. I have a delicious chiffon creme, or perhaps a delightful sponge that has left the ovens not five minutes ago."

Ellie followed Joy through the room, trying not to notice the discreet but avid interest following their progress.

"There now." Joy sat down and smiled around them. "It's a mercy to be off my feet for a moment."

"Joy." A woman dressed in a gorgeous lilac afternoon gown appeared at the table. "How lovely to see you."

The woman was beautiful. Honey colored hair was skillfully arranged beneath a beautiful hat festooned with tiny lilac blossoms. Her bone structure was classically beautiful and made warm and inviting by a pair of large brown eyes.

"Victoria." Joy rose and kissed the other woman's cheeks. "You look well."

"As do you." Victoria's glance shifted to her.

Joy slid smoothly into the gap. "Ellie Pierce, allow me to introduce you to Victoria Bonnington."

"How do you do, Mrs. Pierce?" Victoria took her hand.

"I'm well." Ellie nearly forgot her manners. "And you?" Victoria was perfect. Perfect for this place, perfect for New York, and perfect for the man Cole was determined to be once again.

"Ellie joins us from Denver," Joy said.

"Denver?" Victoria raised a delicate brow. "How very courageous of you. I'm sure I could never have survived such a feral place."

Ellie felt like she needed to defend herself and Denver. "It's not so bad."

"Hmm." Victoria's smile didn't reach her eyes, and she turned to Joy. "You must be happy that our Cole has reappeared from that savage place and in one piece."

Savage seemed a bit much, and Ellie hadn't missed the *our* either. Somehow, she didn't think she was part of that *our Cole* club.

"I am." Joy's entire being lit up. "And he looks so well."

Victoria tittered. "He certainly looks robust enough. He cuts quite the brawny figure of late. His tailor must be quite at a loss as to how to make him look more the gentleman."

"I think he looks extremely well." Joy's tone cooled. "I think he looks the better for the meat on his bones."

Ellie agreed with Joy, not that she'd seen Cole before.

Victoria smiled and rushed into the silence. "Of course, you are quite right. It's just that in my mind, he's the man I was engaged to, and I hold that memory dear." Her gaze drifted over Ellie. "You did not say how you and Cole knew each other."

"Friends," she blurted. Victoria made her feel like her face was smudged and her dress grubby. "We're old friends."

"Indeed." Victoria raised her brow. "We must have tea, and you can tell me all about it."

Ellie made some noise of agreement, which she had no intention abiding by. She sipped her tea as Victoria and Joy chatted easily about mutual acquaintances and places they both knew.

Here was the reason she had kept Cole out of her bed this morning. Ellie had a mirror, and she knew she wasn't a coyote, but Victoria was lovely. Tall, slim, elegant and beautifully spoken, the way she moved through her world was refined and graceful in a way Ellie would have to be three days a ghost to mimic.

After a bit more chatter, Victoria said her goodbyes and glided out of the tearoom.

"So." Joy studied Ellie. "That was Victoria. The Victoria."

Ellie tried to find a brave smile but lost. "No wonder Cole never forgot her."

"Hmm?" Joy stared out the window at Victoria being helped into her carriage by a footman. "She is beautiful. But twelve years is a long time, my sweet Sugar Ellie, and a lot can change in that time."

CHAPTER
THIRTY-THREE

Ellie was surprised to find Cole in when she returned to the hotel. She had invited Joy to join her for dinner, but she'd declined, and Ellie was alone with Cole for the night.

"Dinner." Cole stepped aside to reveal a white-clothed table set with crystal and silver by the window.

Ellie stopped and stared at the beautiful table. It was a table set for romance, and it made her want to cry.

"Hey?" Cole bent to peer into her face. His voice gentled. "Sugar? This was supposed to be a celebration."

"Celebration?" She forced her tears back and took a careful breath. "I'm just tired."

Cole looked like he might argue, and then took her hand and led her to the table. "Tonight, we are celebrating your new venture."

"It's not a venture yet." She laughed at his enthusiasm.

Looking suspiciously arch, Cole held out the seat for her. "That's what you think."

"Cole?" Ellie tried to give him a stern look as she sat. "What have you done?"

"So suspicious." He clicked his tongue at her and held a glass up. "Champagne?"

"Yes, please." She didn't trust the hint of smug to his smile. "You may as well tell me, because I'll get it out of you eventually."

"Where's the fun in that, Sugar?" He whipped the domed silver top off a plate. "Oysters?"

Ellie had never seen an oyster, and she stood and stared at them. "Are you sure we're supposed to eat those? They don't look like anybody should put that in their mouth."

"Trust me." Cole scooped up one of the shells and poked at it with a strange looking fork. "Open up."

Still not sure about eating that thing, Ellie opened her mouth. The oyster slid into her mouth briny and slimy and she nearly spat it out. Shuddering, she swallowed it. "Ugh! Cole!"

"Not an oyster lover?" Cole was doing a bad job of hiding his amusement. He took an oyster, tipped it into his mouth and followed it with a sip of champagne. He took another silver dome off a second plate. "Try the smoked salmon."

Not on her life was she letting him put another food she hadn't tried before in her mouth. Taking a sliver, she squeezed lemon juice over it as Cole instructed and tried it.

He could keep his oysters, but she liked the smoked salmon. "Are we going to get to the celebration part?"

Cole stood and took away their first course. He pushed a dining cart with more silver domes on it over to the table. "Not before we eat."

She was hungry anyway, so Ellie let him feed her and fill up her champagne glass. By the time they'd made their way through the duck, the steak, and the lobster, and Cole had opened a second bottle of champagne, Ellie had a full belly and a golden glow to the world.

"Now." Cole took out a sheath of papers and put them on the table in front of her. "We get to the celebration."

"What's this?" Ellie peered at the top sheet.

"This"—Cole tapped the top page—"is the lease to your new store."

She'd only looked at the store yesterday. "How did—Joy!"

"My mother did, indeed, tell me." Cole grinned and flipped to the next page. "This is our business agreement drawn up legally. I will fund the store until such time as it can stand alone, and then I will take a share of the profits."

Ellie traced her name on the document. Seeing it like that made it seem real for the first time. Finally, she had the chance to put Sugar Ellie behind her. She could walk away from that part of her life and reinvent herself.

The feeling overwhelmed her, a wave of so many emotions she couldn't speak. Happiness for certain, and apprehension about her new beginning, but the sadness surprised her. She had always hated Sugar Ellie, and now putting her aside was tearing a part of her out and casting it aside.

"Ellie?" Cole took her hand and tugged her to her feet. "What's going on?"

She shook her head, not able to put all that was going on inside her into words.

Cole wrapped his arms around her and tucked her into his front.

When Cole held her, Ellie could imagine a world in which nothing could harm her again, a happy place where she could be truly loved and adored. Except the practical side of her knew Cole would take his arms away and the harsher world would intrude again.

"Thank you." She wasn't ready to leave the warmth and security of Cole's arms, and she wrapped hers around his waist and breathed in the leather and sandalwood of him. It was hard to imagine a time when those two scents wouldn't make her ache for him. "You did so much more than I expected you to."

"I wanted to, Sugar." He kissed the top of her head. "I need to know you're safe and taken care of."

Ellie thought it better not to ask why. Pearl had always said never to ask questions you didn't really want to hear the answer to. When she was settled, she'd like to be able to send for Pearl. She would find a way to do it without alerting her brothers.

"I took another liberty." Cole's voice rumbled though his chest. "I didn't want you alone in your store, so I sent for Molly."

"From Denver?"

Cole nodded. "She was more than happy to come. She has family in New York."

Company would be nice, and Ellie pressed her face into his neck. "Thank you."

"You're so welcome, Sugar."

Neither of them made any move to disentangle. Candle-light played over the silent room and caught them in its golden glow.

What Ellie wouldn't give to stay there forever, but that was never possible, and she wouldn't ask Cole for something he couldn't give her. God knew he was a good enough man to try to give her the next best thing, but after you'd had Cole "Whisky" Mansfield make you glad you'd been born a woman, there wasn't anything else to replace him.

They had tonight, now, and Ellie wanted one more night with him before she let Victoria have him forever.

"Ellie?" The husky rasp to his voice gave him away. Cole was having similar thoughts.

She looked up at him. "Yes, Cole. More, Cole."

"Yes?" He looked triumphant as he scooped her into his arms. "You're dug beneath my skin, Sugar."

Ellie wrapped her arms around his neck. She didn't need words from him. She craved his touch.

Laying her on the bed, Cole came down over her. "Ellie." He bent and kissed her.

The taste of his mouth was so familiar it rushed through her, triggering a sensory wave that Ellie surrendered to.

His weight pressed her into the soft mattress. His kiss consumed her. His hands knew all the places on her body that made her senses spark.

Sitting up, he pulled his shirt over his head and dropped it.

Ellie spread her hands over the muscle of his torso. His skin was hot silk against her palms. His body was a delight to her touch, and she tried to draw the memory of his skin deep into her. When she left his bed this time, she really would stay away. Her hands would never again touch the flesh she was touching now.

It wasn't enough, and Ellie sat up. She pressed her mouth to his chest and pushed him back.

Cole lay back for her, his eyes dark and secret in the shadows, but she could feel their heat on her skin.

She trailed her lips over his stomach. The muscle contracted against her tongue as he sucked in a breath. "Sugar."

"Let me." She opened his pants and slid them down his hips. Cole helped her get rid of them and lay down for her again.

She'd never done this before, but her girls had sure told her enough about it.

His erection jerked in her hand as Ellie lowered her mouth to him. She slid him into her mouth.

"Jesus!" Cole jerked beneath her, throwing his head back.

Ellie let his reaction guide her as she worked him with her mouth.

"Sugar." His muscles tensed and her name sounded like a tortured groan in his mouth. "You need to stop."

No, she didn't, and Ellie took him to his finish.

In the aftermath, he lay with his eyes shut, relaxed and flushed. "Damn, Sugar." Those whisky eyes opened and found her. "That was not how I saw this going."

She had done this to him, and she took satisfaction in that. "Complaining?"

"Ah, hell no." Chuckling, he sat up and drew her to his shoulder. "Gimme a minute or two and we'll get back to my plan for the evening."

Ellie liked the sound of that and snuggled into his chest.

It took Cole less than his requested minute or two before his big hands went exploring. He rolled her to her back and removed her clothes one piece at a time. Reverently, he exposed her to his view, caressing and kissing the skin as he revealed it. "You're so soft," he whispered to her belly. "So soft and beautiful."

"Cole." She arched into the heat of his mouth.

He drew her skirts down and off. "I need to say something to you, Sugar."

"What?" Ellie was struggling to keep her wits about her as he spread her thighs and settled between them.

"I regret nothing." Cole kissed her inner thighs. "This thing between us, Sugar, it's the best thing that's happened to me in years, maybe ever."

Her heart twisted and tears threatened to spill. Ellie tried to swallow them away. Nothing in her life would ever compare to her time with Cole. She wasn't a romantic dreamer. Eventually her heart would heal, and she might even move on, but her life would always be a little emptier without him.

He made love to her then, with his mouth and then as she was drifting down from an intense climax, he joined them.

Pushing her hands over her head, he twined their fingers as they moved together.

Their eyes met and held. Ellie let him see in her eyes what she would never say, what she had no right to ever say. This was the best Cole could give and she, starved for all she could get, would take what he offered.

Their skin grew slick with perspiration, their breathing labored. Ellie both craved and dreaded her completion. She wanted it desperately, but it would also mark an end.

Cole drove them both forward, eyes locked on hers, hands gripping her as if he too struggled to let go.

"Sugar," he whispered.

Ellie went over the edge into bliss with his name on her lips.

He followed her over and lay against her, his weight welcome and heavy. She would have given anything to stay there forever.

Eventually Cole sighed and rolled to his side. He tucked her against him and kissed her head. "Why is that I find it so fucking hard to let you go?"

THIRTY-FOUR

H e did let her go. Three short, busy days later, Ellie moved into her apartment above her store. The next day Molly arrived and stood in the center of the store with her eyes shining.

She gave Ellie a nod. "This will be grand."

"I think so." Ellie concentrated on the store and shoved thoughts of Cole as far back in her mind as she could. It helped that she had barely seen him since she'd woken in his bed.

Neither of them had spoken that morning, but they had both known it was done. Time to move forward with their separate lives.

Over the next three weeks Joy was at the store constantly dismissing any attempt Ellie made to economize on getting the store set up right. After nights of agonizing with Molly, Ellie surrendered and named her store the only name she could: Sugar's.

She got her living space set up, and she and Molly agreed to share until one of them could afford to move elsewhere. At night when the busy city still bustled outside her door, Ellie was glad for the company.

A week before they opened, the fabrics she and Joy had ordered arrived.

Joy was on hand to chivy the deliverymen into putting them where Ellie wanted them and complain about their boots on the new floors.

"There!" She brushed her hands together and grinned at Ellie and Molly. "We're ready."

And they were.

The sign was hung above the door, pink on a white background at Molly's insistence. The bright displays of fabrics were in the windows and ready. Everything in its place, and a little over two months since Ellie had arrived in New York, Sugar's opened its doors.

COLE MISSED HIS SUGAR ELLIE, simple as that. Even when he was strolling along on a beautiful morning to meet Victoria, Sugar lurked in his thoughts, pushing her way to the forefront if he gave her the smallest gap.

Like the way the bright explosion of flowers in the hanging baskets outside a restaurant reminded him of her. Ellie was vivid, brash and bold and without a word insisted on attention. But she was also sweet and had a softness to her she kept well guarded.

New York seethed around him. He joined the bustling sidewalk and merged into the human flow. Still, he didn't feel part of it as he used to. The younger version of himself had loved New York, felt like it was his place. Now he was distanced from it in some inexplicable way. Like a fond visitor, he liked the city, was enjoying it, but it didn't resonate as home to him.

Of course, he'd been there less than three months and the home part would come. Three months since he'd been in New York and two of those since he'd seen Ellie.

He swerved to avoid colliding with a group of girls chattering and giggling in his path. Their mothers stood by, gimlet gazes on any man passing.

Mother seemed to be making up for Ellie's lack of a mother of her own. Maybe he'd have more luck forgetting Ellie if he didn't hear all about her and what she was up to at dinner. Yet, he let Mother talk, getting the strong sense that if he stopped getting his news of Ellie that way, he would fold and go and see for himself.

He'd moved back into his childhood home, and while it was great to have his mother close at hand, he and Brett were too old to share a house, so he was looking for somewhere of his own.

He leaped the portico stairs of Victoria's mansion and rapped with the head of his cane.

The butler opened the door and bowed. "Mr. Mansfield. Won't you come in?"

He supposed it was progress that the man no longer pretended not to know his name.

Following the man at a stately pace across the tiled foyer, he was hard put to tamp his impatience. This slow progression to a destination known to him struck him as ridiculous. Informal manners had become more familiar to him than those he'd been raised with.

He waited in Victoria's blue and gold salon. She could take anything from five minutes to an hour, depending on her mood. This morning was a good day, and she appeared ten minutes after his arrival looking lovely in soft gray silk that highlighted her creamy skin and clung to her curves.

She and Bonnington hadn't had children, and he wanted to ask her, but Victoria didn't invite personal questions.

"Cole, darling." She held her elegant white hands out to him.

Responding to her raised cheek, he bent and kissed it. All this hand and cheek kissing was wearing a hole through his patience as well. It wasn't that he thought Victoria owed him anything more, but she gave every indication of being interested in more and disinclined to allow it. As much as it frustrated him, however, he didn't push anything.

"You're looking lovely," he said. Victoria always looked lovely, but he said it because it was expected he would. Even courtship had a rule book to it. Living in Denver, he'd forgotten the thousands of steps in the complicated courtship dance.

"Thank you, Cole." She glanced at him from beneath her lashes. "And you are looking rather...burly."

Burly? *Burly?* Whatever the hell that meant. Yesterday, she'd made some crack about his tan and then compared him to a dockworker or a farmer. Good luck living out west and keeping your lily-white complexion. Also, he preferred the man he was now. All that sitting on his ass doing not much of anything was making him antsy. He needed to find a better way to spend his days than waiting until it was time to dance attendance on Victoria. The indolence and pleasure seeking had been him in New York as a young man. This version of Cole couldn't respect a man who did nothing with his days but let other people wipe their butts for them.

"I had a particularly interesting evening yesterday." Victoria settled on a chaise, moving her skirts for him to sit beside her.

Cole perched on the shiny fabric, anchoring himself with his feet firmly on the ground. Fucking thing was like trying to sit on a greased hog. "Tell me about your evening."

"Do you remember Becca Yates?"

Not even a bit. "Becca?" He hummed. "Remind me."

"Oh, Cole." Victoria laughed, and she had a great laugh. It tinkled in the air and made her even more beautiful. "You were always horrible at names. We really must do something to get you better *au fait* with polite society again."

Polite society could go and *au fait* itself. "I still am terrible with names."

"Becca was a redhead, tall and thin, with an alarming propensity to freckle."

Cole nodded, but an image popped into his head of another woman, a whore he'd met in his wandering gambling days. Also redheaded and skinny, her face covered in tawny freckles. He couldn't recall what they'd called her, but he did remember her singing. That plain, homely woman had transformed into an incandescent beauty when she sang. More than her voice, she'd been able to weave a spell around her listeners as she sang from the soul.

Lark. They'd called her the Rusty Lark, and she'd gotten caught in the crossfire between two aspiring fast guns. The entire town, respectable folk and saloon rats, had walked behind Lark's casket.

"...and you'll never guess what he said next." Victoria leaned forward and tapped his knee.

For sure he wouldn't because he'd lost most of what she'd been saying. Cole made an encouraging noise and Victoria went off on her story again.

Funny, he hadn't thought about Lark for years. Watching her casket being lowered into the ground and knowing that voice would never ring pure and passionately again had made him madder than hell. It was the sort of senseless loss you got hardened to out west.

Victoria's stick up the ass butler slunk into the room. "I beg your pardon, Mrs. Bonnington, but a message has arrived for Mr. Mansfield."

"For Cole?" Victoria blinked at the butler.

"Indeed, madam, from Mrs. Mansfield, I believe."

Cole got to his feet and took the note from the butler.

Darling. His mother's easy, looping scrawl spread over the page. *I know you're busy, but I think your intervention is needed at Sugar's. Ellie is threatening to shoot some man's pecker off. I'm hoping you can dissuade her (although probably not as fervently as the man.) J.M*

He could no more stop his grin as he read the note than he could pause the tide. Mother often regaled the dinner table with Ellie's antics as well as news of her progress. Cole had even caught Brett leaning forward for a new Ellie story the other night. The thought of never seeing Ellie again fit Cole like the wrong skin.

"What is it?" Victoria stood and approached him. "Bad news?"

For some poor bastard, if he didn't get there. "Just a Colorado hellcat who needs dealing with."

Striding down the street, he let the belly laugh building inside him go. That his mother had actually written the word *pecker* no small part of his amusement.

After hailing a cab, he arrived at Sugar's about thirty minutes after receiving the note. He hadn't been there in weeks, and he took a moment to appreciate what Ellie had achieved. The pink and white awning stood out in a street of dark green and maroon trim. A beautiful pink confection of a dress stood in the window.

The bell tinkled over his head as he entered.

Mother, Ellie and a tow-haired, grizzled man in overalls were sitting on the sturdy chairs Ellie had chosen for her store and eating sandwiches.

They all stopped and stared at him as he entered.

"Mother?"

Ellie looked a bit pale. She was probably working too hard. He'd have a word with Mother about that and see if she could get Ellie to slow down. She also looked so damn beautiful it took his breath away.

Mother stood and held her hands out to him. "Darling! Thank you for coming, but I owe you the hugest apology."

"Nobody's...parts in peril then?"

The man put down his sandwich and guffawed. "Tell you what, this little firecracker had me worried about the wedding tackle for a moment."

Ellie rolled her eyes at him. "It wasn't like I was going to really shoot."

"Begging your pardon, Ellie." The man toasted her with his teacup. "But that's not a chance I was going to take."

"Nor I." Mother tucked her hand through his arm and led him closer to Ellie and her new friend. "But I was a bit alarmist to send the message."

Ellie turned her bottomless chocolate eyes his way and gave him a sweet, tentative smile. "Cole."

"Ellie." It had been forever since she'd caressed his name as she spoke it. "The store looks good."

She flushed and put her sandwich on the plate. "Would you like me to show you around? You do own half of it."

"Later." He nudged her sandwich closer to her. "You look like you need to eat."

The man, his mother, the store all receded as she met his gaze and held it. "It's good to see you."

"And you." So good that his answering smile came from his core. "Mother keeps me informed on what you're getting up to."

"She's a terrible spy." Ellie threw his mother a fond glance.

"But she makes a good sandwich and an even better cup of tea."

"Best I've had all week." The man sipped his tea and smacked his lips.

Ellie kept her gaze on him.

Maybe it was his conceit, but he thought she was looking at him like she'd missed the very sight of him.

"Are you hungry?"

He was about to deny it, but those thick wedges of fresh bread looked delicious. "What's on offer?"

"Ham, cheese, fresh tomatoes and bread Molly baked this morning," Mother answered.

Cole took a seat beside the man. "Sounds perfect." He motioned the teapot. "Any more in there?"

"I'll get you a cup." Ellie stood.

"No, you won't." The man pressed her back into her seat and stared at her sandwich. "Cole is right, you should eat. You work harder than any man I know, and you're only a tiny bit of a thing."

"Don't make me get the gun, Sal."

Sal threw back his head and guffawed. He winked at Cole. "Don't she beat all?"

Yeah, she did. Sugar had this way of lighting the world around her. "And she's a crack shot." Cole winked at Ellie.

She laughed.

And Cole couldn't drag his gaze away. Ellie laughed like she would never get the chance to do it again. Her eyes crinkled into half-moons over her flushed cheeks, and the sound boomed from her, all the more surprising for her size.

God, he'd missed her.

She bit into her sandwich.

Mother brought him a sandwich and took a seat beside him. "Sal and Ellie had a dispute over cotton," she said.

"Who won?" Cole was hungrier than he'd thought, and he took most of the sandwich in one huge bite.

Mother raised her brow at him. "Who do you think won?"

"Sorry, Sal, but the smart money is on the lady." That was a good sandwich. The bread was so fresh it almost fell apart, the cheese was sharp, the ham succulent and the tart bite of fresh tomatoes finished it off. In the months he'd been in New York, Cole had eaten all kinds of fancy meals, but not one compared to that sandwich and cup of tea.

Sal waved his teacup around. "Of course, she did. My oldest boy could do with a smart, strong woman like this one."

"I'm not getting married, Sal." Ellie shook her head at Sal.

Jealousy, cold and hard, twisted through Cole, and he bit into his sandwich before he stood and bellowed that Ellie would never marry Sal's son. Not a fucking chance.

THIRTY-FIVE

Ellie was running out of lies to tell herself as she dragged herself out of bed and opened the store a couple of mornings after Cole's visit. Part of her wished he'd never come, and an even bigger part of her had hoarded each precious moment and pressed it between the pages of her memory.

Molly had gotten an early start running errands. She already suspected what Ellie was being forced to accept. It had been three months since her last monthlies. That alone, she could put down to opening the store, the hard work and the determination to make her store a success. The sensitive, swollen breasts and the tiredness, however, could not be so easily explained away. At the Four Kings, she'd had this conversation with more than one girl.

Outside the store, a gloomy day greeted her. The folk of this big, exhausting city were up and about, paying no attention to the threatening gray clouds. Already, the weather had begun to cool in the late evenings and early mornings. Fall was on its way. Back home, they would be taking a break from the crushing, dry heat of summer and praying fire didn't break out in the parched brush.

Cole's man came by every few weeks and let her know how the search for Theo was going. They'd traced him to San Francisco, from where he'd taken a mule train to the gold fields, and they'd lost track of him, but Cole's man remained hopeful.

Sputtering raindrops hit the sidewalk outside the store. People moved faster to get out of the damp.

She was pregnant. Knocked up, in the family way, expecting, with child, a bun in the oven, gravid.

And with not a damn clue what to do about being that way. Her conscience whispered that Cole needed to know, had the right to know, but she hesitated to tell him. Twelve years Cole had waited to have his dream, and now that it hovered within his grasp, she couldn't be the one to take it away from him.

As much as Cole had played the high roller and done it well, his heart had never been in it. Maybe that's what she'd recognized in him when they'd first met. Despite the slick duds and the smooth talking, gun toting charmer he appeared to be, perhaps she had always known there was a lot more to him than that. Who could tell? It was all water under the bridge now, and she was going to have his child.

Unmarried and pregnant had all the makings of disaster, but she didn't regret it was Cole's baby she carried. She had no idea how she was going to make the store, the baby, her life work. It was really difficult to attribute her baby to her dead, and nonexistent, husband.

A woman opened the door and stepped out of the drizzle. "Good morning."

"Can I help you?" Ellie recognized Victoria the moment she looked up.

Victoria strolled into the shop taking everything in. "I feel sure you can."

Ellie waited, refusing to give in to the desire to explain her store, to excuse it for not meeting Victoria's standards. Instead she watched Victoria fiddle with a heavy claret velvet ribbon they used for trim, pick up and replace a lace collar.

As a woman who had run more than fifteen whores, Ellie recognized the signs of a woman bent on trouble. If she waited, Victoria would spit it out.

It took less than five minutes for Victoria to get to her reason for being there. "You're Ellie Pierce, and you came from Colorado with Cole."

"I did."

The glitter in Victoria's eyes spoke of a woman determined to draw blood.

Ellie braced for it. "And you know this because we've met before."

"Right." Victoria fingered a raw silk and dropped it with a curl of her lips. "I never heard the story of how you met."

For a glorious second, Ellie toyed with the idea of telling Victoria the truth. Cole had offered five hundred dollars to fuck her. Instead she said, "Then you should ask Cole to tell you."

"We both know he won't do that." Victoria gave her a tight smile. "So, I'm asking you, woman to woman. I'm assuming you know something of my past with Cole?"

"I know he never forgot you in all the years he lived in Colorado. I also know he came back to New York for you." It cost her a chunk of her heart to say as much, but she didn't have the energy to get into a territorial war with Victoria. Victoria had already won, and the only person who didn't know that was Victoria.

"Oh?" Victoria blinked at her.

Ellie almost laughed. Victoria had come here for a catfight.

She'd probably spent the carriage ride getting her ammunition all lined up, and now Ellie had frustrated all of that by refusing to play. "Did you think I didn't know that?"

"I'm not sure what you mean." Victoria tittered and wound her reticule straps around her fingers. "I'm sure I had no thought to what you did and did not know."

"Really?" God, this woman would need to grow a tougher hide. "So, you didn't come here to make sure I was no threat to you?"

Victoria gaped at her and then blushed. "I have no idea what you're talking about."

"Yes, you do." Ellie was tired of her game already. Victoria had won, and won the greatest prize of all, and she hadn't the strength to stand there and pretend. "You came here to look the enemy in the eye and warn them away from your man."

Victoria struggled for words.

Ellie marched to the door and opened it. "I have good news for you. You've won. Cole is yours, and I'll stay out of your way."

To give her due, Victoria tried to come back and ended on a huffed, "Well, I never."

Ellie opened the door. "Make him happy, Victoria. Make him happier than I ever could, and you'll never see me again as long as you live. He deserves that and so much more, and if you can't do that, then you need to start worrying yourself over me."

Still opening and shutting her mouth, Victoria marched out the door. She stopped on the step into her carriage and almost marched back into the store but decided against it and let her footman hand her into the coach.

"Well done." Molly leaned against the doorjamb from the workroom into the front of the store. "You told her all right."

"Let's get the store ready for the day."

Folding her arms, Molly stared her down. "It was a wonderful speech, great, in fact, but I must have missed the part where you told her you're having Cole's baby."

CHAPTER

THIRTY-SIX

I f Cole had been carrying his Colt Double Action, he would have shot the painted, pinned and primped opera singer screeching away like an awl to his temples.

The noise coming out of her mouth was god-awful. That much he might have been able to bear, but the way his fellow occupants in the opera box insisted they were loving every second of it had pushed him over the edge.

Someone needed shooting, and he was in the right sort of mood to do it.

"Isn't she marvelous?" Victoria whispered to him behind her fan.

Cole huffed ostrich feathers out his mouth. Not able to manage a civilized sound, he gave a noncommittal grunt.

"She's from Paris, you know." Victoria made a face like that was supposed to send him into giddy swirls of delight. "They say she was all the rage in Paris."

"We should send her back," he said.

Victoria tittered and tapped him on the arm with her fan. "Cole!"

That was another thing. That fucking fan needed to get fed to a goat. Victoria waved it around like there was some kind of bug infestation swarming around her face.

Paris Opera Girl sucked in a breath deep enough to swallow the Hudson and let go with a shriek that almost stripped the wallpaper.

Cole shifted on his seat. "Jesus."

"Cole?" Victoria's smile was brittle. "Are you not enjoying Madame Eloise?"

Like a punch in the family jewels. "I'm not much for opera."

"But, Cole." Victoria frowned, or as near to it as she came, which was a slight flesh pinch between her eyes. "Everybody agrees she is incandescent. To hear her sing is to be transported."

At that moment, Madame did him the favor of her life and stopped singing. She stood there, flushed, eyes sparkling and expectant, and peered down her large nose at her peons.

Relief made him applaud at least as loudly as the rest of their party.

"We are invited to join Digby and the rest of his party for a late supper." Victoria stood and twitched her silk skirts straight.

"Fine." It irked him the way she assumed he would fall in with whatever plans she made.

She smiled over her shoulder at him. "I am famished."

Which meant she would nibble the corner of something and call it a meal. "Me too."

"Oh." Her eyes sparkled. "Mimi Rochester is here. It's been an age since I saw her. I simply must say hello."

Off she bustled.

"Mimi!" Victoria squeaked.

"Victoria, darling!" A robust blonde in a red dress so low her bosom was threatening to escape threw her arms open.

"Cole." Brett sidled up beside him. "Didn't expect to see you here."

Since Mother had locked them in together, he and Brett had established an uneasy truce. By tacit agreement, they stayed away from controversial subjects, which left the weather. "I didn't expect to see me here either."

Brett nearly cracked a smile. "Not a music lover?"

"Is that what we witnessed?"

This time Brett grinned. "It was a near thing," he said, folding his arms and surveying the room. "My life passed before me."

Cole laughed. He couldn't help it. He'd always thought of Brett as part of Victoria's crowd, but Brett spent more time at the office than he did socializing. It had given Cole a grudging respect for him. Brett had taken what their father had left him and quadrupled it.

"We're going for a late supper." Inviting his brother was a first for him. "Would you like to join us?"

"Who's us?" Brett eyed him suspiciously.

"Digby and whatever his sister's name is."

"Chloe."

"Right and the Arbuthers, and that Mimi woman in the red dress." At least he assumed so because Victoria was tugging her his way.

"Jesus!" Brett flinched. "Not Mimi Rochester."

Mimi caught sight of Brett and waved like she was flagging down the only stagecoach for three weeks. "Brett! Brett Mansfield." She charged straight for Brett and latched on to his arm. "You sly thing, I swear you've been avoiding me."

The look of misery Brett tried to conceal made Cole laugh even harder. His brother shot him a glare.

"Say you'll join us, Brett?" Mimi batted her lashes at Brett. She pouted and giggled. "I refuse to take no for an answer."

"Perfect." Victoria clapped her hands as if she was gathering a group of children. "Our table is waiting."

In the carriage on the way to the restaurant, Cole sat back as Victoria and Mimi chattered away. Only the knowledge that Brett was suffering the same silent misery provided comfort. Propped in the carriage corner, arms folded and his chin on his chest, Brett looked like death couldn't come too soon for him.

They reached some restaurant that looked a lot like the one they'd been to the night before and the night before that. The same interchangeable maitre d' led them to a starched linen clothed table in the midst of a sea of beautifully dressed, jewel laden people, most of who had some urgent piece of gossip to share with Victoria.

As he took his seat, Cole had to face an uncomfortable truth. It wasn't Mimi, Victoria or even that shrieking Parisian woman. The problem was him. He had come back to New York determined to be the man he had been before. That man, however, had died long ago in the scorching Colorado sun, and he couldn't be resurrected. Truth be told, Cole didn't even want him back.

The Cole who had left New York had been a spoiled child, throwing his blessings away by the handfuls. He hadn't needed to take part in the duel that had led to his banishment. Instead of behaving like a man, his boyish conceit and arrogance had made him imagine some insult he couldn't even remember anymore.

Mother had been heartbroken, Victoria had seen her dreams smashed, and he'd made an enemy of his only sibling. His actions that day had left ripples in other people's lives, and he couldn't fix those.

Of all the things he'd believed about coming back to New York, his feelings for Victoria changing hadn't been one of them. But three months since their reunion and the words to propose to her still wouldn't come.

Across the table, she was laughing at something Digby was saying. The jewels in her ears and at her neck caught the light and sparkled. She was a beautiful woman. No doubt about it. She would be the perfect wife, but for another man, a man who appreciated what she had to offer and existed in her world.

"What?" Brett nudged him. "You have a strange look on your face."

Cole bet he did. He didn't love Victoria, perhaps he never really had. "Thinking."

"About?" Brett sipped his champagne, his gaze intent on Cole.

"Change."

Brett nodded and put his glass down. "You have changed."

Cole didn't think Brett would have noticed. "So have you."

"When you left, I had to step up." He shrugged. "And really, I should thank you for that, because I loved it. I loved having a real purpose to my day. I like being involved in business."

"So do I." Cole was having a night for realizations. What had started as a form of survival, building up a steady income, had become a passion. It still was, and he wasn't ready to let it go. "I need to tell her."

"Yeah, you do." Brett held his hand up for the waiter. When one appeared, he said, "My brother and I will have a whisky."

The waiter hurried off and Cole pushed his champagne away. "Ever thought of expanding?"

"Out west, you mean." Brett tilted his head and studied him. "I might, if I had someone I trusted to deal with."

"Someone who knew how business was done in that part of the world?"

"That someone would make me look seriously in that direction." Brett nodded. "She'll be fine, you know." He met Cole's gaze. "I think she's halfway to realizing the same thing you did, and Digby is hovering and waiting to pick up the pieces."

Head close to Victoria's, hanging on every word, Digby certainly did look like a man infatuated. Victoria looked flushed and happy too. She deserved someone who could understand and appreciate her.

That did make him feel better. Cole didn't relish failing Victoria another time. Going forward with this relationship, having it end in marriage, would be an even worse mistake, however. He needed to set them both free.

He and Brett chatted a bit more about opportunities in the future and supper passed quickly.

In the carriage on the way home, Victoria turned to him. "You were quiet tonight."

"Opera is really not for me." He was also tired of pretending they fit. "Or late suppers. Somewhere I've lost my taste for a lot of what New York has to offer."

She sucked in a soft breath. "What are you saying, Cole?"

"I think you know." He looked at her. "We're different people, Victoria."

"Cole." Her eyes filled with tears. "Please tell me you're not doing this to me a second time?"

He flinched because that was exactly what he was doing. "I know you've noticed." Dark glances shot at him over drinks when he said something she didn't approve of and the way she determinedly laughed off the parts of him she didn't understand spoke volumes about where their relationship was. "I don't fit in, and it bothers you."

"No, I—"

"Vic." He looked at her, willing her to admit the truth they both felt. "Half the time you look like you'd happily kick my ass."

"Cole!" She jerked as if he'd struck her. "Your profanity offends me, and yet you continue."

"Partly, it's the way I speak now," he said. "It fits this version of me."

"That's an excuse and a pathetic one." Victoria shifted in her seat, smoothing her skirts. "You make no effort because you choose not to."

She had him there. "Perhaps so."

"And." She straightened her shoulders and thrust her chin out. "If you must know, there are things about you that make me want to scream."

This was better than her pretending to be soft and wounded.

"I wish you'd make more effort to think about what comes out of your mouth." She threw a hand in the air. "But you don't. You open your mouth and say the first thing you think." She gathered more steam on a sharp in-breath. "Like tonight! Madame Eloisa is a musical treasure, and you snorted. Snorted!"

He let her run. It was the least he could do.

"And when you told Chadwick Arbruther that he couldn't shoot worth sh—" She cleared her throat. "That word."

"You mean shit."

"Cole!" she yelled. "You can't say that word in front of me. I'm not like your cozy little whore."

Everything in him stilled. He kept the question light, because he got the distinct feeling he really wanted to hear what she said next. "What are you talking about, Vic?"

"Ellie." Victoria tossed her head. "Or should I say Sugar Ellie Pierce." She twitched her cloak together. "Frankly, Cole, I'm surprised you had the sheer gall to bring her amongst us. To introduce her to Joy."

"Mother likes Ellie." Victoria had been busy. "How did you find out who she was?"

She gaped at him. "You don't even try to deny it."

"Would there be any point?"

"No." She sniffed. "My Pinkerton man knows what he's about."

"You sent a Pinkerton man to find out who Ellie is?" He kept a tight rein on his fury.

"What else could I do?" Victoria shrugged. "You were back, but you weren't the man I knew before, and you brought that woman with you. I like to know whom I allow into my life."

"Did he go to the Four Kings?" Jake was no fucking idiot, and a Pinkerton agent would tell him all he needed to know. Following that man back to where he came from would be child's play to Jake and the twins.

Clueing in to his anger for the first time, Victoria frowned, and eyed him warily. "Of course he did. They were quite open about who she was. Apparently, she's been missing for some time, and they're desperate to find her."

"Victoria." He took deep, steadying breaths. "Once more I have injured you through my actions, which is probably the only thing holding me back from snapping your neck."

She gasped and shrunk from him. "How dare—"

"Your vulgar curiosity has exposed Ellie to danger. I acquit you of doing so deliberately." He leaned closer to her. "But if Ellie gets hurt, somebody is going to pay the price, Colorado style, and I'm going to be the one to collect."

THIRTY-SEVEN

Ellie stood and stretched her back. Across from her in the workroom, Molly looked up and grimaced. They'd been working most of the night on a rush order for a new client.

The women who came to her store knew what they wanted and could be rather demanding about it. With her trying to build a strong client base, she needed to do what it took to assure their business.

"Bugger it." Molly sucked her finger.

Ellie empathized. She'd made more holes in her fingers than she thought possible. "We'll need to think about getting help soon."

"We could really do with it right now." Molly grimaced and stretched her fingers. "I could see if one of my cousins is looking for work."

"I'm not sure I could pay for someone else yet." Ellie had been making steady money, but she was not at the point she could expand.

Molly gave her a firm look. "You could always go and see Cole about what you need. I'm sure he wouldn't be happy to hear how you're working yourself to the bone."

Ellie flushed. Molly never minced words, and it was one of the things she liked about her, but sometimes it made her uncomfortably blunt. "You know why I can't do that."

"I know why you think you can't." Molly snorted. "All because he's pining for that uppity bitch." She dropped her work to her lap and jabbed a finger at Ellie. "Have you thought a woman like that might not make him happy. She might nag him into an early grave."

"She may well do." Ellie was tired of having this conversation with Molly. "But it's not up to me to say what he wants."

"No, indeed." Molly rolled her eyes. "Because the fact that you're carrying Cole Mansfield's baby gives you no rights where he is concerned at all."

"Ellie?" Jake stood in her workroom door.

"Jake." Ellie thought she must be imagining him.

Standing, Molly glanced between her and Jake. "Jake?"

"Yes, Jake," she said, pulse thundering in her ears. Molly already knew the story.

Molly screamed and threw her sewing box at him.

Ducking out the way, Jake stepped into the light.

Ellie stood and stared. She couldn't believe it was really him, but there he was all right, dodging the scissors Molly threw at him. "Jesus, woman, stop!"

"Get out." Molly grabbed up Ellie's scissors and brandished them at him. "I will stab you before I let you near her."

Ellie found her voice. "What are you doing here, Jake?"

Jake kept his attention locked on Molly. "The door was open."

"Son of a bitch." Molly lunged at him. "You tried to sell her, you pecker."

"Stop, Molly." Ellie grew lightheaded and dropped into her seat. Some part of her mind reminded her she should be running for her life, but her legs refused to move.

"Ellie." Jake grimaced. "There are things I need to say to you."

"Then say them." Theo crowded into the room behind Jake. "Say what you need to say and then we can talk about Ellie's newest surprise."

"Theo?" Ellie stood, her spine gave out, and she slumped on her stool. After all these months of missing him, worrying about him and trying to find him, he was standing right there and looked as well as he ever had. "Theo!"

"That's Theo?" Molly curled her top lip. "I thought he'd be taller."

Theo threw Molly a confused glance and then aimed back at Ellie. "Hey, Ellie." A gentle smile softened his hard face. "Looks like I can't leave you alone."

"Theo." The room blurred as tears filled her eyes. She stumbled to her feet and straight into a hug.

Theo tightened his arms around her, and her world stopped shifting. Since she'd been a tiny one, Theo could always wrap her in security. As her big brother, he'd really been more of a father to her. Until that moment, she hadn't realized how truly frightened she had been that Theo was dead.

Once opened, the floodgates refused to shut again, and she cried and cried. All that she'd held in through escaping from Jake, then ending up with Pete and Isaac, her relationship with Cole, her heartbreak and her terror about what the future meant for this child. Safe in her big brother's embrace, she cried it all out. Theo was there, and she was safe. Theo was there, and he would help her untangle the dreadful snarl she'd made.

It took a while for everything to calm down. Molly made tea and placed it on the workroom table, along with a batch of fresh scones, butter and jam. Molly didn't believe any crisis should be tackled without sustenance.

Ellie sat beside Theo. She couldn't stop staring at him. He was leaner and tanner, and he looked well, better than when he'd left.

Jake sat opposite her and looked everywhere else but at her. She'd said nothing to him since she'd first seen him.

Looking at his sullen face, she wanted to shake him and demand answers. Why had he turned on her like that? She wanted to demand the answer for the betrayal that had begun all of this.

Theo sipped his tea, his eyes tracking Molly as she moved about making something else to sustain the conversation.

He'd gotten to San Francisco safe and sound and then followed a potential opportunity inland. He'd been fine all along and setting up their next fortune. He was tired of saloon life and running girls. Theo wanted to make his living ranching.

"You? A rancher?" Ellie tried to picture it. Theo had more fallen into the saloon than made a choice to do so. He'd been left with four siblings to care for and no way to make money other than to supply the miners with his home-brewed hooch.

"Why not?" Theo shrugged. "I've been working out west as a ranch hand, trying to learn the business." He sipped his tea and looked as if he'd rather drink anything but.

Ellie laughed and fetched the one bottle of whisky Joy had stashed there in case Cole ever came to visit. She poured a glass for Theo and then looked to Jake.

Jake shook his head. "Actually, Ellie, there is something I need to say."

"Damn right you got something to say to her." Theo glared at him. "Get on with before I break your fool head."

Jake looked at her. He was different somehow. "Minnie is gone."

"Good." Ellie was relieved for Pearl and the girls. "Why?"

"I threw her out." Jake cleared his throat. "After."

"After what?"

Jake flushed. "You know...the...um."

Leaning over the table, Theo cuffed him. "Spit it out, you fucking idiot."

"I'm sorry, Ellie." Jake's flush deepened. "I should never have done it."

Molly stood over him with her arms folded. "Which bit shouldn't you have done?"

"All of it." Jake scowled at Molly. "I shouldn't have done any of it."

As far as apologies went, Jake wasn't even half done. "You mean about auctioning me off to the highest bidder?"

Theo growled. "I should shoot you for that alone."

"Not in here." Molly sniffed. "That saffron silk is for Mrs. Lewis's daughter's wedding, and I haven't got time to make another dress if that one gets splattered with blood."

"I wouldn't have done it, Ellie." Jake shifted his chair away from Molly. "Even before we found out you were missing, I'd changed my mind and was going to call the whole thing off."

Ellie wasn't so sure. "I guess now we'll never know, but I wasn't going to wait around for you to have an attack of conscience."

"It was Minnie." Jake swallowed. "Minnie got in my head and made it sound harmless."

"Harmless?" Molly picked up a kitchen knife and attacked a loaf of bread.

Gaze on the knife, sweat slid down Jake's temple. "It was only her virginity. At least that's what Minnie said. She said every woman has to lose it sooner or later, and at least this way someone would make money at it."

"I'm still going to shoot you," Theo said. "As Ellie is still alive, I'll make sure it's not gonna kill you, just hurt. A lot."

"Theo!" Jake scrambled to his feet.

Theo palmed a gun and Jake sat right back down. "I brought this fucker here to apologize to you in person," he said. "In the circumstances, you deserved to hear it face to face. What I'm gonna do about him is still undecided."

"You said all I had to do was apologize to her." Jake nearly shot out his chair again but thought better of it.

Theo showed him teeth, more snarl than smile. "I lied."

"You said." Sweat beaded on Jake's top lip. "I told you about Minnie, and you said I needed to stop thinking with my pecker."

Molly slammed a plate of sandwich fingers on the table. "Never met a man who got that right."

"Excuse me?" Theo narrowed his eyes at Molly. "Do you even know me?"

"I know Ellie." Molly folded her arms. "And I know her brothers didn't do right by her." She gathered a head of outraged steam. "You made her pretend to be a madam. An innocent girl. You exposed her to untold danger."

Theo blanched. "I was trying to protect her."

"No!" Molly went nose to nose with him. "Protecting her would have been taking her away from there and making a life somewhere else."

"That wasn't possible." Theo didn't back down. "And don't you think I know I made a bad choice?"

Molly opened and shut her mouth.

"I turned my little sister into a whore." Anguish crept into Theo's voice and over his face. "If I could wave my hand and go back to that time I would, but I was twenty-one, and all I saw was a quick fortune and an even quicker way to take care of the younger ones." He looked at Ellie. "I am sorry, you know, Ellie. If I had to do it again, I would load all of you in that stupid wagon and get the hell out of there. We had strong backs; we could have tried something else."

Ellie also remembered that time. "Theo." She took his hand. "We were hungry all the time. Whatever Pa mined went straight into a bottle. We were starved, filthy, and that old wagon wouldn't have made it to the end of our row of tents."

"You may be right about the wagon." Theo gave her a sad smile. "But Jake might never have done what he did if I hadn't put you at risk."

They could go round and round about this endlessly. "It's done now."

"Yeah." Jake stuffed a scone in his mouth. "All said and done, now let's move on."

Molly snatched her scones away. "Don't you eat my food. I've not forgiven you yet. You make some pathetic apology that didn't count for anything, and put all the blame on a woman, and expect me to feed you."

"I—" Jake dropped his head and breathed deep. Then he looked up at Ellie, and he looked like the brother she'd grown up with. The same one who had taught her how to tie her laces. "I lost my mind, Ellie. I should never have even thought that stupid auction would work. Yes, it was Minnie's idea, but you weren't her sister. It was my job to stop it all, and I didn't." He cleared his throat. "I sent Paul and Patrick out to find you. Not to bring you back and force you into anything, but to bring you back safely."

"You did?" Ellie glanced at Theo.

"That's what he says." Theo shrugged. "And I wouldn't have believed a word of it, but Pearl says it's the truth. He and Minnie had a fight that woke up everyone the morning they discovered you were gone. He tossed Minnie out right off."

Molly filled his whisky glass and Theo nodded his thanks,

"But he still had to deal with all those low lives who had come for the auction. And things got nasty there for a while. He needed the twins to get rid of them all." Theo chuckled. "They weren't too partial to being told the whole thing was off."

Jake stared into his tea. "They nearly burned down the Four Kings."

"Is everyone all right?" Ellie had no sympathy for Jake and the twins about that. They'd created the mess in the first place. "Pearl, the girls, everyone got out safely?"

"Everyone is fine." Jake nodded. "We...ah... let the girls go. We're turning the rooms into boarding, and Pearl's gonna run it."

"What will the girls do?" Her girls had become whores in the first place because they had no other way to feed themselves.

"A couple are staying to work with Pearl, the rest I set up in the old boarding house on Aspen street. Maisy took them over. Even Kitty agreed to stay with her," Jake said. "I paid to set it up right for them."

Ellie got the feeling Theo had a lot to do with that new direction. "How did you find me?"

"I knew about Cole's businesses in Denver," Theo said. "When Jake told me Cole had been seen with you, I started there."

"Then some Pinkerton man showed up and started asking about you." Jake smirked. "We persuaded him to tell us who had sent him."

"Do you know a Victoria Bonnington?" Theo looked at her. "And why does she want to know all about you?"

Molly snorted and gave Ellie a significant look. "Told you."

"She's Cole's..." She didn't know but guessed it had progressed by now. "She's Cole's fiancée."

"Fiancée?" Theo looked thunderous. "Then he's going to have to get himself unengaged and do right by you."

THIRTY-EIGHT

Cole stared at Mellor. The butler looked frazzled, his jacket disheveled and his hair standing on end. He stood in the doorway of the dining room.

"Who did you say?" He wasn't sure he'd heard right, and also that those bastards had dared put a foot inside his mother's house.

Mellor jerked his lapel straight. "There are a Mr. Jake Pierce, a Mr. Patrick Pierce and a Mr. Paul Pierce here who are most insistent on seeing you. They are refusing to leave. I could send for the—"

"No." Cole stood. "Could you fetch my—"

"Coat." Mellor handed him his coat. "I thought you might have need of this."

Mother looked at Mellor and then him. "Pierce? Those are Ellie's brothers?"

"Yeah." Cole drew his Colt from his inside coat pocket.

Blinking at him, Mother paled. "What are you doing?"

"That looks like you could do with some help." Brett stood

and dropped his napkin on the table. "Could you fetch my pistol? It's in—"

"The study." Mellor nodded. He looked at Mother. "Mrs. Mansfield?"

"For certain!" She threw her napkin on the table and shot to her feet. "Fetch my derringer. No way in hell are my sons walking into this alone. I fancy a shot or two at Ellie's brothers myself."

Shocked into immobility, it took Cole a precious moment to catch up with his ears. By which time, Mother was marching through the foyer, cocking a small Derringer Mellor had produced from God knew where.

"Right." She threw open the front door and aimed her pistol.

Jake's hands shot in the air, followed by Paul and Patrick. Theo looked at the gun and bowed. "Good evening. Mrs. Mansfield, I presume?"

"Yes." Mother locked her gaze on Theo. "Which one are you?"

"Theo." He bowed.

Mother aimed at the other three. "He gets to live. Which one of you is Jake?"

Brett came up beside Cole. "I'll cover the big one."

"That's not the one who needs covering." He pointed his Colt at the twins. "Those two are the worst, and I believe our mother is going to kill Jake for me."

"Mrs. Mansfield." Theo stepped forward.

Cole covered him. He didn't think Theo would have had anything to do with Jake's schemes, but he still didn't like the bastard that close to his mother.

"While I appreciate your desire to shoot Jake"—Theo clapped his hand on Jake's shoulder hard enough to make Jake flinch—"he is my brother, and I haven't completely given up on him." Then he looked up at Cole, barely concealed fury in his eyes. "But if we could shelve Jake's shooting for the moment, we have something more important to discuss."

"Ellie's going to kill you," Jake murmured.

Theo kept glaring at him, and Cole could think of only one reason an older brother would be that pissed at him. A man who he had always gotten on well with. "Ellie will get over it," he said. "Come in."

Mother gaped at him. "This is not your house, Cole Mansfield. I decide who comes into this dwelling."

"Fine." Cole grit his teeth. "Mother, would—"

"By all means." Mother gave Theo a tight smile. "Please come in." She waved her pistol at Jake and the twins. "But this vermin stays on the porch."

"Fair enough." Theo stepped into the house. "You can put the guns away."

"That remains to be seen," Mother said. She nodded at Brett. "Keep an eye on those three out there."

Brett nodded and cocked his gun.

"You." Mother pointed at Theo. "Get in there and explain what's happening to Ellie."

Theo stopped in front of him. "Ellie will be fine. Ellie will be more than fine because I'm going to ensure your boy makes it so."

HER ARMS FULL OF CLOTHES, Ellie had to step around Molly to get to her suitcase. Ellie seemed to have amassed more black dresses than any one woman needed since her time in New York.

The problem was that when she got a new fabric, she often tried it out in a garment for herself or Molly first. If anybody was rude enough to ask about the size of her wardrobe, that's what she would tell them. By anyone, she meant her brothers. Who she was currently furious with.

She tried to shove a bombazine day gown into her trunk. A trunk she had sent Molly out to buy this morning.

"Stop that." Molly rescued the gown and folded it. "I'm not sure why you won't wait for your brothers."

Ellie nearly growled at her. "You know why."

"Because they went to demand Cole do the right thing?"

"But it's not the right thing." Suddenly exhausted, Ellie plopped on her bed. "Cole is in love with Victoria, and he wants to marry her. He's wanted to marry her since he left New York years ago."

Molly snorted and picked up a satin evening gown that Ellie had no use for before and would certainly have no use for once she began showing. But she could always take the seams out, and her gowns were a part of her. She was taking them with her, and she didn't care how much her brothers complained about all her luggage.

"You know he'll probably chase after you." Molly finished the gown and sat beside her.

"No, he won't." And that made her sadder than she had any right to be. "Cole needs to stay here and pursue his dream. He deserves it."

Molly pulled a face. "How is it that he deserves his dream and you don't deserve yours?"

"I have my dream." Ellie managed to say the words without sobbing. "This is my dream." She waved her hand to indicate the store. "Sugar Ellie is long gone, and the respectable Widow Pierce makes lovely dresses for ordinary girls."

"Hmm." Molly looked around her. "And yet you're going to run away?"

"Well, this rather changes things." She looked at her belly.

"Unless you think people will believe my husband magically rose from the grave."

"Er...no." Molly shook her head. "And that is going to be difficult to explain anywhere you go."

Ellie had this part covered. "I've thought of that. I can say my husband died without knowing I was with child. It will make me even more of a pitiful figure."

Molly looked skeptical. "And what about the store?"

"You'll be the face people see until I can come back." Ellie stood and dug a sheaf of papers out of her desk drawer. "I need to lie low until the baby is born."

Molly stared at the papers as if they might bite. "I'm absolutely certain Cole will not be happy with that arrangement, and as your partner, needs to approve it."

"Cole had no use for this place." Ellie shrugged. "And only Joy comes around to check on how we're doing. I'm sure she will see that you're the best person for the job."

"What if I don't want the store?" Molly folded her arms. "What if I want to come with you?"

Ellie hadn't thought of that. "Do you? Want to leave?"

"No." Molly rolled her eyes. "I like it here, and I'm close to my family again."

It was true. "You're good at this, Molly. I've watched you with the customers, you're at least as good as I am with them, and I will be mailing you designs."

"You've said all this." Molly sighed. "But I don't know why you're in such a hurry to leave now."

"Because my brothers went to see Cole." She couldn't remain still anymore, and she went to the window and looked out. "I don't want to be forced on him."

The normal morning bustle carried on outside her window. Now, however, the bustle had divided into familiar parts. The boy running with his cap pulled low over his eyes was Silas from three stores down. His dad owned a printing business, and Silas often ran messages and whatnot around the city. On the corner, Maria sold her delicious fresh bread that she baked every morning. Across the road from her store, the Gillespie brothers were arguing again. No matter the subject, the brothers would argue.

It felt familiar, but not like home. Perhaps with the baby coming, home took on a special importance for her. Theo had asked her what she wanted to do, stay in New York, return to the Four Kings, even come with him to California. That was before he announced he was off to see Cole, and all hell had broken loose.

For once in their lives, all four of her brothers had united against her. Cole needed to be told. That's where opinions split. Patrick and Paul were in favor of beating Cole senseless, particularly Paul, who was looking for some payback. Jake had tried hatching a scheme to use her baby to extort money from Cole and the rest of the Mansfields. Theo had beat Ellie to it and punched Jake in the mouth for that one.

Theo wanted to fetch the preacher. Fetch the preacher indeed. Ellie went back to her packing. As if a woman like her would ever need a preacher for anything other than the last rites.

"You really must hate that bonnet." Molly rescued the crepe bedecked bonnet Ellie had been mangling into a hatbox. "Ellie." She stood in Ellie's path until Ellie looked at her. "Your brothers are right. Cole needs to know about his child."

Right now, Theo could be telling Cole. He would be horrified, destroyed, see all his hopes and dreams crumbling. That's if he recognized the child. The thought snuck into her mind and punched the breath out her lungs.

That's what she was really scared of. Cole would find out she was carrying his baby and not care. He would carry on with his life, even marry Victoria in some lavish society wedding, and never once think about a girl who had loved him enough to give herself to him, and the child she had brought into this world.

Ellie had seen it happen more times than she'd seen saloon brawls. Dammit! Half the girls who had worked for her had started like this and ended up being tossed out of home to fend for themselves. It wasn't fair, and it darn sure wasn't right, but she had lived in the real world for too long for girlish dreams to survive.

Men walked away once they'd gotten what they wanted, and they didn't look back.

Cole hadn't walked away from her. She could acquit him of that. They had ended things by mutual agreement. If anything, she'd been the one pushing that agreement for the sake of her poor, battered heart. She was the one who had told him not to come and see her. Of course, Cole had gotten around that by sending Joy, but he'd abided by the letter of their agreement.

Molly was right. He did deserve the chance to know this child. The man who had rescued her from Jake, and then Pete, brought her all the way to New York, and set her up in a business was a man who would want to know he had a child. She pressed her palm to her belly. Cole had made this life with her and he deserved the chance to be a part of the baby's life.

"What is it?" Molly was by her side immediately. "You don't feel good?"

"I feel fine." Physically at least. "I need to tell Cole about the baby."

"I—"

Hammering at the door startled the two of them.

"Ellie!" Cole yelled from the street. "Open this door."

"Well." Molly peered out the window. "The good news is I don't think you need to tell him anymore."

THIRTY-NINE

After weeks of not seeing Cole, Ellie took a long moment to drink him in.

Molly had let him in and then left them alone in the workroom.

With wind-ruffled hair and his cravat askew, he reminded her more of the Cole she used to know. He had that rakish air that drew women to him. At least it drew this woman like a magic spell he cast over her.

"Ellie." Cole studied her, his gaze lingering on her midsection. "Is it true?"

"Yes." He was there, strong and tall and dependable, and she wanted to collapse into him and weep. Except she'd given up the right to do anything of the sort.

Cole shoved his hands in his pockets. "You should have told me."

"I was working up to that."

"Why?" He raised his voice and then lowered it immediately. "I don't understand why I had to hear this from Theo."

That Cole was more bothered about the delivery of the

news than the news itself threw her off, and she had to find her voice. This wasn't the question she had thought to be answering first.

If she had given herself time to think through the possibilities, the scene might have played out like this: Cole arrived puffed up with righteous indignation and demanded how she had allowed such a thing to happen.

Except, Cole never did what she expected him to. "You want to marry Victoria," she said. "I couldn't take that away from you. It's been your dream for so long, and I want you to have that."

Cole studied her in silence for a while and then he said, "Why, Sugar? Why is it so important that I have my dream?"

It was similar to what Molly had asked, and she still couldn't answer it fully. "Because you waited all those years for her. You loved her, Cole. I want you to have the love and happiness you deserve."

"I did love her." Cole closed the distance between them. "When I was young and spoiled. She was young and spoiled too, and we fit together perfectly in our world."

For a moment, Ellie struggled to catch a breath. That hurt more than she would have thought possible. Also, hearts really did feel like they were snapping in two. "There, you see." She cleared her throat to loosen it. "That's why I haven't told you."

Cole stopped in front of her. "Would you ever have told me?"

"I don't know." Ellie answered as honestly as she could. "I know you had the right to know about your child, but I didn't want to do anything to jeopardize your engagement to Victoria."

"What engagement?"

That surprised her, but she maintained her line. "Well, if you're not engaged now, you soon will be."

"I'm engaged as of this moment." Cole caught her by the waist and tugged her closer.

"Cole!" Ellie tried to free herself. "What are you doing?"

"Making sure my fiancée can hear me good and clear." He wrapped his arms around her waist.

He'd brought Victoria? Ellie peered around him, but the workroom was empty.

"Are you listening, Sugar?" He tightened his hold. "Say 'Yes, Cole' if you can hear me."

"Yes, Cole." Her mind had blanked.

"I am not, nor have I been, engaged to Victoria since my return." He leaned closer to her ear. "Ask me why, Sugar?"

Her pulse drummed in her throat. She didn't want to think too hard about what was happening. Her everything hung in the balance. "Why?"

"A week ago, I admitted Victoria and I did not suit." One hand rested on the curve of her spine, the other slid into the hair at her nape. "I haven't seen her since, but I have it on good authority she's not suffering alone."

"Oh." All this man ever had to do was touch her, and she melted for him. Surely, a woman should have more backbone than that.

"Now ask me where I was going before your brothers interrupted my breakfast?"

"Where?"

"Here." He nuzzled her neck. "I couldn't stand not seeing you anymore. Now ask me why."

And Ellie discovered her gumption by sheer force of will. "I tell you what." She drew back enough to meet his gaze. "How about we stop the guessing games, and you lay it out for me?"

"There's my Sugar Ellie." Cole smiled, and in his eyes was an expression that made her breath stop and her heart miss a beat. He looked at her as if there was nobody he'd rather be looking at and nowhere he'd rather be. "Here we go then. I love you, Sugar Ellie Pierce. I think I've been half in love with you for years. No man offers twenty thousand dollars for a woman he's fond of."

It had always been Cole for her. Deep in that place within that she steered clear of, Cole was nestled in burr-like and forever. "You were never serious about that."

"No, I wasn't." He kissed her forehead. "But I would have paid every cent I owned to have you look at me like you're looking at me now."

"How am I looking at you?" It was past time for Ellie to ask the questions.

"Like you love me." Cole held her gaze. "Do you, Sugar? Do you love me?"

"Yes."

"Good." He wrapped her into him and surrounded her with the scent and feel of him. "Because you're the dream I've been chasing all these years." He kissed her temple. "It wasn't Victoria at all. I was chasing the dream of a woman to share my life, love me like I loved her, and make the sun come out every day for me."

Ellie glowed from the warm happy place inside. "Ask me if I want the same?"

"Do you, Ellie?" He rested his head atop hers. "Do you want the same?"

Snuggling as close as she could, she said, "I do, Cole. In every way I possibly can, I do."

EPILOGUE

Ellie huffed and puffed alongside Cole as they walked into the Denver Pacific Railway station. They were running a bit late on account of there being so much more of her to dress and get moving these days.

"I still think you should have stayed at home." Cole stared at her huge belly pointedly.

As they waited for their baby to make its appearance, Cole had been getting more and more antsy and protective.

"Not with Bridget there," she said. "And besides, I wanted to be here to meet the train."

"Sugar." Cole raised his eyebrow at her. "When are you going to start the obeying part of your vows?"

Ellie giggled, because they both knew the answer to that. "Never."

They'd both decided New York was nice for a visit but the red dirt of Denver was baked soul deep into both of them. Cole had kept his beautiful house when he had left for New York and Roberts was delighted to have them back. He was still trying to turn Silas and Caleb respectable. Caleb had taken to working in a smart house just fine, but Silas still missed his days of tending bar.

Ellie still got the occasional person from the Four Kings recognize Sugar Ellie, but it didn't bother her anymore. Sugar Ellie was a survivor and part of who she was. Cole had tracked down the old oil painting of her that used to hang above the bar and it now hung in their bedroom.

Isaac had brought Bridget to Denver for the birth of her first baby. They'd arrived on Cole's doorstep two nights ago with the news that Pete had sent them to make sure the birth went well. Roberts had taken charge and moved them to a room as far away from Ellie and Cole's as the mansion allowed.

Ellie would not have thought it possible, but Bridget had gotten even lovelier, and she was ridiculously happy. Of course, that meant she chattered more than ever. Isaac, and he must really love her, listened to every word she said as if it came straight from the lips of God.

"At least you've stopped working until little Mansfield is born." Cole guided her around a cart laden with goods on the platform.

A second Sugar's had opened in Denver four months earlier. Having decided she wasn't the type who liked running a boarding house, Pearl had sold up and come from Rattler's Gulch to run Sugar's for her. A dress shop was much more Pearl's thing, and she'd only threatened to shoot one customer so far. To be fair, the woman had made one of Pearl's seamstresses cry. Of course, the new Sugar's catered to the needs of the women out west, while Molly ran the New York store.

Joy had been more than happy to keep her eye on the New York operation, and she and Molly worked well together.

Theo was making noises about her starting a third store in California, close to where he ranched, but plans would have to wait until little Mansfield was born. Theo had also made a few trips to New York, and Ellie strongly suspected Theo's interest in Sugar's was more in the nature of his interest in Molly.

Three days after her and Cole's hasty marriage in New York, Jake and the twins had disappeared. They couldn't say for sure, but they'd heard rumors about three men matching her brother's descriptions raising hell in Kansas City.

"Here it comes." Ellie pointed as the Cheyenne train steamed into the station.

Amidst hissing steam, and clanging bells, doors opened, and passengers stepped onto the platform.

Ellie caught sight of Brett first, standing taller than the disembarking passengers around him. Mansfield Bros. had become Denver's leading shipper of goods between the east and west. As long as Cole and Brett stuck to business, they got on fine.

They heard her before they saw her. "Get out my way before I shoot your pecker off."

A cowpoke leaped out of the way as Joy charged down the platform.

Brett walked behind her, eyes rolling. "Dear God, Mother. Must you?"

"Yep." Joy patted the Colt at her hip. Somehow, she made it work with her fancy New York traveling gown. "I've been wanting to say that since I heard Ellie say it."

She caught sight of them and grinned and waved. She had insisted on coming west for the birth of her first grandchild. "There you are."

"Joy." Ellie hugged her mother-in-law around her huge belly.

"And how is my Sugar Ellie?" Joy smiled at her mistily.

Ellie smiled back. "Sugar Ellie is doing sweet."

If you're an historical romance fan, check out Sir Arthur's Legacy, a medieval romance series, also by Sarah Edwards. Or join my newsletter to read the Prequel to The Betrothal Melee, The Marriage Parley for free (links below the Sweet Bea excerpt).

Sweet Bea, #1 Sir Arthur's Legacy

Is love sweeter than revenge?

Dreamy, impulsive, and spirited, the Lady Beatrice embarks on a mission to save her family from losing everything.

Unfortunately, she chooses as her savior the very man who hates her family the most.

Angry and sworn to vengeance, Garrett will see Sir Arthur pay for destroying his life. He has chosen as his instrument Sir Arthur's youngest daughter, Beatrice.

Both intent on their missions and drawn together by an undeniable attraction, can Sweet Bea teach Garrett that love, not vengeance, is the greatest reward of all?

Chapter 1

Beatrice had a secret. A secret of the most delicious sort.

She was being wooed. Wooed with honeyed words and sweeter touches. Tingles spread to Beatrice's fingertips, rushed back again, and pooled in her stomach.

Ducking her head, she kept her pace to a saunter. There was nothing amiss with her. No reason for anyone to pause their day and watch her.

Spring filled the air with scents of new grass and wildflowers. The sun beamed from a cloudless arc of blue above her. Birdsong serenaded her as cornflowers merrily bobbed beside the path. Even the insects buzzed encouragement. She was young, she was in love, and the world could not be more perfect.

Garrett. Just his name made her shiver.

For first dibs on news, deals, and giveaways, and so much more, join the @Home Collective

Or if Facebook is more your thing, join the Sarah Hegger Collective

Anything and everything you need to know on my website http://sarahhegger.com

ABOUT THE AUTHOR

**Sarah Edwards is also published under the name
Sarah Hegger**

Born British and raised in South Africa, Sarah Hegger suffers from an incurable case of wanderlust. Her match? A hot Canadian engineer, whose marriage proposal she accepted six short weeks after they first met. Together they've made homes in seven different cities across three different continents (and back again once or twice). If only it made her multilingual, but the best she can manage is idiosyncratic English, fluent Afrikaans, conversant Russian, pigeon Portuguese, even worse Zulu and enough French to get herself into trouble. Mimicking her globe trotting adventures, Sarah's career path began as a gainfully employed actress, drifted into public relations, settled a moment in advertising, and eventually took root in the fertile soil of her first love, writing. She also moonlights as a wife and mother. She currently lives in Ottawa, Canada, filling her empty nest with fur babies. Part footloose buccaneer, part quixotic observer of life, Sarah's restless heart is most content when reading or writing books.

f

PRAISE FOR SARAH EDWARDS

Sarah Edwards also writes as Sarah Hegger

Drove All Night
"The classic romance plot is elevated to a modern-day, wholly accessible real-life fairy tale with an excellent mix of romantic elements and spicy sensuality."
Booklife Prize, Critic's Report

Positively Pippa
"This is the type of romance that makes readers fall in love not just with characters, but with authors as well."
Kirkus Review (Starred Review)

"What begins as a simple second-chance romance quickly transforms into a beautiful, frank examination of love, family dynamics, and following one's dreams. Hegger's unflinching, candid portrayal of interpersonal and generational communication elevates the story to the sublime. Shunning clichés and contrived circumstances, she uses realistic,

relatable situations to create a world that readers will want to visit time and again."
Publisher's Weekly, Starred Review

Hegger's utterly delightful first Ghost Falls contemporary is what other romance novels want to grow up to be." –
Publisher's Weekly, Best Books of 2017

"The very talented Hegger kicks off an enjoyable new series set in the small Utah town of Ghost Falls. This charming and fun-filled book has everything from passion and humor to betrayal and revenge." –
Jill M Smith, RT Books Reviews 2017 – Contemporary Love and Laughter Nominee

Becoming Bella
"Hegger excels at depicting familial relationships and friendships of all kinds, including purely platonic friendships between women and men. Tears, laughter, and a dollop of suspense make a memorable story that readers will want to revisit time and again."
Publisher's Weekly, Starred Review

"...you have a terrific new romance that Hegger fans are going to love. Don't miss out!"
Jill M. Smith – RT Book Reviews

Blatantly Blythe
"Ms. Hegger has delivered another captivating read for this series in this book that was packed with emotion..." Bec, Bookmagic Review, Harlequin Junkie, HJ Recommends.

Nobody's Fool

"Hegger offers a breath of fresh air in the romance genre." –
Terri Dukes, RT Book Reviews

Nobody's Princess
"Hegger continues to live up to her rapidly growing reputation
for breathing fresh air into the romance genre." – Terri Dukes,
RT Book Reviews

"I have read the entire Willow Park Series. I have loved each of
the books ... Nobody's Princess is my favorite of all time."
Harlequin Junkie, Top Pick

Also by Sarah Edwards

Sarah Edwards also writes as Sarah Hegger

Urban Fantasy

The Cré-Witch Chronicles

Prequel: Cast In Stone

Vol l: Born In Water

Vol ll: Purged In Fire

Vol III: Raised In Air

Vol IV: Cradled In Earth

Vol V: Joined In Spirit

Sports Romance

Ottawa Titans Series

Roughing

Hooking

Contemporary Romance

Passing Through Series

Drove All Night

Ticket To Ride

Walk On By

Running On Empty

Ghost Falls Series

Positively Pippa

Becoming Bella

Blatantly Blythe

Loving Laura

Hunter Brothers

Nobody's Angel

Nobody's Fool

Nobody's Princess

Medieval Romance

Sir Arthur's Legacy Series

Sweet Bea

My Lady Faye

Conquering William

Defying Roger

Henry's Honor

Love & War Series

The Marriage Parley

The Betrothal Melee

Western Historical Romance

The Soiled Dove Series

Sugar Ellie

Standalone

The Bride Gift

Bad Wolfe On The Rise

Wild Honey